How could sh... ...nd? Amelia stood and app... ...ed him. "And if you cannot? 'Forsaking all others,' the rector said. Your wife is to have all your love and devotion."

"And a husband should have all his wife's," John replied. "Do you tell me you've held nothing back?"

She stiffened. "No, nothing! I've never loved another."

"And do you claim to love me?"

Amelia swallowed, her gaze falling to the black-and-green carpet even as she halted a few feet from him. "Perhaps not yet." Her voice sounded so small. "But I'm trying."

He moved to close the distance between them and touched her cheek, drawing her attention back to his face. Standing so close, she could see that gold flecks danced in the dark eyes, as if some part of him still clung to light, to hope.

"I know you are trying, Amelia," he murmured. "You've turned this place into a home. You may well have saved Firenza's life. I admire your efforts."

A tear slid down her cheek. "Admiration is not love."

Books by Regina Scott

Love Inspired Historical

The Irresistible Earl
An Honorable Gentleman
*The Rogue's Reform
*The Captain's Courtship
*The Rake's Redemption
*The Heiress's Homecoming
†The Courting Campaign
†The Wife Campaign
†The Husband Campaign

*The Everard Legacy
†The Master Matchmakers

REGINA SCOTT

started writing novels in the third grade. Thankfully for literature as we know it, she didn't actually sell her first novel until she learned a bit more about writing. Since her first book was published in 1998, her stories have traveled the globe, with translations in many languages, including Dutch, German, Italian and Portuguese.

She and her husband of over twenty-five years reside in southeast Washington State with their overactive Irish terrier. Regina Scott is a decent fencer, owns a historical costume collection that takes up over a third of her large closet, and she is an active member of the Church of the Nazarene. You can find her online blogging at www.nineteenteen.blogspot.com. Learn more about her at www.reginascott.com, or connect with her on Facebook at www.facebook.com/authorreginascott.

The Husband Campaign

REGINA SCOTT

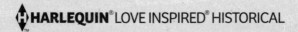
HARLEQUIN® LOVE INSPIRED® HISTORICAL

Recycling programs
for this product may
not exist in your area.

LOVE INSPIRED BOOKS

ISBN-13: 978-0-373-28258-6

THE HUSBAND CAMPAIGN

www.Harlequin.com

Printed in U.S.A.

A new commandment I give you: Love one another.
As I have loved you, so you must love one another.
—*John* 13:34

To my dear Kris, who knows what it's like
to rearrange a life for those you love,
and to the Lord, who is so much better at
arranging things than I'll ever be

Chapter One

Hollyoak Farm, Peak District, Derbyshire, England
July 1815

Why was the most beautiful woman of his acquaintance sleeping in his stable?

John, Lord Hascot, pushed a lock of rain-slicked dark hair out of his eyes and raised his lantern to peer more closely through the shadows. He hadn't visited the crumbling, thatched-roof outbuilding near the River Bell since he'd first purchased the Derbyshire property five years ago. He and his horse Magnum wouldn't be out this direction now if his horse Contessa hadn't gone missing. Only a chance late-afternoon thunderstorm had driven him to seek shelter.

He hadn't expected to find the place inhabited, and by Lady Amelia Jacoby, daughter of the Marquess of Wesworth, no less. Even if he hadn't recognized the plum-colored riding habit of fine wool, he would have known those elegant features, that pale blond hair. In the light from the lantern, he could see golden lashes fanning her pearly cheeks.

He'd never mastered the rules of London Society, but he was fairly certain they didn't cover how to properly react to a lady found sleeping in the straw. Some might expect him to take Magnum out in the rain from the opposite stall where he'd made his horse comfortable and leave her to her peace. He rejected the idea. For one, he refused to mistreat Magnum. For another, how could he call himself a man and abandon a defenseless woman in a storm?

John snorted. What, was he being chivalrous? He'd thought that habit long broken. He ought to wake her, order her to take her troubles elsewhere. Lady Amelia's concerns were none of his affair.

The storm made the decision for him. Thunder rolled, shaking the stable. With a squeal of fear, a white-coated mare threw up her head from the next stall. With a cry, Lady Amelia jerked upright. It was either comfort her or her horse.

He had more faith in his ability to comfort the horse.

As she climbed to her feet, he handed her the lantern, then turned to the other stall before she could question him.

"Easy," he murmured, moving slowly toward the mare. He kept his muscles loose and his face composed.

Out of the corners of his eyes, he saw Lady Amelia staring at him. He didn't dare take his gaze off the mare. He stroked her withers, murmured assurances in her ears. He could feel the horse relaxing, settling back into the stall.

Turning, he found Lady Amelia's pretty mouth hanging open. Very likely no one had ever favored her horse over her.

Then her eyes widened in recognition. "Lord Hascot?"

John inclined his head. "Lady Amelia."

Lightening flashed, and she glanced up with a gasp. John came around the wall before thinking better of it.

"Easy," he said, putting a hand on her arm and taking the lantern back from her before she dropped it in the dry straw. "It's just a storm."

She nodded, drawing in a longer breath this time as if trying to settle herself, as well. Odd. He could feel the dampness in the wool of her habit, yet the mare had been dry, and now he noticed a sidesaddle slung over the low wall separating the stalls. Had she seen to her horse's comfort before her own?

"Forgive me," she said. "I shouldn't be so timid. I simply wasn't expecting such a storm. Will it pass soon, do you think?"

The quick recitation sounded breathless. He couldn't blame her if she was nervous. Very likely he wasn't the most comforting sight to a well-bred young lady. He didn't bother with navy coats and cream trousers when working. His tan greatcoat covered a rough tweed jacket and chamois breeches that were more practical for a horse farm. And he'd been told more than once that his black hair and angular features could be intimidating. Particularly when he scowled.

He could feel himself scowling.

"Summer rains generally pass quickly in the peaks," he told her. "Best to wait it out."

She nodded, then hurried to the other stall. "Did you hear that, Belle?" she murmured, stroking the mare's mane. "We'll just wait a moment, and then we'll be able to go back to Lord Danning's. There's my sweet girl."

She talked to her horse as if the mare was a person. She might be the only one besides him who treated a horse like a friend, but that didn't mean she wasn't the typical Society miss, self-absorbed, fixed on marrying the finest. She would have no use for a country baron, which was all for the best.

"Why are you here, Lady Amelia?" he asked, locating a nail in the beam above his head and hanging the lantern from it.

Her hand fell away from Belle, but she didn't look at him. "I was caught in the rain and sought shelter."

In an old building that contained only straw left over from the last cutting? And she stated the fact carefully, as if unwilling to offer more information. Yet he wanted more. He wanted to understand her as he understood his horses. "Where is your groom?"

She met his gaze, arching delicate brows more golden than the hair gathered in a bun behind her head. "I haven't needed a groom when riding since I was five, sir."

Neither had he. Yet the rules were different for women. That much he knew. "Even so far from Lord Danning's lodge?" he argued. "He's still hosting that house party, isn't he?"

"Yes," she said, so faintly he had to move closer to be certain. "Yes," she repeated with more conviction, as if to forestall other questions. "We visited your farm early in the stay, so I expect the party to last another week."

He could not help remembering that visit. He didn't care for people who came to visit his farm merely to ogle the horses, with no true concern for the animals' well-being. That sort of visitor reminded him of the shallow Society he had left behind when he'd exiled himself to Hollyoak Farm two years ago. Then he'd wanted only to escape, away from the woman he'd loved, away from the brother who'd betrayed him. But he'd known Whitfield Calder, Earl of Danning, since they'd been boys together at Eton. Calder understood the value of a good horse, and something about his friend's note requesting a visit had hinted of despair. John knew something of despair. He could not be the agent to visit it upon another, nor would he walk away without attempting to resolve it. So he'd agreed to the visit, and five women and four men had descended upon him, expecting entertainment.

He was never entertaining.

His guests, to his surprise, had been. Over the years, he'd learned to watch people, to know what he might expect from them, to be prepared to respond. A man who insisted on riding with spurs was often a man who mistreated his horses. There was never enough gold for John to sell to him. And a lady who fluttered her lashes and smiled behind her fan was to be avoided at all costs. She was too much like the woman who'd preferred his brother to him.

Lord Danning's lady visitors were not like that. Two were older wives, one with a doting husband in tow. The other three were clearly eligible misses, and unless he was off his game, their quarry was the earl himself. Indeed, Danning seemed to have his hands full with an outspoken redhead.

And choosing the redhead, John had thought at the time, was a mistake. He knew bloodlines—strength in the limbs and a loyal heart—would tell in a person's behavior, and it was clear to him which lady had those traits in abundance.

Lady Amelia Jacoby.

She'd been so far above the others that John could only wonder why she was even part of the group. He wondered the same thing now. Had she set her heart on marrying Danning and been so crushed when he preferred another that she'd run away? The drops he saw glistening on her cheeks now that he was closer could as easily be from tears as rain. Why else would a woman who had everything—family, wealth, beauty— cry herself to sleep?

"Has Lord Danning made his decision, then?" John asked.

She drew herself up. "I am no gossip, sir. You would have to ask the earl that question."

She might not be a gossip, but she had answered the question. The stiffness in her shoulders said Danning had chosen a bride, and it wasn't her. Why should that fact please him?

Thunder rumbled again, drawing nearer. She set about soothing Belle once more. John glanced at the big stallion across the way, and Magnum raised his head as if with pride. He trusted John to care for him, what- ever happened. And John would never let him down.

At the moment, however, he could do nothing more for the horse. John knew Magnum had eaten plenty ear- lier that day, for rich pastures surrounded the farm. As soon as the rain let up, John could send Lady Amelia on her way and take Magnum back to the main stables and bed. With any luck, the others would have found Contessa by now. He had never met a horse who knew more ways to escape a fenced pasture, or one more de- termined to do so. Normally his men kept an eye on her, but a new groom had been preoccupied with learning his duties, and the mare had slipped away.

Now lightning set shadows in sharp relief, and he saw Lady Amelia shudder. "You would be wise to sit down," he advised.

She glanced about as if trying to determine where. What, did she think stables came with gilded chairs or cushioned benches? To John's mind the most likely spot to sit was on an old grain bin along the back wall. She must have reached the same conclusion, for she went to settle her skirts about her on the bin as if ready to pour tea.

"Won't you join me, my lord?" she asked, patting the other side of the wooden slats.

She was only being polite. He could not conceive that she would truly wish his company. But he moved closer and convinced himself to sit beside her. Through the musty scent of earth and straw came the incongruous perfume of orange blossoms. Was that the scent of her hair? Surely it was poor manners to bury his nose in the silky-looking tresses as if they were a feed sack. Yet some part of him was tempted to do just that.

"I didn't realize this was your property," she said by way of conversation. "How far do your holdings stretch?"

It was an expected topic, and a gentleman was supposed to prose on at great length, he was certain. He didn't prose. "Far enough to provide food and a good run," he replied.

"I'm sure that must be very gratifying for your horses," she said. "What brought you out in the storm, my lord?"

Thunder boomed, and she shuddered again. In fact,

he could feel her least movement, the moment she yawned behind her hand, the shiver that went through her. Was she cold? Hungry?

Whatever you did for the least of my brothers, you did for me.

The remembered verse demanded his attention. But he couldn't believe the Lord would answer a prayer half formed. He hadn't answered any of John's prayers since before his brother had died.

Still, John pulled his greatcoat from his shoulders and draped it around her.

"Oh, Lord Hascot, I couldn't," she protested.

"Take it," John insisted. "I must see to my horse."

He slid off the box and started forward, but he couldn't help glancing back at her. Her fingers, as long and elegant as the rest of her, clutched at the wool as she pulled it closer. Her sigh of thanks was as soft as a kitten's.

Something inside him melted.

John lifted his head, turned his back on her and forced himself to march to Magnum's stall. His horse eyed him.

"Don't start," John said. He sank onto the straw and put his back against the stone wall. Drawing up his knees, he crossed his arms over the top of his chamois breeches.

He didn't have to speak with Lady Amelia, tend to her like a nursery maid. He'd play the gentleman and protect her, but nothing more. He'd already had his heart carved from his chest by a beautiful woman who'd claimed allegiance. He wasn't about to offer the knife to another, even the lovely Lady Amelia.

* * *

Amelia didn't remember falling asleep. Certainly, she knew it her duty to keep Lord Hascot company, though he had abandoned hers. She tossed out a few polite questions, all of which were met with terse responses from the other stall. She might have thought she had offended him, only he'd been as short with everyone else when she'd visited his farm with Lord Danning a few days ago. Apparently Lord Hascot did not like people nearly as much as he liked his horses.

But one moment she'd been yawning on the grain bin, and the next she was waking up on a bed of straw. She frowned at the change and couldn't help wondering how she'd reached this spot.

Then the day's events rushed back at her. She'd been at Fern Lodge keeping Mr. Calder busy so her new friend Henrietta Stokely-Trent could chaperone her other new friend Ruby Hollingsford on an outing with their host, Lord Danning. She thought she'd done rather well to follow Mr. Calder's instructions and affix a creature of feather and horsehair he called a fly onto a brass hook and toss it into the river by way of a long, jointed pole. But Mr. Calder had forsaken his fishing lesson to search for Henrietta, and Amelia had been disappointed with herself for failing to keep him occupied and away from the courting couple.

Her disappointment was nothing to how her mother had reacted.

"And why are you keeping company with Mr. Calder in any regard?" she'd demanded after she'd found Amelia changing into her riding habit with the idea of going after the group. "He is the son of a second son, a nobody. We came here for Danning."

Her mother had come for Danning. Lady Wesworth had decided the wealthy earl held promise for her daughter. Amelia had had hopes Lord Danning might have the makings of a good husband. He was kind, considerate and affable, everything her father was not. It had been rather exciting to be one of three women invited to a house party to determine which was best suited to be his bride. But it was quickly evident that he favored Ruby Hollingsford, and why not? Ruby was outspoken, fearless, bold.

Everything Amelia was not.

But some of Ruby's boldness must have rubbed off, for Amelia had answered her mother, "I do not intend to marry Lord Danning. If I marry, I will marry for love."

Her mother had puffed up like a thundercloud gathering. It was truly a fearsome sight, and one Amelia had witnessed only a few times in her life and never with good results.

"Your father will have something to say about that," her mother had threatened.

The subsequent argument had so overset Amelia that she'd run for the stable at Fern Lodge, called for Belle and ridden as far and as fast as she could, seeking only escape.

Escape from a mother who could not understand.

Escape from a father who could not care.

Escape from expectations she could not meet.

Only when she'd felt the rain cooling her tears had she sought shelter, which was where Lord Hascot had found her.

She sat up, and his greatcoat slid down her form.

"Lord Hascot?" she asked, climbing to her feet and tucking her riding train up over one arm.

The door of the stable stood open, a shaft of sunlight stabbing through the darkness. A man stepped from the shadows into the beam of light. She recognized him immediately—that thatch of midnight-black hair, the sharp planes of his features, the still way he held himself as if ready for anything.

"Easy," he said. "There's no need for concern."

Oh, there was every reason for concern. She knew what must happen next. If she hoped for any peace, she would have to apologize to her mother. She had long ago learned the many ways to turn criticism into commendation.

Unfortunately, this time would be more difficult. She knew what her mother wanted, what her father expected. They insisted that she marry a wealthy, titled gentleman who would bring further acclaim to the name of Jacoby, the House of Wesworth. No amount of positive thinking, prayer or discussion had changed their minds.

But wealthy, titled bachelors of marrying mind, she had learned, were not at all plentiful, and the competition to secure them was stiff. While she'd enjoyed the glittering balls, the witty conversations that were part and parcel to a London Season, she had not liked participating in the marriage mart. Men were quick to praise her beauty, but their attentions seemed shallow.

Indeed, it was rather degrading to have to parade herself, gowned in her best, hair just so, smiling, always smiling. Sometimes she felt as if she was one of the horses at Tattersalls, the famed horse auctioneers in London. She would not have been surprised if one of the gentlemen asked to examine her teeth!

"Thank you for your thoughtfulness, my lord," she

told Lord Hascot. She bent, retrieved his greatcoat and held it out to him. "And thank the Lord the storm has ended."

He came forward and accepted the coat as solemnly as if it were a royal robe. "You'll want to be on your way, I suspect."

"Yes, thank you." She slipped into the box next to hers and reached for Belle's headstall, which was hanging from a hook at the end of the box. "My mother will be worried."

"I sent word to Fern Lodge this morning," he said.

Her fingers froze. Indeed, she was surprised she could even blink. "This morning?"

"It is past dawn," he said. "One of my grooms just came in search of me. You slept through the night."

She clutched the leather of the reins and managed to turn and look at his scowling face. "And where did you sleep?"

"I didn't. I was over there." He lifted his chin toward the far wall. "You were not disturbed."

She nodded. She had to nod, for every part of her was shaking. She'd spent the night alone with a gentleman. It didn't matter that nothing untoward had happened. It didn't matter that he had merely kept watch over her from the opposite side of the stable.

She was ruined.

Ruined.

No one of consequence would offer for her now. All her father's expectations, all her mother's hopes for an alliance with a highborn family were utterly, irrevocably dashed.

She was free!

Thank You, Lord!

Her joy was singing so loudly she almost missed hearing Lord Hascot say, "I will, of course, do the expected and offer for your hand."

Chapter Two

What could possibly have forced those words from his mouth? John had known he was taking a chance by staying with her. He'd expected one of his staff to come looking for him long before dawn. But his men had all assumed he was out searching as they were for Contessa amidst the pouring rain. John had already sent the groom back to the house with Magnum and instructions to contact Fern Lodge, for very likely the Earl of Danning was equally concerned for his lost guest, and her mother must be frantic.

Lady Amelia looked nearly as frantic, standing before him, gaze flickering about the old stable as if she hoped to spy a stray chaperone perched in the corner. She knew the penalty for spending the night with him, even on the opposite side of the stable. Yet he had no interest in bringing a near stranger to Hollyoak as his wife. He'd worked hard to make this farm the best in England. A Hascot colt was widely recognized as the mark of a prosperous man. Having a wife would be little asset there.

As for preserving the line, at times he was certain

the idea was inadvisable. He knew weak stock when he saw it. Perhaps a long-lost cousin of stronger stuff could be found to take over the barony when John died without issue.

So why had he just made the ultimate sacrifice and offered this woman a place at his side?

"How very kind of you, Lord Hascot," she said, interrupting his thoughts and pausing to bite her petal-pink lip a moment as if choosing her words with care. "But there's really no need. You were merely being a gentleman to watch over me during the storm."

Relief at his narrow escape from parson's mouse-trap was not as strong as it should have been. He told himself to be glad she was so practical, so quick to spot the truth. He hadn't the time, patience or inclination to make a decent husband. His feelings ran too deep; he never expressed them well.

"As you wish, Lady Amelia," he said with a nod. "I offer you the hospitality of my home, such as it is, before you return to Fern Lodge."

Her hand touched her hair above her ear, where the strands had come loose from her pins. A piece of straw stuck out like the ostrich plumes she must wear to her balls in London. Straw speckled her riding habit as well, clinging to the fabric as the wool outlined every curve of her slender form. John forced his gaze to her face, which was growing decidedly pinker, as if she'd noticed his scrutiny.

"Thank you, my lord," she replied with obvious relief. She turned to Belle, then paused as if wondering how to put the saddle back into place.

"Allow me," John said.

She stepped aside with another smile.

But in this he wasn't being chivalrous. She'd done well to remove the tack the previous night, but in his experience, few women knew how to take care of their own horses. They'd never had to learn. Grooms attended them, beaux helped them in and out of sidesaddles. He personally thought sidesaddles ridiculous contraptions that hampered a woman's ability to control her animal, but he doubted any word from him would make the fashionable change their minds.

So he laid the saddle on the mare's back and cinched it up from long experience. He slipped on the headstall, checked that the brass was properly buckled. All the while the mare stool docile, placid. For all her good lines, he sensed very little fire in her.

He'd always thought the horse reflected its rider. Lady Amelia had called herself timid in passing. Was her polite demeanor truly a sign of a timid heart?

For she stood waiting as well, a pleasant smile on her face as if she was quite used to gentlemen serving her. He bent and cupped his hands, and she put her foot in his grip. It was long and shapely, even in her riding boot, and she lifted herself easily into the saddle, where she draped her skirts about her. With a cluck, she urged Belle into a walk out of the stall.

And John walked beside her, feeling a bit like a stable lad attending the queen.

"What a lovely day," she said as they exited the building.

In truth, it was a fine day. The storm had carried off the last cloud, and the field sparkled with the remaining raindrops. Dovecote Dale stretched in either direction, following the chatter of the River Bell, the fields lush and alive. He always felt as if he could breathe easier here.

But not with the woman beside him. She was trying to initiate conversation, just as she had last night. He remembered the London routine: mention the weather, ask after a gentleman's horses, talk about family or mutual friends. Had she no more purposeful topics?

When he did no more than nod in reply, she tried again, gesturing to where several of his animals were out in the pasture. "Your horses look fit."

John nearly choked. "Fit, madam? Yes, I warrant they could make it across the field without collapsing, particularly in such excellent weather."

Her cheeks were darkening again, the color as pink as her lips. "Forgive me. I didn't mean to give false praise."

"No," John said, forcing his gaze away from her once more. "Forgive me. I haven't mixed in Society for a while. I find the forms stifling."

"I quite understand."

The certainty of the statement said she found them equally so, but he suspected she was more in agreement with the assessment of his social skills.

"Is there something you'd prefer to discuss?" she asked politely.

None of the banal topics London appeared to thrive on. In fact, he had only one question plaguing him. "Why exactly were you out in the storm yesterday?"

She was silent a moment, her gaze on the house, which could now be seen in the distance. Her head was so high the straw in her hair stood at attention. Finally she said, "I had a disagreement with my mother. Riding away seemed the wisest course."

He'd met her mother when Danning's guests had come to tour the farm. A tall woman like her daughter, with a sturdier frame and ample figure, she had a way of making her presence felt. And it didn't help that she had a voice as sharp as a cavalry sword. Riding away probably had been the best choice.

"You never answered my question last night, either," she reminded him. "What brought you out in the storm?"

"One of my horses is unaccounted for," he said. "I thought perhaps she'd made for the river."

She reined in, pulling him up short. "Oh, Lord Hascot, if she is missing you must find her!"

Her eyes, bluer than the sky, were wide in alarm, her cheeks pale. John raised his brows. "I have grooms out even now. I've no doubt they'll bring her in."

"Are you certain?" she begged, glancing around as if she might spy Contessa trailing them. "This place is so wild."

If she thought his tended fields wild he did not want to know what she'd make of the grasses of Calder Edge, the grit stone cliff above his property.

"Hollyoak Farm is bounded by the river to the south," he explained, pointing out the features as he talked, "and Calder Edge to the north. If Contessa goes east, she'll run into the Rotherford mine, and they know where to return her. West, and she'll eventually hit Bellweather Hall. The duke's staff will send for me. Either way, I'll fetch her home."

She seemed to sag in the saddle. "Oh, I'm so glad."

"Why do you care?" John asked, catching the reins before she could start forward again. "Most people treat a horse as nothing but a possession."

Her pretty mouth thinned. "For shame, sir." Her hand stroked her horse's crest as lovingly as the head of a child. "Belle is no possession. I'm honored to call her my friend. I assumed you felt the same way about your horses, even that black brute I heard you call Magnum."

John's face was heating, and he released the reins as he looked away. "You would not be wrong. Sometimes I'm certain I spend more time in conversation with him than anyone else. Perhaps that's why I'm so bad at conversing with a lady."

"I'm not much of a conversationalist myself," she admitted, urging Belle forward once more. Her look down to John was kind. "I always seem to say the wrong thing at the wrong time. Please forgive me."

Either she was too used to taking the blame for the failings of others or she was trying to impress him with her condescension. Still, John found it all too easy to forgive her. For one thing, he had the same affliction when it came to conversation. He found his horses easier to converse with than people. And for another, there was something utterly guileless about Lady Amelia.

Part of him protested. He'd been down this road before and been left standing alone at the end. It was probably best to walk the other way this time.

Amelia had always prided herself on her congenial demeanor, honed by years of criticism from her parents and her governess. But Lord Hascot challenged even her abilities. He reminded her of a cat that had been petted the wrong way—fur up and claws extended.

Hollyoak Farm was nearly as unwelcoming. When she'd visited with Lord Danning a few days ago, she'd thought the red stone house a boxy affair, as angular as its owner. Even the bow window of the withdrawing room sat out squarely as if giving no quarter. Now all the drapes were drawn and the doors shut. Lord Hascot led her to the stable yard, a gravel expanse between the two flanking stable wings, where he helped her alight on a mounting block. Taking Belle's reins himself, he nodded toward the house.

"You'll find a maid waiting to attend you," he said. "If I do not see you again before Lord Danning comes to collect you, know that I am your devoted servant."

Though his voice was gruff and his statement an expected one, something simmered under the words, the echo of concern. Amelia smiled at him.

"Thank you, Lord Hascot," she said, trying for a similar sincerity in the oft-used phrase. "I appreciate everything you did for me and Belle."

One of his hands strayed to Belle's nose, the touch soft, and those stern lips lifted in a smile. Why, he could be quite handsome when he smiled, his dark locks falling across his forehead and the sunlight brightening his brown eyes to gold. Before she could say anything more, he turned away, and she fancied she felt the chill of winter in the summer air.

Such an odd man. Amelia shook her head as she made for the house. He acted as if he was much better off without people around. Still, he had been kind to stay with her and offer for her when needed. Now she had to prepare herself to face the true consequences of the night's events: her mother's disapproval. *Help me, Lord!*

She was thankful to see the young woman waiting for her in the corridor, just as Lord Hascot had predicted. The maid had light brown hair peeking out of her white lace-edge cap, a round face and a firm figure swathed in a gray dress and white apron. On seeing Amelia, she immediately bobbed a curtsy.

"Dorcus Turner of Rotherford Grange, your ladyship," she announced. "His lordship sent for help, seeing as how he has no lady on staff. How might I be of assistance?"

Another oddity. Surely a house this size required several maids to keep it clean. Or did Lord Hascot disdain even the services of a female?

"Thank you for coming all this way, Turner," Amelia answered. "Is there somewhere I might tidy up?"

Turner wrinkled her nose. "I haven't been told, but I imagine there must be some spare room in this dismal pile." Amelia's surprise at her outspoken manner must have been evident, for the maid dipped another curtsy. "Begging your pardon, your ladyship. This way."

She led Amelia down the dim corridor paneled in squares of dark wood, and Amelia soon agreed with the maid's assessment of the house. Though it was now midmorning, every velvet drape remained closed, every candle unlit, making the place a house of shadow. Combined with the dark paneling that covered at least half of every room she glanced into as they passed, she could easily imagine the mistress of the house curling away in a corner to cry. Small wonder Lord Hascot rarely smiled!

She followed Turner up a set of stairs with a brass-topped banister to a room on the chamber story, where the maid set about taking down Amelia's hair.

"I warrant you're the first lady to set foot in this house for a long while," she said as she worked. "I hear tell Lord Hascot never lets his visitors closer than the stables."

Perhaps because he knew the house to be so uninviting. "I imagine most of his visitors come to see the horses, in any event," Amelia replied. Certainly that was why Lord Danning had brought his guests to Hollyoak Farm.

"Oh, aye," Turner agreed, pulling a silver-backed brush from the pocket of her apron and proceeding to run it over Amelia's long, curly hair. "Everyone around here knows he's a great one for the horses, but not with the ladies. It won't take much for you to turn him up sweet, your ladyship."

Amelia stiffened. "That will do, Turner. I have no interest in being courted by Lord Hascot."

She had never spoken so sternly to a servant. She'd never had to. The staff at home was too afraid of her father and mother to ever speak out of turn. Turner, however, merely grimaced before setting about repinning Amelia's hair.

"Sorry, your ladyship," she said. "You might as well know that I tend to speak my mind. This could be a fine house, and I warrant his lordship could be a fine husband, for a lady with a bit of grit and a lot of determination."

Grit and determination. She'd never considered herself particularly gifted in either. And after spending a little time in the gentleman's company, she could only wish his future bride luck, for it would take quite a campaign to turn Lord Hascot into the proper husband.

Chapter Three

John was certain he'd seen the last of Lady Amelia. Her family had no reason to interact with his. He'd already refused her father's attempt to purchase a horse, twice. Something about the Marquess of Wesworth struck him as cold, calculating. Any kindness in the man had obviously been passed to his daughter.

Yet as John checked with his head groom and learned that Contessa was still missing, he could not seem to forget the woman he'd found sleeping in the straw. Perhaps that was why he hurried out of the stables at the sound of carriage wheels on the gravel.

A lavish landau sat on the yard, brass appointments gleaming in the morning light. The four matched grays pulling it had the sleek, well-kept look of carriage horses. He would not have allowed one in his stable, and he was none too sure the same might not be said of the lady perched on the leather-upholstered seats of the open carriage. Lady Wesworth's back was ramrod straight in her serpentine pelisse, the peacock feather in her bonnet waving in the breeze.

Most of his grooms were still out searching for Contessa, but his veterinarian, Marcus Fletcher, must have heard the carriage as well, for he came out of the opposite stable block. A tall, gangly fellow with a riot of curly red hair and gold-rimmed spectacles, he was generally good with people for all he'd chosen to be a horse doctor instead of a physician. By the imperious frown on Lady Wesworth's face, however, John thought even Fletcher's good nature might not be sufficient.

"Lord Hascot," she said as John approached, Fletcher falling into step beside him. "What have you done with my daughter?"

She made it sound as if John had stolen Amelia from her home. Luckily, he was spared an answer by the opening of the rear door of the house and the entrance of the lady herself, followed by the maid John had requested from Rotherford Grange.

"Amelia!" Lady Wesworth cried as her daughter drew closer. "Are you hurt?"

A reasonable question, but it was said with a note of accusation, as if only injury would allow her mother to condone her actions.

"Good morning, Mother," Lady Amelia answered pleasantly, as if she usually started the day in a strange house. "I'm very sorry if I concerned you. I'm fine."

Indeed, she looked quite fine. The maid had done an excellent job of smoothing her platinum hair, brushing out the plum habit. Her blue eyes sparkling, Lady Amelia was nothing short of perfection.

Unfortunately, her mother did not appear to agree. Her chilly gaze swept over her daughter, as if seeking any fault.

"Of course you concerned me," she all but scolded. "You are my daughter, our only child." She affixed her gaze on John and held out her hand in a clear order to help her from the carriage.

He ignored her and turned to Lady Amelia. He had done his duty and delivered her safely back to her family. Surely that would silence the nagging voice in his head that he should do more.

"I trust the rest of your visit to Dovecote Dale will be unmarred by further unpleasantries, your ladyship," he said with a bow. "Safe travels."

Was it his imagination, or did her smile warm at his gesture? "Thank you, Lord Hascot. I hope you find your missing horse."

Despite everything that had happened, she remembered Contessa. That alone made her remarkable in John's eyes. As his head groom brought out a brushed and watered Belle, her smile only grew.

So did her mother's frown. Indeed, she had turned an unbecoming shade of red.

"Lord Hascot," she said, eyes narrowed, "my husband will expect you in London within the week. Come along, Amelia."

Lady Wesworth obviously expected not only instant obedience but humble gratitude for being given the benefit of her exalted command. John knew a sprightly mare generally resulted in a sprightly colt, but he found it difficult to believe Lady Amelia shared much in common with her mother.

And he no longer danced to anyone's tune.

He bowed to Lady Amelia, then turned his back on her mother and strode to the stables. The Jacoby women no doubt had a social calendar filled with appointments, and he had work to do. But he had only reached the door of the main stables before Fletcher caught up to him.

"She'll have to pay for this, I fear," he said.

John eyed his veterinarian. Marcus Fletcher had been in his employ since John had first bought Hollyoak Farm and started raising horses. He very nearly hadn't hired the fellow, for Fletcher did not exude confidence. His hands, however, were large and capable, his smile generous and his good nature without limit. Now, by the way he kept glancing back toward the house, he was concerned for their departing guest.

"I've no doubt she's well acquainted with her parents' strictures," John said, pulling open the door and heading inside. As always, the cool air of the stable welcomed him, brought him the scent of fresh hay, clean water and well-cared-for horses. Most of his stock had already been let out to pasture, and his footsteps rang against the cobbles as he made his way down the center aisle.

"Oh, assuredly," Fletcher agreed, following him. "She seems a very obedient daughter. But you didn't see her face as they left. It was as if she'd lost her last friend."

Something was tugging at him again, but he pushed it down. He'd been chivalrous enough where Lady Amelia was concerned. He had no reason to go haring off to London to fight the lady's dragon parents. And nothing to be gained by it. Lady Amelia, like other women of her class, married for position and power, and he was certain her father would agree that John as a baron had too little of either.

He glanced at the empty stall partway down the row. Where could Contessa have gotten to this time? "We have more important matters at hand," he told his veterinarian. "Send word to the village—a one hundred pound reward for Contessa's safe return."

Fletcher's red-gold brows rose. "Generous. You do realize, however, that the last horse you sold went for a thousand pounds. There is money in a Hascot horse."

"Only if you can prove it's a Hascot horse," John countered, heading for the rear of the stables. "No more than a few know her bloodlines. And with that game leg, she can't have gone far. I'll take Magnum out again. They generally find each other in the fields."

"And what of Lady Amelia?" Fletcher pressed, following him. "I suspect some would say you owe her a duty, as well."

Magnum nickered in greeting. John stroked his horse's nose and nodded to the groom who had hurried up with the tooled leather saddle. "I offered, she refused. That's all that need concern you."

Magnum shook his head as if he quite disagreed. Fletcher went so far as to jerk to a stop on the cobbles. "You offered?"

John crossed his arms over his chest as the groom laid on the saddle that had been made especially for the broad-backed horse and set about cinching it in place. "It was expected."

"If I may," Fletcher said, pausing to clear his throat, "you are not known for doing the expected."

John dropped his arms, put a foot in the stirrup and swung himself into the saddle. "Then be glad."

"She is lovely," Fletcher ventured, looking up at him.

She was beautiful—a porcelain princess and apparently nearly as fragile. John didn't answer as he took the reins from his groom.

"Sweet natured," Fletcher continued as if to encourage him. "And accomplished, too, I hear."

"So are half the mares in my stable," John replied, "and you don't see me running to court them."

Fletcher made a face as he stepped back out of Magnum's way. "Certainly not! But, my lord, you must admit you could do far worse than Lady Amelia."

John gathered the reins. "And you must admit that she could do far better. I'll start in the east and work my way west. Send word if you find Contessa."

"But, my lord," Fletcher protested.

John didn't wait to hear another word. He'd already determined that he would likely never see Lady Amelia again. The sooner he forgot about her, the better for all concerned.

She was in disgrace. Amelia kept her usual smile as she rode Belle alongside her mother's carriage. The harangue had started before they'd even cleared the drive from Hollyoak Farm, and it continued now as they took the bridge over the River Bell that marked the edge of Lord Danning's property. She was certain a few days ago she would have been crushed by the complaints.

Today she could only watch as the doves vaulted from the trees at the sound of her mother's strident voice. Amelia took strength in her position. Her motives to marry for love were right and pure. Surely the Lord would honor them. She merely had to suffer through, and all would be well.

Her new attitude, she suspected, was a result of her acquaintance with Ruby Hollingsford, that bold young lady Amelia had met at Lord Danning's house party. Amelia knew less was expected of Ruby, who was the daughter of a prosperous jeweler. Her father did not expect her to marry a titled gentleman—although he clearly had hopes of a match between his daughter and Lord Danning. Ruby's father seemed to dote on her every word, her least action.

Amelia's father did not dote. On anyone. Neither did her mother.

So Amelia answered her mother's questions about the situation and Lord Hascot calmly, agreed that they should return to London immediately and made her excuses to Lord Danning and Ruby. Ruby seemed the only one truly saddened to see her go.

"You stick to your guns," she said, giving Amelia's hands a squeeze. "You promised me you'd only marry for love."

"Never fear," Amelia told her. "I won't forget."

But her promise was easier to keep with Ruby nodding encouragement than when she faced her father in London.

"You are a very great disappointment to me, Amelia," he said.

He had called her into his study the day after she'd returned. His perfectly organized desk sat before floor-to-ceiling windows overlooking the boxed-in formal garden behind the house. Every book was lined up properly on the white-lacquered shelves, every paper neatly filed away. Her father stood at the window, addressing the tops of the trees. Not a single strand of his sandy hair was out of place; his dove-gray coat had nary a crease. He wouldn't have allowed it.

She was aware of every least wrinkle in her muslin gown, of the crumb of toast that had fallen on her lacy sleeve as she'd hurriedly quit the breakfast table to answer his summons. She wasn't sure why she'd been so quick to answer. She'd known what he'd say. And she should be used to his disappointment by now. It had started the day she hadn't been born a boy.

But the truth was, it hurt. When she was younger, she used to think she could earn his love. If she wore her hair perfectly combed, if she curtsied without wobbling, if she played a sonata with no mistakes, he would recognize her as having worth. But he never noticed her hair, paid no attention to her curtsy, was too busy to listen to a sonata. If her governess praised her French, he would ask why she hadn't mastered Latin, as well. If she rode with the hunt, he would ask why she hadn't led the field. There was no pleasing her father.

And yet she could not seem to stop trying.

"I'm very sorry, Father," she said to his back, attempting to stand as still and composed as he was. "But I can assure you that nothing untoward happened at Hollyoak Farm. Lord Hascot offered for me and I refused. The matter is settled."

He turned from the view at last, his pale blue eyes showing not the least emotion. "I fear the matter cannot be settled so easily. Hascot would be a decent alliance for you. I intend to have him."

"A shame you're already wed, then," Amelia said.

Her father stiffened, and she wanted to sink into the floor. Where had that come from? How could she be so disrespectful?

"Forgive me, Father," she said. "I suppose I meant that as a joke, and it was a poor one. I merely thought we would have more discussion when it came time to choose a suitor."

"Your mother and I have discussed the matter," he replied as if that were sufficient. "I have written to Hascot and requested that he attend me."

His note might have been couched as a request, but it would have been an order. She felt as if something was crawling up inside her, choking her, making her fists clench. Her parents were going to force her to wed.

Lord, show me how to stop them!

Calm welled up. She would prevail. And Lord Hascot would have something to say in the matter. For one thing, he knew he and Amelia had settled things. For another, he bore her no love. How could he?

She'd read a number of stories in which the hero conceived undying devotion for the heroine the moment he saw her, but in her experience it took a bit more time and proximity to develop lasting emotions. At least, that was what she hoped. For if men were supposed to wish to marry her on sight, something was very wrong indeed.

"Please don't press me on this, Father," she said.

Her father was watching her with a slight frown, as if he wondered what woman was masquerading as his daughter. "If it is that business with Lady Hascot that concerns you," he said, "I can assure you her interests lay elsewhere."

"Lady Hascot?" Amelia asked, confused. "Lord Hascot's mother?"

"His older brother's widow, the former Lady Caroline Musgrave," her father corrected her, with a look that said she should have known that. "As the wife of the previous titleholder, she is beholden to the Hascot estate for her living. I understand there has been a question about whether Lord Hascot intends to honor his brother's wishes, but his actions should have no bearing on you."

The only thing she'd seen about Lord Hascot that could make her admire his character was his care for his horses. He might be handsome, in a dark, brooding sort of way, and he had been kind to assure her safety that night in the stable. But he was stiff in conversation, sharp in manner, rough in voice and dismal in attitude. Now it seemed he could not even care for a poor widow!

"His actions have no bearing on me at all," Amelia said. "I don't intend to see him again."

Her father's look was enough to make her knees start shaking under her petticoat. "Make no mistake, Amelia," he said. "Bringing the appropriate son-in-law into the family is the one consolation for having a daughter. Hascot may not have the fortune or influence in Parliament I wanted, but his reputation as a horseman is unparalleled. I can make use of that. Therefore, you will accept him when he offers."

She dipped a curtsy. Better that than to let him see the frustration surging up. She didn't want to be angry at her father, didn't want to be a disobedient daughter. But she had seen enough of John, Lord Hascot, to know that he was a man as cold as her father, and she would not wed him. And she would tell the horseman that in no uncertain terms if he bowed to her father's demands and came calling.

Chapter Four

John hadn't intended to call on Lady Amelia, even after her father's imperious note demanding his presence in London. He generally came to town once a year for one of the larger sales at Tattersalls, and then he was careful never to cross paths with Caro. He was never comfortable dealing with the woman he'd thought to marry, especially now that she was his widowed sister-in-law, but it wasn't as if she had scared him out of town. Hollyoak Farm had ever been more of a home to him than London. He'd only spent the Season in town to humor his brother.

He had no interest in humoring Lady Amelia's father. The Jacoby family and the Wesworth title were well known for their pretensions. He had met the current titleholder twice, both times when Wesworth had come seeking a mount. Both times he'd made it seem as if John should be honored to receive him.

The letter Lady Amelia's father had sent him held the same tone, but something in it hinted of consequences. John very much doubted the marquess could do anything to diminish the reputation of Hollyoak Farm.

Hascot horses led the hunting field from Cornwall to
Carlisle. They had, to John's dismay, carried Hussars
into battle. It would take more than the sneer of the Ja-
cobys to sway the horse-loving gentlemen of the *ton*.

But even as he was tempted to dismiss the letter,
he couldn't help wondering about the consequences
to Lady Amelia. Surely Society wouldn't shun her
for sleeping in his stable one night. And marrying her
would hardly improve her standing with the *ton*. He
wasn't known for his cutting wit or dashing style.

Still, Fletcher's prediction that she would pay for
her lapse refused to leave John, so he rode to London
with the idea of assuring Lady Amelia's father that the
marquess need not concern himself for her reputation.

But the meeting with Lord Wesworth did not go as
he had expected.

"We are practical gentlemen," Lady Amelia's father
said when he received John in his study. "This emo-
tional business associated with marriage does not become us."

John could not argue with that. He'd grown emo-
tional about marriage once. He still bore the scars. He
took the seat his lordship indicated before the desk.
"Then you had another reason for writing to me."

Wesworth perched behind the desk, his lips twitching as if he could not decide whether to smile. Or perhaps he was simply unused to the gesture. A spare man
with a balding pate, he was so still and pale that he reminded John of grain left too long in the rain.

"I see this contretemps in Derby as an opportunity
for the both of us," he explained.

John cocked his head. "I don't follow you."

He rearranged the quills laid out on his desk, from

longest to shortest, the sharp ends all pointing inward. "I am speaking of a connection between our houses. You are a man who understands breeding, sir. You know my daughter's worth."

Would he compare his daughter to a horse? John must have frowned, for the marquess looked up and elaborated.

"She is beautiful, well trained in the art of managing a household, a talented singer, I'm told. You would be aligning yourself to a powerful family, able to arrange matters in Parliament to your liking."

John leaned back. "The last time I checked, Parliament had enough on its hands settling the affairs in France to worry about the regulation of the horse trade."

"Ah," the marquess said, hands stilling, "but there is more of interest to a horse breeder, say the right to enclose certain property."

Enclosure gave the landowner the right to keep the local citizens from using property once held in common. Some of his pasture was unenclosed land. His frown grew. "Are you threatening me?"

Still the marquess did not smile. "I should not need to threaten you, Hascot. You wronged my daughter. I merely seek restitution."

"I wronged no one," John insisted, pushing himself to his feet. "Good day, my lord." He turned for the door, but the quiet words stopped him.

"You'd have her shamed, then."

John looked back at him. He remained calm, as if he had no more than commented on the weather. "She's your daughter, Wesworth," John reminded him. "A word from you would likely cure any ill in Society."

The marquess was watching him. "And what if I

should refuse to say a word? Or worse, be sadly forced to agree that you ruined her?"

John felt his hand fisting and forced his fingers to relax. "Why?" he demanded. "What would be gained by such actions? I might lose a few sales to ladies outraged by my supposed lack of morals, but the gentlemen will still come for my hunters. Your daughter stands to lose the most."

His fingers set to rearranging the quills once more, shortest to longest this time, and now the points were aimed toward John. "My daughter's situation is immaterial. This is a discussion between gentlemen." As if assuming John had capitulated, he leaned forward and raised his gaze. "For the privilege of marrying into my family, I expect a colt every other year."

Anger was overtaking him, and he was thankful it only came out of his mouth. "If you treat your own daughter like cattle, sir, I wouldn't trust you with one of my horses."

The marquess recoiled, color flushing up his lean face at last. "How dare you!"

John returned to the desk in two strides, leaned over, braced both hands on the polished surface and met the marquess's cold gaze straight on. "I will marry your daughter, but you will only receive one of my colts when you can treat it and her with the respect they are due. That is my offer. Take it or leave it."

"Done," the fellow said, as if he'd just commissioned a new coat and was haggling over the buttons. "My wife is waiting in the withdrawing room. You may pay your addresses to my daughter."

John quit the study before he said anything further.

If he truly was going to marry into this family, the less time he spent with Amelia's father, the better.

Standing in the withdrawing room of the Wesworth town house, however, he had to convince himself not to squirm. The spindle-legged, gilded chairs that rested against the papered walls looked as if they, too, feared to sully the cream-patterned carpet. Every picture, every knickknack was placed precisely in the center of whatever space it had been given. Lady Wesworth, seated on a white satin-striped sofa with a square back, did not even look as if she was breathing.

But that might have more to do with her fear that she was about to give her daughter away to a lesser being.

The paneled door opened, and Amelia entered the room. Somehow, life seemed to come with her. Though she wore one of the frilly white muslin gowns that remained the fashion, her color was high. Her smile as she approached him, however, was more strained than welcoming.

"Lord Hascot," she said, inclining her head so that the light from the window gilded her pale hair. "What a surprise."

Had her mother and father kept their machinations from her? "You did not know I was coming?" He glanced at her mother, who rose and came forward.

"Lord Wesworth and I find it best to make decisions without concerning Amelia," she informed John.

Amelia blushed. "How kind, Mother, but some decisions concern me more than you know."

Her mother frowned as if she could not imagine such a circumstance.

He certainly could. Amelia had a right to decide who to wed, and her choices must be legion. He was mad to even consider proposing. But hearing her father attempt to bargain for her future—never questioning whether John would make a good husband, whether she'd be cared for, appreciated—had touched something inside him. He could not willingly leave her to her fate.

He should assure her he meant the best for her, that he would give her a secure future. Yet the words refused to leave his mouth. It had ever been this way. When he was a child, he'd stammered, and his already shy nature had combined with the trait to keep him largely silent. Even though the stammer had faded with maturity, he still found it remarkably hard to make conversation, particularly when he was the center of attention, as now.

Lady Wesworth was obviously losing patience with him, for as the silence stretched, she moved to assist. "Lord Hascot has something he wishes to say to you, Amelia," she announced with a pointed look to him.

At this, Amelia straightened, her composed face tightening as if it mirrored her convictions. "Lord Hascot and I have nothing further to say to each other."

She had little use for him, and he could not blame her for it. "I had a similar reaction when I read your father's note," he assured her. "I came to London to make certain you had taken no harm from your short stay at Hollyoak Farm."

Her color was fading, but she spread her hands, graceful. "As you can see, my lord," she said, "I am fine. Perhaps if you could explain that to my mother and father, we can put all this behind us. You know I already refused you once."

And would do so again. She did not have to say it aloud. He could see it in the height of her chin, hear it in the strength of her voice. Just contemplating his next move made him as jittery as a colt taking its first steps.

Her mother moved to her side, the rustle of her skirts loud against the carpet. "Things have changed, Amelia. Lord Hascot has already spoken to your father. He is aware that this is not the match we wanted for you, but we are persuaded that he will make you a good husband."

Were they? He wished he had that confidence. He was certain he'd make a wretched husband, but after meeting Lady Amelia's father, he could only pray that life with him would be an improvement for her.

Now, how was he to convince her of that?

So it was true. Her mother and father had somehow persuaded themselves and Lord Hascot that he should wed her. No doubt the thought of aligning himself with her father had sweetened the pot.

"I hope Father at least laid claim to a Hascot colt for his trouble," she said.

Oh, but why did those unkind words keep coming from her mouth? Yet even as she regretted them, she saw Lord Hascot's face reddening, and she knew her accusation was true. Her father had traded her for a horse! And this man, this lord who clearly preferred horses to people, had agreed to it. Words failed her.

They did not, of course, fail her mother.

"You are, no doubt, overcome by the thought of marrying, Amelia," she said, jaw tight, "so I will forgive you for that outburst." She turned to Lord Hascot. "Please know that Amelia is normally obedient in all things, my lord. You need have no concerns that she will make you an excellent wife."

Of course she'd make an excellent wife. She'd been trained since birth to manage a household, to oversee the education of children, to sing and play and dance, to make her husband happy. She was docile, sweet natured, eager to please.

"Yes, I'm quite the catch," she said, hysteria forcing out a high, brittle laugh. "I dare say I'm a great deal more biddable than his stock."

"Excuse us a moment, my lord," her mother said. She seized Amelia's elbow and drew her back toward the door.

"What is this?" she hissed, blocking Lord Hascot's view of Amelia by turning her back. "You run away, spend the night in a stable like a milkmaid and then dare defy your father's attempt to salvage your reputation? What has happened to you, Amelia?"

What was happening to her? She felt the image she'd held of herself melting like silver purified, and she wasn't sure yet what shape it might form.

"I don't wish to marry him, Mother," she tried. "I don't love him. Nor does he love me."

Her mother sighed. "Love, again. I wish you had never met that Hollingsford girl! You must think logically, Amelia. Lord Hascot has five thousand pounds per annum, his horses are widely admired and he was willing to take you. Be happy with that."

She did not wait for Amelia's reply but only turned to Lord Hascot once more. "I would prefer Amelia be married here, my lord. A quiet ceremony with a few friends and family, by special license."

Her mother would even dictate the ceremony. *Think!* There had to be something she could say, something she could do, to make them all change their minds. *Please, Lord, help me!*

No inspiration struck. But now that her mother had moved away a little, Amelia could see Lord Hascot standing tall and proud where they had left him.

"Impossible," he said to her mother's dictates. "We will be wed in a church, after the banns are read."

"The banns?" Amelia could hear the confusion in her mother's voice. Common folk married by banns, their names read out for three Sundays in a row in their home churches. The aristocracy married by license or special license, away from prying eyes, among their own kind.

"The banns," he insisted. He met Amelia's gaze. "That way, if anyone chooses to object, he can."

He was giving her a chance. She didn't understand why, but she knew it. He would not force himself on her after all. By having the banns read, he gave some other gentleman who cared about her the opportunity to come forward, protest the wedding, state his former claim on Amelia's affections.

If only she had such a gentleman to defend her!

A quiet voice inside her urged her to defend herself. But how? Her father had made his wishes clear. She could run away, but how would she live? She wouldn't be old enough to marry without consent for another three months, even if she found a man she could love. No other relation would take her in, knowing she'd defied her father. And with no reference, who would hire her as a governess or teacher? Sadly, she wasn't trained to be useful in any other legitimate profession, and she refused to think of the illegitimate ones.

In fact, the only person who would support Amelia's position was away on her honeymoon. Ruby Hollings-

ford and the Earl of Danning had wed by special license
and were off on their wedding trip to Yorkshire, where
the fishing was supposed to be excellent.

Still, she thought and prayed as the next three weeks
passed, but no solution presented itself. Each Sunday,
she sat in church, listened to her name and Lord Hascot's being read aloud, endured the stares and murmurs
that inevitably started anew. She kept her head high,
accepted the congratulations offered her, fended off the
questions, the conjectures. The *ton* was agog that the
beautiful, talented Lady Amelia, daughter of the powerful Marquess of Wesworth, had settled on a taciturn
provincial baron. They expected her to confess an undying devotion, a sudden passion.

She refused to lie. So she said nothing.

But she didn't stop thinking. She thought while
her mother had her measured for a wedding gown of
creamy satin. She thought while she embroidered the
last pink rose on the lawn nightgown for her trousseau.
She thought as she directed the servants in packing her
belongings—clothing, books, sheet music, favorite fur-
niture, watercolors she'd painted—for the trip to Hollyoak Farm.

She had two choices she could see—to convince her
father that Lord Hascot wasn't the right son-in-law to
bring credit to the Wesworth title or to convince Lord
Hascot that marriage to her served no one. She thought
she'd have better luck with Lord Hascot, but he had immediately decamped for Derby, intending to return just
before the wedding, and it was not a subject to be presented by a letter. That left her father.

She'd never had luck simply wandering into his study
for a conversation. For one, he was more often to be

found at his club or Parliament. For another, even when he was home, he always had more important matters that required his attention. To Amelia's mind, nothing should be more important than his daughter's marriage, so she lay in wait for him in the breakfast room three days running before finally catching him.

"Is there a problem?" he asked as he looked up from that morning's *Times* to find her standing by his side.

Every other man of her acquaintance rose in her presence. "Yes, Father," she said, forcing herself to say the words she had rehearsed. "I am convinced that Lord Hascot will not be an asset to the family. He lacks address, he has no influence on Parliament, as you pointed out, and his title is far inferior to yours. We can do better."

He took a sip of his tea before answering her, fingers firm on the handle of the gilt-edged cup. "No doubt. But plans are in place, Amelia. Promises have been made. I need this alliance. If he treats you badly, you can always come home."

He seemed to think that a kindness, and she did not know how to tell him that home had always been where she was treated worst of all.

That night, she threw herself on her knees beside her tester bed, hands clasped and gaze on the gold drape of the half canopy. "Father, help me! I don't know what else to do, where else to turn. Surely this isn't Your will."

Yet what if it was, that voice inside her whispered. God could turn ashes to beauty, make good come from tragedy. Could He make something from this marriage?

The answer came the night before her wedding and from an unexpected source.

Amelia had not seen Lord Hascot since the day he had proposed, but her mother assured her he had returned to London and was staying at the Fenton. How she knew this, Amelia didn't question. All the servants reported to her mother anything they saw or heard. That was one of the reasons Amelia intended to leave her maid behind if she married Lord Hascot. The outspoken Dorcus Turner would suit the woman Amelia was becoming much better than the cowed creatures her mother seemed to hire. In fact, it was her mother who came to tell Amelia that Lord Hascot wished to speak to her.

"I tried to dissuade him," her mother complained, pacing in the bedchamber where she'd come to announce their visitor. "You are far too busy with preparations at this time to speak with him."

All the preparations were made for the wedding at St. George's Hanover Square at nine o'clock with a breakfast to follow at the house. All Amelia had to do was convince herself to go through with it. What, was her mother worried that she'd take this opportunity to refuse him?

The very thought forced her to her feet, had her eagerly following her mother down to the withdrawing room, thanking God for the opportunity and praying for the words to persuade her unwanted betrothed to cry off.

Lord Hascot was waiting, standing by the hearth, though his gaze was on the door. At the sight of her, he stood taller and inclined his head in greeting. Some of his coal-black hair fell across his forehead. He must have been in a hurry, for he hadn't even given his greatcoat to their servants. She remembered the soft wool that had covered her that night in the abandoned stable.

She hadn't realized she'd be trading it for a wedding ring.

"Good evening, my lord," she said, following her mother into the room.

"Yes, good evening," her mother said, as if remembering her own manners. She hovered around as Amelia seated herself on the sofa, asking about refreshments, his activities in London, the state of his stock. Odd. She had never known her mother to chatter.

When she stopped for a breath, he said, "I'd like to speak to Amelia. Alone."

Her mother visibly swallowed, skin paling. She was afraid! Her stubborn, demanding mother was afraid to see her plans dashed. Pity stung her, and Amelia put a hand on her arm.

"It's all right, Mother. I'm sure Lord Hascot simply wishes to speak of things that will follow our wedding."

Now her mother's color came flooding back, and she hurriedly excused herself.

"Nicely done," Lord Hascot said as the door shut behind her.

Amelia managed a smile. "Thank you. But I wasn't trying to mislead her. Why else would you come but to tell me your expectations?"

He licked his lips. Like the rest of his features, they were firm and sharp, as if chiseled that day from fresh marble. But what surprised her was that she saw a sheen of perspiration under the fall of his black hair.

"Are you certain you want to go through with this?" she marveled.

She wasn't sure how he would respond. Perhaps some

part of her hoped for a declaration of secret devotion. The rest of her could only pray she'd given him license to beg off. Instead, he motioned her to the sofa and came to sit next to her, so gingerly she wondered if he thought he might stain the white upholstery.

"I'm not in the slightest certain," he told her. "But I see no other way. I have given my word."

Could it be so easy to rid herself of this stone-cold lord? Amelia found it hard to breathe with the possibility. "If you don't wish to marry me, sir, simply tell me."

He took a deep breath as if he fought for air, as well. "It is not what I wish, but what you wish."

The statement was so far beyond anything she had ever experienced that Amelia blinked. "What?"

He rubbed his hands along his coat, gaze on the movement of his fingers. "I never planned to marry. I have no time to be a doting husband. But if you wish to be my wife, you are welcome at Hollyoak Farm. I will keep the stables and the horses. The house will be yours to command. And I will expect you to manage any visitors who come merely to look."

He made it sound as if she was accepting a position. "And the payment for my services?" she couldn't help asking.

He frowned as if he didn't understand her. "You will have a home, the funding to furnish and decorate it as you like and as much as you could want for dresses, though I can't imagine you will need many out in Derby. Know that I will honor my vows, and I will treat you with respect."

Respect. Not love, not devotion. It was less than what she'd prayed for, but the new woman who was emerging seemed drawn to it. It was something she'd never had after all. And if he intended to honor his vows, then someday she might hope for children.

Something fierce and strong rose up inside her. She would have children to love, to dote upon as surely as if she had wished it for herself. That would be the good to come from this marriage, that would be God's blessing for her trials.

"Very well, my lord," she said. "I accept your offer. We will marry in the morning. And may God smile upon our union."

Chapter Five

And so she was married. She stood before the rector, her parents and a few friends among the dark wood paneling and soaring stained glass windows of St. George's Hanover Square. She repeated her vows and listened to John repeat his in that gruff voice. It wasn't until she said, "Till death do us part," that a tremor ran through her. She could only hope no one else noticed.

She continued smiling as they returned to her parents' home and the receiving line down the corridor as guests progressed to the wedding breakfast at tables her mother had had erected in the withdrawing room. She accepted congratulations, thanked the noble guests for their good wishes. She counted three dukes, two marquesses and an earl who was related to the king. And all of them seemed far more interested in making her husband's acquaintance than in wishing her well.

John did not appear the least bit humbled by the attentions paid him. He stood beside her, nodding, exchanging few words. His sharp features and hooded gaze reminded her of a falcon she'd seen once. That bird had been wary, gaze sweeping the grassy lands for prey. She didn't like the thought that perhaps this time she was the mouse.

"Well done," Lord Danning said, next in line to congratulate them. A tall man with golden hair, his ready smile to her and John eased her tension. But it was the sight of Ruby beside him that truly raised her spirits.

Marriage obviously agreed with her friend, for Ruby's green eyes positively sparkled, and her mouth was stretched wide in a grin. Her red hair was tamed under a fashionable chip hat, an ostrich plume curling down around her ear to tease her cheek.

"As soon as you're finished," she said, giving Amelia's arm a squeeze, "come find me. I can't wait to hear all."

Amelia wasn't sure how much she dared relate with so many other people about. But after the guests had been seated for the wedding breakfast, she managed to slip away with Ruby into the gardens behind the house.

"I know the two of you met when you were up at Fern Lodge with us, but I won't believe it was love at first sight," Ruby declared in her forthright manner. She linked arms with Amelia as they strolled the white-rocked paths among the low boxwood hedges. "So what happened? Did he follow you to London? Plead his case on bended knee?"

"Not quite," Amelia admitted, going on to explain the situation. When she finished, Ruby's face tightened.

"Not the most auspicious of beginnings," she agreed. "Do you at least admire him?"

Amelia thought hard. He was cool but generally considerate in a rough sort of way. He was not much of a conversationalist. He did not seem to be particularly devoted to family.

"He is by all accounts good with his horses," she finally said.

The faint praise hung in the sunny morning air a moment. She glanced at Ruby, and suddenly they were both giggling.

"He looks presentable in a jacket and trousers," Ruby offered.

"His nose is not offensive," Amelia countered.

"He does slip out of services on Sunday to race his carriage," Ruby assured her.

"And he isn't an avid fisherman," Amelia proclaimed triumphantly.

Ruby hugged the sides of her emerald gown as if to hold in her laughter. "Oh, so true! You are very fortunate there, you know. On my honeymoon, I learned fifteen different ways to entice a trout to rise. Who would have thought the silly things so fussy!"

"Or so determined," Amelia agreed.

Ruby sobered. "Indeed. I never thought I'd give the time of day to a trout other than to gobble him down for dinner. But I have come to care about such things as fishing because *he* cares about them. I'm sure it will be the same with you and Lord Hascot."

Amelia could only hope her friend was right. In truth, she'd always enjoyed riding. Why shouldn't she enjoy helping John with his horses? Perhaps they could find companionship of a sort, at the very least.

Her doubts returned the moment they stepped out of the house for the carriage.

She had changed into her travel attire, a corded surge gown of navy blue with a feather-trimmed bonnet, and John had changed into a rough tweed coat and brown trousers. Her mother took one look at his scuffed boots and turned her back on him. But Amelia could see him frowning at the lumbering travel coach and wagon standing behind his trim carriage.

"What's all this?" he asked.

Before Amelia could answer, her mother drew herself up. She'd been far too busy with her other guests the past few hours to pay much attention to her daughter or new son-in-law. Now she affixed him with an imperial glare.

"These are Amelia's belongings, her contribution to your home, sir," she informed him.

He eyed the chair leg poking out of the canvas covering the back of the wagon. "My home is sufficiently furnished, madam. You may keep your castoffs."

"Well, I never!" her mother cried, face reddening.

Amelia stepped in the middle from long practice. "They are not castoffs, my lord, but a few pieces of which I am very fond. Being a bachelor household, your home likely lacks some of the things a woman needs."

Now he frowned at her. As frowns went, it was fairly formidable. His dark brows drew down over his long nose in a V that made his deep brown eyes cavernous. She imagined his staff must duck and scurry when they saw such a look. Being her father's daughter, she had seen worse.

"Such as?" he demanded.

"A jewelry case?" Amelia guessed. "A dressing table? Poetry by Shakespeare and Everard?"

His brow cleared. "Very well. But it will all have to come later. I intend to make Dovecote Dale by dinner tomorrow, and I won't be held up by the pace of that wagon."

"Now, see here," her mother started, but Amelia's father came out of the house just then, approaching them with measured tread. As if Amelia's mother saw defeat coming, she called to her servants to do as Lord Hascot requested.

That necessitated a rush among her parents' staff to ensure Amelia had what she'd need for the next three or four days before the coach and wagon reached the farm. Then it was time to say goodbye.

Her mother went so far as to hug her, her arms wrapped around Amelia's shoulders, her head resting against Amelia's. She couldn't remember the last time her mother had been so demonstrative, and tears pricked her eyes.

Then her mother whispered, "Remember your vows, Amelia."

Her vows? Did her mother think she would be unfaithful? The very idea hurt so much that the tears overflowed. Her mother must have noticed them as she disengaged, because she patted Amelia's hand.

"There now, it shouldn't be so hard," she said, voice unusually quiet for her. "You were always an obedient child, until recently. Just see that you treat your husband with a similar level of agreeability."

Obedience. Agreeability. That was what her mother expected of her. Normally, it was what Amelia expected of herself, as well. "Honor thy father and mother," the Bible said. She would continue to honor them, but she was no longer their child. And though she was Lord Hascot's wife, she could not help feeling that perhaps she might at last become her own person.

Her father merely extended his hand, and she accepted it in farewell.

"I trust we will see you in London this fall," he said, and Amelia could tell by the way his pale blue gaze shifted to John that he was addressing her new husband.

She couldn't help glancing at John, as well. He stood next to the open door of the carriage, waiting for her to climb in.

"I come to London in the spring for a sale at Tattersalls," he said. "Amelia is free to come whenever she likes."

Her father released her hand and turned to offer his arm to his wife. That was all that need be said. She blinked back the tears and went to join John in the carriage. When would she learn that nothing about her warranted her father's attention?

Would it merit her husband's? And if it did, would she want his attention?

She watched him as the coach sped out of Mayfair. He had taken the rear-facing bench with his back to the driver, leaving her the leather-upholstered forward-facing seat. With the curtains drawn back from the windows, light flooded the compartment so that she could see every plane of his face, the way his coat draped his tall frame, the grip of his gloved fists on the edge of the bench. This was the man with whom she would spend the rest of her life.

The man who would sire her children.

Heat flushed up her face. Surely they needn't discuss children so soon. They had just wed. He was in a rush to return home. But he'd said he wished to reach the farm by tomorrow dinner. That meant they would spend the night together along the way.

Lord, help me! I don't think I can do this.

Across the coach, John watched Amelia. Her face had turned that delicate pink it did when she was concerned about something, and now she took a deep breath and folded her hands in the lap of her dark blue gown. She was frightened and trying to pretend otherwise. He'd seen similar behavior in a horse new to the herd.

Of course, she'd been tense all day. In the pale satin gown beside him at the altar she'd stood so still she'd looked as if she was made of fine crystal. He'd felt the tremor pass through her when she'd said her vows. She was still no surer of their decision to marry than he was.

He leaned back, but the leather behind him was less forgiving than the look on her face. "You will make an excellent wife, you know."

She raised a brow. "On what do you base that assessment, sir?"

She seemed to think his confidence a complaint. Given the man who was her father, he could understand why.

"It is my impression that all young ladies in Society are schooled in the efficient running of a household," he explained.

She continued to regard him. "So you lack a housekeeper, a butler."

"I have a butler." Why was the seat feeling harder every moment? John shifted, trying to get comfortable. "I have an entire staff, but they have received little attention with my efforts focused on the horses. I'm sure improvements could be made."

He thought she relaxed a little. "I'd be happy to help there. And I'm looking forward to helping with your horses, as well."

His muscles stiffened as if in protest. "I need no help with the horses."

She inclined her head. "I didn't mean to imply that

you did, my lord. I trust you located the one that had disappeared the day you found me in the stable."

John nodded. If she intended to merely talk about his horses instead of attempting to manage them, he could oblige. It was the one topic of conversation where he actually felt confident. "We did. She crossed the bridge and wandered toward town. A farmer alerted us, and we brought her home."

"Do they wander a great deal?" she asked, surprise in her voice.

"Not at all. Horses are herd animals. They feel safer together. But Contessa is another matter."

"Contessa." She smiled as if the name pleased her. "Quite a lady, I take it."

"Our queen. She leads the herd. Contessa is a direct-line descendent of the Byerley Turk and one of the finest animals you'll find in England."

"I've heard of the Turk," she said, eyes wide as if the relationship impressed her. "Father has several descendants. They are all exceptionally fine animals. Did Contessa race?"

"No," John said, and even now the memory hurt. "She was the first horse I bought myself when I was still at university. My father thought I was becoming too attached. Maudlin sentimentality, he called it. He sold her to a colonel who took her to the Peninsula."

Her hand pressed against her pretty pink lips a moment. "Oh, no! Did she see action, then?"

"A great deal. She was finally pulled down on the Spanish frontier. The colonel thought enough of her to send her home to recuperate, but it was clear she'd never support a cavalry run again. And I was able then to buy her back. She was the first horse I brought to Hollyoak."

Could she hear the pride in his words? Did she appreciate its source? He'd never met anyone who could understand his devotion to his horses. He knew most men saw them as nothing more than transportation, perhaps an acknowledgment of their prestige. They were far more to him. No horse had ever spurned his friendship, lied to his face or stabbed him in the back.

"Small wonder you went looking for her in a thunderstorm." She smiled at him, and even though he'd felt justified in his efforts for the mare, his work suddenly felt noble. It was as if Amelia approved of him.

Dangerous stuff that, his emotions turning on her smile. He refused to be so easily led again.

"You needn't be concerned I'll set you a similar task," he assured her. "You'll have enough to keep you busy without dealing with the horses. Buyers appear frequently, often without warning. As I said, I expect you to deal with those who come merely to look. That includes keeping the wives and daughters occupied."

"And safely away from the horses," she said.

It was in him to agree, but something in the way she said it told him agreement wasn't wise.

"I'm more than happy to show a lady my stock," he said instead. "But I've found most have little interest."

"Perhaps if you asked," she replied, gaze dropping at last, "you might find them quite interested indeed."

Was she talking about his buyers or herself? She certainly seemed interested in the conversation. She had looked out for Belle as best she could that night in the stable, and she had risen to Contessa's defense when she'd initially heard the mare was missing. Still, he could not believe his horses would ever be as important to her as they were to him.

She seemed to think the conversation finished, for she lapsed into silence. Her gaze went to the window as if hoping to see their destination in the distance. He knew they had far to go yet. Gazing backward from where he sat on the rear-facing bench, he could see that the stone buildings of London were disappearing to be replaced by golden fields of grain and neat hedgerows. As they took a bend in the road, he spotted another fellow following them. John frowned.

"Something wrong, my lord?" Amelia asked.

Had she been watching him? John shook his head, as much at his vanity as to answer her question. "There's someone behind us," he said. "Cob of a horse, sway-backed, hollow sides, which generally means poor pasture or not enough grain. And he pulls too hard on the bit."

Amelia turned to eye the road back. "You can tell all that at a glance?"

John shrugged. "You can tell a lot about a horse and his rider if you know where to look. This fellow isn't comfortable riding. He's holding the reins too far out from his body and using his heels over much."

"I see what you mean." She turned to eye John now. "Is he following us?"

Was that worry he heard in her voice?

"Anyone can use the king's highway," he replied. "But there have been no reports of highwaymen along this route. I wouldn't be concerned."

She nodded, but he wasn't sure she believed him.

The afternoon stretched. John busied himself planning an extension to the main stable block, but when the coach finally pulled into the yard of the Fox and Hound Inn that evening, Amelia still sat primly across the coach, hands folded in her lap. He offered her a smile as the carriage stopped. The smile she returned was small and tight.

What had he done to offend her? Had she expected scintillating conversation after their other encounters? Or was she a woman who held a grudge for every little slight? He didn't like thinking about his future in that case. The good Lord knew there were all too many ways John had found to offend people, even without trying!

"Lord Hascot, Lady Hascot, welcome!" the innkeeper warbled on seeing them, his broad smile at odds with his lean frame. "Your rooms are ready, just as you requested, my lord. May I serve dinner in the private parlor in an hour?"

"Make it a half hour," John told him. "I'm famished. This way, my lady."

"Rooms?" she whispered as he led her toward the stairs, and something trembled in her voice. "Separate rooms?"

"Of course," he said.

Then she finally smiled at him, and he nearly missed a step from the blinding brilliance.

She'd thought he'd intended them to sleep together, and she clearly wasn't thrilled with the idea. He should have expected that. Caro had cooed over him, calling him her brooding darling, but he had never been sure that was a compliment. Certainly he'd never mastered the flowery language that was supposed to set women dreaming of sweet kisses. Perhaps he should have let Amelia bring her poetry in the coach.

Then again, he wasn't ready to consummate the marriage, either. He would have to be six feet under not to find those platinum tresses, that lithe figure attractive.

But people were not as simple as horses, and it took more than attraction to make a good marriage, the kind that nurtured children.

His father might have questioned John's attachment to his horses, but John thought a proper father would take an interest in his offspring, show them how to get on in the world, introduce them to important things like prayer and riding. Right now he stumbled over the former and would probably be too critical of the latter. And he would certainly never condone raising a hand to his child.

"Never fear, your ladyship," he said as he left her at her room, the scent of orange blossoms hanging tantalizingly in the air. "I do not intend to claim my matrimonial rights until we are both satisfied it is the best course."

If he was not the man he was, he might have taken exception with how happy that seemed to make her.

Still, he could not fault her that evening. Now that she was no longer concerned about how they would spend the night, she was pleasing company.

She presided over the meal; he could think of no other word for it. She folded her elegant hands once more and recited the grace with bowed head. As if she was honoring him as a guest in her own house, she served him from the ragout of beef the innkeeper brought, offered him seconds when he gulped it down and made sure he was given the largest piece of the peach tart that accompanied the meal. Through it all, she kept up a steady stream of polite conversation that required no more than a nod from him unless he wished otherwise.

Indeed, the evening and the next day passed in such

undemanding comfort that he was surprised to hear the rumble of the wheels as they crossed the River Bell, which marked the edge of his property.

He had purchased Hollyoak Farm on his twenty-fifth birthday with monies left him by his mother and immediately set about improving it. Now solid stable wings stretched parallel to each other out behind the house, pasture and planted grain waving away in all directions. He could see Contessa dashing across the nearest field with the odd gait the old lady had conceived to compensate for her injury. The very air smelled sweeter as he opened the carriage door in the yard behind the house.

Across the back of the building, his staff had lined up to welcome him and his new bride in the glow of a setting sun. John walked beside her, told her names and positions, nodded his appreciation for their gesture. Amelia smiled graciously, greeted each person by name after John had introduced him and made an appropriate remark about their positions.

By the time they reached the end of the line, he couldn't help noticing that half his men were grinning like idiots and another third were blushing like debutantes at their first ball. A few, however, frowned, clearly skeptical of the success of this newcomer in their ranks.

He was not nearly so skeptical. In fact, he had a feeling that, unless he was very careful, Amelia was going to be entirely too successful—at managing his life.

Chapter Six

So many people, and all here to greet her. It was rather gratifying. Amelia turned her smile on her new husband, who did not look nearly as happy as she felt.

"And may I see the stables?" she asked sweetly.

If anything, his scowl deepened. "Perhaps another time."

As he took her arm, his men melted into the background, away from his scowl. They knew to be obedient. She was beginning to think obedience to be overrated. It was clear that if she wanted to learn more about her husband's horses, she would have to insist.

For now, she focused instead on the house. She knew from her previous visit that the corridor from the rear door led straight through to the front. As she entered this time, she smelled garlic as if from a recent meal emanating from the room to the left.

"The kitchen," John confirmed with a nod in that direction. "And the staff hall. My library is opposite."

An odd place for a library, but then she supposed it gave him a clear view out to the stables while he worked.

The way along the dark-paneled walls and through an arch under the main stairs was familiar. The man waiting by the front door was not. He was not as tall as John, his arms and legs stuck out as if someone had sewed them on carelessly and his red hair was so curly it looked as if a rouged puff sat on his head. His smile was the widest she'd seen at Hollyoak Farm.

"Lady Hascot," he said with a bow so deep he nearly lost his spectacles. "Welcome home."

"This is our resident veterinarian," John said as he straightened. "Marcus Fletcher."

"Dr. Fletcher," Amelia said, offering him her hand, which disappeared inside his long-fingered grip. "A pleasure to meet you."

"Fletcher has his own quarters on the property," John explained as the man released her hand. "He generally takes his meals with me."

"If that pleases you, your ladyship," the veterinarian hurried to add.

She imagined some brides would be highly incensed to find another person sitting daily at the table. All she could think was that at least she and John would not be stuck trying to converse with one another again. "I'm sure that will be delightful, Doctor," she told him.

He beamed at her. "Excellent! Not tonight, of course. I have a patient I must see to."

John stiffened beside her. "One of the horses is ill?"

"Firenza," his veterinarian replied with a grimace. "I think she may have found some water hemlock by the creek. I noticed it last week and had Peters root it up, but she may have stumbled on a stray patch. All the symptoms are there."

"Is it deadly?" Amelia asked, but John had already stepped away from her to take the doctor's arm.

"You've purged her, of course? Good man. Can she stand? We should walk her about the stables to keep her breathing."

"She's still having convulsions." Dr. Fletcher was moving back the way they had come, John pacing him. "I've taken the liberty of clearing out the other horses near her to keep from frightening them."

Would they simply leave her standing there? "My lord?" Amelia tried.

"Good thought," John agreed. "I can't believe she'd eat the hemlock. She turns up her nose at apples! I've never seen such a picky eater."

They were nearly to the arch. Amelia took a step forward and raised her voice. "John!"

He stopped and looked back at her as if surprised to find her in his home. "Yes, your ladyship?"

"I understand this is an emergency," Amelia said, keeping her voice calm as she always did when her mother made unreasonable demands. "But perhaps you could show me to my room first?"

He waved a hand up the stairs beside her. "Next floor up, first door on the left. That maid should be waiting." He disappeared under the arch with his veterinarian.

Well! Amelia shook her head, gathered her skirts and marched up the stairs to the next floor. Four doors opened off the U-shaped corridor, and she easily found the room he'd indicated. His staff must have been apprised of the arrangements, for the trunk and bandboxes she'd been able to bring with her were waiting at the foot of the bed.

So was Turner. The maid also gave Amelia a big

smile before spreading her gray skirts in a curtsy. "Welcome home, your ladyship. I'm honored to be serving you again."

She seemed so glad to see Amelia that the room felt warmer. "Thank you, Turner," Amelia replied. "I shall have to write to your mistress to thank her as well for allowing me to make use of your skills."

Turner's smile faded. "My mistress was moved to London, your ladyship. And the new mistress of Rotherford Grange chose another girl for her maid."

Amelia didn't know the situation, but she couldn't help thinking the mistress of Rotherford Grange had made a mistake. The maid clearly knew her job. She proved it by setting to work unpacking Amelia's things.

As Amelia helped, she studied her new bedchamber. Like much of the rest of the house she'd seen so far, the paneling on the walls was so dark it was nearly black. The hangings on the walnut bed were navy chintz, the carpet forest-green. She felt as if she had wandered into the woods on a moonless night. It was not a promising beginning.

So she set to work to improve things. She lit all the lamps, brightening the space, and unpacked her toiletries and arranged them on the highboy dresser along one wall. The gleaming glass of the perfume bottles reflected in the polished wood.

The dark covering on the bed would have to stay until the rest of her things arrived in a few days, but she envisioned it with the white lace edging her mother had had made. Even better was the pocket door Turner discovered on the other side of the bed, leading to a decent-size dressing room with space for all Amelia's gowns.

Having a few of her things around her made the room

feel even more welcoming. Turner helped her change from her travel attire into a day dress and brushed and repinned her hair, which made her feel better, too. She could do this. She was born to do this. *Mistress of Hollyoak Farm* had a fine ring to it.

A protest from her stomach reminded Amelia that she hadn't had dinner. She checked the black-lacquered ormolu clock on the serpentine marble fireplace and frowned. What sort of hours did they keep here? She'd always heard people complain of the early bedtimes in the country, but surely the members of Hollyoak Farm ate before retiring.

Knowing Turner was as new to the farm as she was, Amelia rang for the footman, who arrived at the door a short time later.

"When will dinner be served?" Amelia asked.

He shifted on the carpet. None of the men she'd met wore any standard attire. His coat was brown, his breeches gray, and his shoes had not been shined in some time. "His lordship never asked for dinner tonight, your ladyship," he offered. "He and Dr. Fletcher will likely be too busy to eat."

This was ridiculous! She might have been ignored at home, but she'd never gone hungry. "Very well. Tell the cook I'll take a tray in my room."

He scratched his head. "Mr. Shanter has already gone to bed, ma'am."

Once she would not even have slumped in disappointment. A lady did not raise her voice after all. She was calm, composed, in any situation. That was how one could tell the aristocracy from the lesser orders.

But even the aristocracy required food. And she knew what good service should look like.

Amelia raised her head and affixed the footman with her most determined look. "Then Mr. Shanter has a choice. He can either get up and fix me dinner or expect me to invade his kitchen and do so myself. Which do you think he would prefer?"

The cook at home would have danced on a pin before he allowed someone else to touch his kitchen. Of course, he would never have refused a request for food, either.

The footman shrugged, but he didn't meet her gaze. "Mr. Shanter likes his sleep. Best not to wake him."

"Your ladyship?"

Bewildered by such an attitude, Amelia turned at the maid's voice. Turner's face was a fiery red, but her tone to Amelia was polite. "If you'd allow me?"

Bemused, Amelia nodded.

Turner stepped forward and shook her finger at the footman. "Now, you listen to me. This lady is your new mistress. She has the run of this household. You go find this cook of yours, and you drag him out of bed to fetch my lady some dinner. And it had better be a good dinner, too, or the two of you will be whistling for your own supper on the road tomorrow." She poked him in the chest. "Understand?"

The footman visibly gulped as he backed up. "Yes, Miss Turner, your ladyship. Coming right up." He ran from the room.

Amelia couldn't help her smile. "Rather forceful for someone new to the household."

Turner grinned. "I won't be staying long, only until you pick a new maid, I understand, so it makes no never mind what they think of me." She cocked her head. "But you can't allow such behavior in your household, your ladyship. Mrs. Dunworthy, my former mistress, she was too harsh in her ways, and everyone hated her for it. But this? This is too gentle. You deserve their respect."

An interesting thought. She'd always been treated well by the servants in her parents' home, but it hadn't been her doing. She doubted anyone would dare misbehave knowing how her mother and father would react.

She'd agreed to marry John because he'd promised to treat her with respect. She hadn't expected to have to deal with a lack of respect from his servants. Just how hard would she have to work to earn the title of mistress of Hollyoak Farm?

Dawn was a thin line of gold over the hills when John returned from the stables. Firenza, a fiery-coated mare, was at least stable, though Fletcher felt she wasn't out of danger yet. John had agreed to catch a few hours of sleep so he could spell the veterinarian later in the day.

He climbed the stairs, intending only to make it to his room and collapse. With any luck, the footman would just be getting up and could help John with his boots. At the first-floor landing, however, he couldn't help noticing that the door to the room he'd given Amelia was ajar.

Guilt poked at him. He'd dragged her from London at a frantic pace, then abandoned her in the entry hall to find her own way. Surely a husband owed his wife more than that.

His mother had died when he and his twin brother were twelve, his father when they were twenty-two. But he remembered his parents together. They'd had a way of exchanging glances that spoke more than words possibly could. He'd always thought when he fell in love, it would be like that.

But when he'd courted Caro, more often than not he'd

found himself staring at her in awe. How could one of the most popular, vivacious women of the *ton* be interested in him? And as for conversation, he'd been content merely to listen.

Amelia would likely require more than merely listening. For one thing, she spoke as little as he did! And he truly should explain how things worked at Hollyoak Farm.

He glanced into her room. A candle was sputtering in its holder next to the bed. Amelia, wrapped in a satin dressing gown of a blue that likely matched her eyes, was slumped against the headboard as if she'd fallen asleep sitting up.

Waiting for him.

It had been a long time since someone had cared about his comings and goings. Oh, his staff was competent, and Fletcher was a good if single-minded friend, focused on his duties to the horses, which was just as it should be. With John and his brother being twins, there had never been a point in his life when anyone had focused on his needs alone. He was a little surprised about how pleasant it felt.

Perhaps he should return the favor. He'd already put her to bed once after all, when she'd slumped on the box in the stable. He'd carried her to the straw, trying not to notice how good she felt in his arms. Now he slipped into the room and moved to her side to settle the pillow under her head. Her hair, freed from the bun she normally wore, spilled like moonlight across the linens.

His wife.

What had he promised at the wedding ceremony? To protect and cherish her all the days of his life. He hadn't made a very auspicious beginning. The trouble was, he wasn't sure he had it in him to do better.

Her eyes opened, met his gaze and widened in surprise. Though he had every right to be there and had only been trying to help, John stiffened.

"My lord," she said, pushing herself upright. "Is everything all right?"

John nodded, backing away from her. "Fine. Firenza is settled. I was just on my way to bed."

She glanced at the clock on the mantel, then back at him. "To bed? But it's morning."

John spread his hands. "Such is life at Hollyoak Farm."

Her lovely lips thinned. "So I am beginning to understand. I take it horses do not appreciate a particular routine."

John couldn't help a smile. "Horses are creatures of habit. We generally start at dawn each morning, watering them, then letting them out to pasture or taking them for exercise. We have to clean the stables, check the pastures for nuisance plants like the one that nearly felled Firenza, confirm the fences are in good repair. Each horse must have horseshoes and harness and saddle. Then there's the training to be the best on the hunting field, with obstacles to jump and learning to get along with hounds, not to mention the planting of hay for the winter."

She frowned. "And you are involved with all of this?"

Very likely her exalted father had never dirtied his hands. Most of the men with whom John had been raised found his need to be involved perplexing. A gentleman accepted the rents from his properties; he did not actually do anything on those properties.

"Yes," he said, head high. "These are my horses. I take personal responsibility for them. Would you turn the care of your children completely over to others, madam?"

That delicate pink was rising in her cheeks again, as bright as the petals on the wildflowers that grew in his pastures. She dropped her gaze, fingers toying with the coverlet on the bed. "No, indeed, my lord. I consider children a blessing from God, a gift to be cherished."

A gift he was denying her. John backed away another step. "Then perhaps you will understand why I take such care of my horses. I'm going to sleep for a time, but if you need me, have the footman wake me."

"Wait." She sat up taller, her satiny hair falling about her. "You told me that the inside of this house was mine to order. Did you mean that?"

John nodded. "Of course. I never say anything I don't mean."

A smile teased her lips. "Very commendable, sir. Then I take it you won't mind if I put the household on as reliable a schedule as your horses."

John felt his frown forming again. "What sort of schedule?"

Those blue eyes held no secrets. "When meals are served, when certain tasks are performed."

Suddenly he knew how Contessa felt. The proud mare disliked any fence and had found ways over and around them, even with her game leg. John felt as if someone was enclosing his pasture before his very eyes.

"Tasks?" he asked. "I wasn't aware a household required laborious tasking."

"Perhaps not as laborious as training a horse," she

agreed. "But silver must be polished, linens washed, flues emptied. That sort of thing."

All indoor things, far away from him. That was what he'd asked her to do after all. Changing should not be so very difficult. And yet it was.

"Very well," John made himself say, but he couldn't leave it at that. She had to know that the horses must come first, always.

"As for the timing of the meals," he continued, finding himself pacing before her, hands behind his back like an Eton don, "we generally have all the animals back in the stables by six, so if dinner were served a half hour later, all the staff should be ready. Barring unforeseen circumstances, such as illness or injury to one of the horses, of course."

"Of course." How could anyone argue with that pleasant smile? "And breakfast, I take it, should be early."

"Very early," John insisted.

Her smile grew. "Then I think tea midday would also be advisable. Very good, my lord. I will see to it immediately. You need have no concerns."

Though something told him the response sounded more like a servant than a wife, he nodded. "I will wish you good morning, then, madam."

"Good morning, my lord," she said brightly. "Sleep well."

He nodded again and turned, but he had a funny feeling that sleep would be eluding him that morning. And perhaps for a number of days to come.

Chapter Seven

Amelia knew the duties of a wife. Her governess had explained them in great detail; her mother had embodied them each day. A wife ordered the running of the household—from setting the times and menus of meals to inventorying the linens. A wife determined the decoration of each room, planned all events. A wife was a credit to her husband, in demeanor, in dress and in her good works. And above all else, a wife bore her husband an heir. Anything less was failure.

She knew how failure presented itself. She'd seen her mother's misery, her father's cool disdain when Amelia had been their only issue. She had no wish to live that way. But she had a great many things to do before this household was ready for a family.

She started that very morning.

"Inform the butler I'd like to discuss staffing," she told Turner as Amelia ate breakfast on a tray in bed.

"Yes, your ladyship," the maid said, picking up the gown Amelia had ordered for the day. Her fingers stroked the soft muslin, brushed out the fine lace at the hem, smile wistful.

"And tell Mr. Shanter, the cook, that I will expect him in the withdrawing room at ten to discuss menus."

Turner laid the gown reverently on the covers, then straightened with a snort. "He's still abed. He left out apples and cold popovers for breakfast. I made your tea and toast myself over the fire in the servant's hall."

Amelia narrowed her eyes. "In that case, tell him I expect to see him at nine."

Turner smiled in obvious satisfaction.

That left Amelia an hour after dressing to take a tour of the house herself. She had already determined there to be four bedchambers on this story, each, it appeared, with its own dressing room. She hadn't looked in John's room. Doing so somehow seemed impertinent.

The floor above held another bedchamber and a suite that included a schoolroom, nursery and quarters for the staff. Downstairs, she found a dining room opposite the withdrawing room, just as John's library sat opposite the kitchen. Every room had a least one wall of the black paneling, and most were covered with it. That would be the first thing she dealt with—if she could not have it removed, she'd mask it with lighter paintings or wall hangings.

But though she felt compelled to open the drapes and let in the light in each of the rooms, she could see that the house had potential. She could find fault with the lack of formal function rooms like a ballroom, but it did not appear she would ever need to host a ball here.

Which was a very good thing, as it became clearer every moment that she hadn't the staff to maintain the house, much less entertain.

The butler met her as planned in the withdrawing room. She'd located a secretary in the corner, lowered the desk and set up paper, blotter, quill and ink, prepared to note anything of use in her plans for the house. But when she asked him about the inventory of linen and silver, he grimaced.

"There's little enough of either," he complained. "Lord Hascot rarely entertains indoors, and he has been reticent to make any changes that affect the household budget. I advise you not to alter the current state of affairs."

She'd noticed that John had stiffened when she'd begun making suggestions about the running of the household. She'd thought he was simply unaccustomed to change. Now she could only wonder whether there was some other reason her ideas concerned him.

The cook had further complaints. Mr. Shanter was a small man with a thin mustache that drooped on either side of his pinched mouth. She could only hope his cooking was more generous than his looks.

"Madam can have no understanding of the responsibility of cooking for so many," he whined, hands waving as if he was swatting flies. "Grooms, stable boys, the indoor staff. And Dr. Fletcher eats enough for two! I do the best I can with limited funds, but only God can work miracles!"

She couldn't understand it. Her mother had said John was well-off, even without the sale of his horses. Why was the household so short of funds?

Despite their protests, she managed to learn enough from the cook and butler to determine her most urgent problem. Besides the lack of a lady's maid, which assuredly they would not have needed before now, the house had only one footman who also served as John's valet. He apparently had the cleaning of the house and was perpetually behind from the amount of dust she'd seen. She wasn't entirely sure what the butler did, with only two other servants indoors. From the number of grooms she'd met last night, John certainly didn't run his stables in so Spartan a manner!

She didn't have a chance to ask him about the matter until dinner. She had had a stern conversation with Mr. Shanter about her expectations on the timing and composition of meals. The cook must have taken it to heart, because dinner was ready precisely at half-past six in the dining room.

At least the space was more inviting than other parts of the house. The dark paneling reached only to the middle of the walls, and the upper section was painted in squares of a soft jade. A painting of a horse's head was framed in the center of each panel. The table was long and polished as brightly as the silver that lay at the place settings. Amelia nodded with satisfaction as she waited.

But neither her husband nor his veterinarian joined her at the table. When Mr. Shanter peered in through the connecting door to the kitchen for the second time to see when the rest of the food should be served, Amelia threw down her napkin and rose.

"I'll be right back," she informed the footman, who was watching her warily as if expecting her to start throwing the potatoes that waited in their jackets, as well. "Keep everything warm."

She sailed out the back door of the house and drew to a stop in the center courtyard. The stables on either side seemed to stretch for miles. Where might she find her husband?

She ventured to the block on the left and peered inside. She had visited Hollyoak Farm with Lord Danning and his guests, so she wasn't surprised by the stone columns that marked the ends of each stall, the white walls that separated them, the troughs of sparkling clean water and baskets of fresh hay. She hadn't actually been inside this particular block before, and now she saw it also held John's carriage and farm implements. This must be where he housed his driving horses and work horses as well, though all appeared to be out at the moment.

The other block was nearly as empty, though she spotted Magnum just down the way. As if he knew she was watching him, he tossed his head, and she heard the ring of a hoof against the cobbles.

"Amelia." John came out of a stall farther down and strode toward her. His coat was rumpled, his hair disheveled even more than usual. "I just checked my watch. I expect I'll need reminding about your new schedule."

Part of her wanted to upbraid him for his rude behavior. A gentleman did not leave a lady to dine alone, yet he had served her that way not once but twice! However, the look on his face stayed her words. His eyes were hollow, his face whiter than the linens.

"Is something wrong, my lord?" she asked.

He managed a tight smile. "A sick horse is always cause for concern. We can't be sure it was the plant. If it's contagious, we could lose all of them."

She glanced around again. So many horses, each one finer than the last. She knew how she'd feel if something should happen to her Belle. How awful to lose all!

"Forgive me, my lord," she said. "You have more important matters to attend to than to cater to my whims. Do what you must. Don't be concerned about me."

He nodded and turned back for the stall.

Other gentlemen would have protested their devotion, promised to remain at her side forever. He had never misled her as to where his attentions lay. Amelia returned to the house.

The evening dragged. She had the footman move a few paintings from one room to another, but the fellow looked as if he was about to fall off his feet, so she sent him to bed. Likely he had to rise even earlier than John to have everything ready for his master.

She stood in the middle of the withdrawing room and felt impotent. She couldn't manage his house; he wouldn't allow her to help with the horses. She had friends who complained their only duty was to look pretty for their husbands. Her husband wasn't around enough to notice!

"Begging your pardon, your ladyship," Turner said, waiting in the doorway. "I wasn't sure your plans for the evening."

"It appears I have none," Amelia replied, and she led the maid upstairs for bed.

She had never been good at schooling her face to hide her feelings, so she wasn't surprised Turner noticed her frustration. And as she was beginning to know the maid's bold attitude, Amelia also wasn't surprised when Turner spoke up.

"If you ask me," she said as she helped Amelia into her nightgown, "a gentleman shouldn't spend two nights in a stable, especially after being wed less than a fortnight."

"Lord Hascot has a sick horse," Amelia explained.

"He has a sick wife, too," Turner replied. "Sick of being alone, I warrant."

"That will do, Turner," Amelia said.

The maid's lips compressed. She said nothing more until she had Amelia settled in bed. Then she stepped back.

"You ought to show him what's what, your ladyship," she insisted. "Just like you did with the butler and cook today."

"Turner," Amelia warned.

The maid drew herself up. "I warned you I can't hold my tongue, your ladyship. Not when I see something amiss, and there's plenty amiss with this house. You can send me back to the Grange tomorrow for saying so, but that man needs you. Everyone in the dale knows he's lonely."

Amelia frowned as she leaned back against the pillow. "Lonely?"

Turner took a step closer. "Yes, ma'am. How couldn't he be, no one but horses and horse-mad folk to talk to?"

She made it sound as if John's servants and buyers were somehow crazy. Or he was. "He seems content to me. I think he simply doesn't like change."

"He's stuck in his ways, you mean." Turner snapped a nod of agreement. "You could help him, your ladyship. Draw him out, make him smile." She grinned. "I warrant he could be a handsome fellow if he smiled."

Amelia had thought the same thing when she'd seen one of his rare smiles. "Thank you for your advice, Turner," she said, unable to still a grin of her own. "That will be all this evening."

With a curtsy, the maid left her.

But Turner's words lingered. Was John as lonely as Amelia? Would he accept her companionship? Or would he even care? How was she to make a marriage when the other half of that marriage had no time or interest?

Do unto others as you would have them do unto you.

As soon as the verse echoed in her mind, she knew what she must do. She and Mr. Shanter had come to an understanding. She was certain he would help her. She put her blue twill pelisse on over her dressing gown and headed downstairs.

In the stables, Fletcher yawned for the third time in as many minutes.

"Go to bed," John told the veterinarian, who was seated across from him in the same stall as Firenza. "I'll stay with her until dawn. Come back for me then."

"By your leave, you should be the one to retire," Fletcher protested, straightening against the white wall of the stall. "You have other matters that require your attention."

John shrugged. "If you mean Lady Amelia, she'll be fine. Society women rarely dote on their husbands in any regard."

Fletcher stretched his long legs across the straw, careful not to brush against the panting mare. "That may be, but I would expect any lady to wish her husband's company on her honeymoon."

John snorted, and Firenza lifted her head to eye him. "Some honeymoon—a night in a wayside inn."

"Precisely my point!" Fletcher shook his head so that his spectacles bounced on his long nose. "You owe your wife your devotion."

John eyed him. "I owe her the courtesy due a wife, nothing more."

Fletcher inclined his head. "You'll get no argument

from me on that score. We simply disagree on which courtesies a man owes his wife." He gathered his legs under him and stood with a groan. "But if you are determined to stay, I'll take you up on that offer. Send someone for me if anything changes."

John nodded, and the sound of his friend's footsteps faded on the cobbles.

What did a man owe his wife? Food and shelter, obviously. Respect, certainly. He had never truly considered the matter before now. When he'd courted Caro, he'd thought of nothing but when he might see her again. Even at the time he'd commissioned the betrothal ring, he'd fretted over what he would say to make her agree to be his bride. Their future at Hollyoak Farm had been a misty thing, hardly more than a dream.

Then Caro and his brother had betrayed him, and he'd found it hard to think of a future at all.

He still remembered the announcement. He'd been spending the Season in London, as usual. His brother had insisted upon it.

"You must do the pretty once in a while," James had teased. "The Hascot name should stand for more than horses."

John had returned to their London town house fresh from confirming that the jeweler would have the betrothal ring ready by Friday, when he'd planned to propose. He'd already imagined the scene a dozen different ways, and each one had ended with Caro in his arms. But he hadn't even touched his foot to the stairs when his brother had called him into the withdrawing room.

James was his twin, older only by a few minutes, and he'd always joked that those minutes meant all the world of difference. James was broader, more powerfully built. His hair was thicker and curlier. At times, John felt like his shadow. That day, he'd stopped just inside the doorway of the ornately decorated room, staring at his brother, who'd stood by the black marble fireplace with one arm about the waist of the woman John loved.

"Wish me happy, John," his brother had said with a triumphant grin. "Lady Caroline has agreed to be my bride."

He couldn't believe it. He'd stood there, frozen. "Is this a joke?"

Caro had turned her gaze, the one he was so used to seeing directed at him, on his brother. "No, indeed, Lord John. Lord Hascot has done me a great honor. I couldn't be happier."

He'd felt as if the world had shifted off its axis and forgotten to take him with it. "But I thought you favored my suit."

She'd blushed as she'd met his gaze, her own filled now with pity. "Of course I admire you as a sister should a brother. But my heart has always been Hascot's."

"Can't expect a woman like Caro to hang after a second son," his brother had said with a laugh. He'd released her to move to John's side, clapping him on the shoulder. Then he'd leaned closer. "Those few minutes make all the difference."

At that moment, he'd hated his brother, hated that Caro would choose position over love. He'd yanked his shoulder away, stormed out of the room. In a brass stand by the door had stood the crop his brother had used on his horse. John had grabbed it, feeling the sturdy leather under his fingers, knowing how surely a strongly wielded crop could damage flesh, bruise bone. Didn't his brother deserve such treatment for what he'd done?

What was he thinking?

John had dropped the crop back into the stand, feeling as if it had burned his fingers. The depth of his loathing had disgusted him, surrounded him in darkness. He didn't want to hate the two people who mattered the most to him. He'd left the house, walking about Mayfair until the sun had set and the lamp lighters had made their way around.

Since then, he'd realized a few things. James couldn't help that he was the better catch. Nor could he help that sense of competition he'd felt with John. John had seen it with horses in the field. Magnum found it difficult to be with another stallion without jockeying for position. John didn't like it, knew it could cause problems, but he understood it.

And Caro had been smart to make sure she married the title. That was where the power and security lay after all. No one had foreseen that James would die of heart failure a year later, leaving the title and a grieving widow to John.

Custom had prevented Caro from attending the funeral, but she'd sobbed against John's waistcoat when he'd visited the house afterward.

"What am I to do, John?" she'd asked. "How am I to get on?"

"Nothing will change," he'd promised, wanting only to escape the memories that assaulted him in her presence. "You have the London house and the Hascot seat. I'll stay at Hollyoak."

"You needn't do that," she'd protested, but he'd known it was the only solution. Spending time in her company was too painful. And the church decreed that by marrying his brother, she had put herself forever beyond his reach.

"How is she?"

John blinked, the memories fading. Amelia was standing at the edge of the stall, pelisse covering her nightclothes. Her hair was unpinned, flowing down her back, her face soft and concerned. In her hands was a tray with several cups and a silver pot that steamed.

"Still laboring," John confirmed, trying to gather his wits. "I told Fletcher I'd stay until dawn." He wasn't so far from Society that he'd forgotten he was to stand in the presence of a lady, so he started to rise. She nodded for him to remain seated.

Her gaze, however, was on the mare below. "I know her. That's the horse that kicked Lord Danning."

John chuckled, remembering. "Yes. She has a lot of fire, this one."

"That's why she's still fighting." She ventured closer, and her gaze met his. "May I?"

John made room for her beside him. As she lowered the tray past his gaze, he noticed several biscuits and some cheese and grapes beside the pot.

"I thought you might be hungry," Amelia said as if she'd seen his look.

All at once he was famished. He grabbed a piece of cheese and bit into it as she poured him a cup of tea.

"Sugar?" she asked as if they were meeting in a cheery sitting room instead of a shadowed stable.

"No, thank you." His mother would have been pleased to know he remembered some of the manners she'd tried to instill in him.

Though there was plenty of food for Amelia as well, she seemed more interested in the mare. Cautiously, she reached out a hand and stroked the horse's hock. Firenza lay down her head with a sigh.

"She's trembling," Amelia whispered, eyes wide as she glanced at John. "Is she in pain?"

"We don't think so," John replied, setting down his empty cup. "And the convulsions have stopped. But she can't seem to settle."

"Perhaps she needs a distraction," Amelia said, pulling back her hand. "Belle likes when I sing to her."

His face must have betrayed his surprise, for she smiled. "It's not uncommon. I've heard of others who sing to their beasts to calm them. May I try?" she asked.

John spread his hands. "It couldn't hurt."

Her mouth quirked as if she was used to such lack-luster encouragement. But she rose onto her knees and began to sing.

Afterward, John couldn't remember the words. He only knew how they made him feel. The pure tone of her voice, the soft lilt of the song, seemed to sink into him. Tense muscles relaxed, concerns drifted away. It was as if he was floating, rising, darkness brightening into light at last.

Is this what it sounds like in Your temple in heaven, Lord?

The thought came unbidden, yet it felt right, and he fancied he knew the answer.

As the last note faded, Amelia sat back, watching the roan's sides rise and fall. Even John could see the rhythm was even, normal. She glanced at him.

"I think that helped," she said, and he could hear the hope in her voice. She wanted his approval. "What do you think?"

"I think, madam," he said, "that you are a very great blessing."

She ducked her head, coloring, but John could see the smile curving her pretty lips. If he leaned forward, he could touch them, perhaps feel them warm under his.

He didn't lean forward. He didn't move. He had no doubt that Lady Amelia was the blessing he'd named her. He simply couldn't believe that blessing was meant for him.

Chapter Eight

He liked the way she sang.

Amelia smiled as she sat in the stall next to John. She'd received any number of compliments on her voice since her debut in Society two years ago, but part of her had always wondered about the sincerity. It was expected to praise a young lady's attempts at the arts. The comments were not necessarily commensurate with her actual abilities, especially if she was pretty or wealthy or the daughter of a powerful family. As Amelia was all three, she had never been certain the praise she received was merited.

But John already had access to whatever dowry her father had granted. There was no reason for him to attempt to impress Lord Wesworth, particularly in a stable so far from London. And she could not mistake the admiration warming his dark eyes.

Besides, it was rather satisfying to know she'd eased Firenza's pain. She could see that the horse was more relaxed, her breathing more regular.

Thank You, Lord, that I could help!

She was quite content to sit here and bask in her accomplishment. But their companionable silence was remarkably short-lived.

"You needn't stay up," John said, shifting on the straw.

Was he trying to get rid of her? Disappointment bit. Surely her company was preferable to sitting alone in a stable that was rapidly growing cooler as night darkened the dale. Or was Turner wrong about his loneliness?

"I don't mind waiting," she assured him.

He frowned. "Is something wrong with your room, the bed?"

She felt her cheeks warming again. "It is a fine room, a comfortable bed. It will do quite nicely until…we decide on other arrangements."

She wasn't sure how else to state the matter. Married or not, one did not ask a gentleman when he would be comfortable enough to sire a child.

As if he understood her cryptic comment, his brow cleared, and his gaze focused on her. It was rather unnerving being the center of his attention. Every line of his body, from his sharp features to his lean muscles, seemed tensed to penetrate her defenses. Was this how the hare felt when the hawk hovered above?

"There will be no need to make other arrangements," he said. "I do not intend to share your bed."

Relief vied with chagrin. It took a moment for the implication to sink in. Then Amelia stared at him. "Ever?"

He grimaced, looking away from her at last. "Let us say for the foreseeable future."

"Oh." The enormity of it settled over her. He did not intend to consummate the marriage. She would have no children to love, no example to set. She'd spend every day as she'd done today, alone in the house. She knew from her time at Lord Danning's that Dovecote Dale boasted only three other houses of the aristocracy, and two were only occasionally occupied. She might as well be living on the moon.

"If you like children," he said as if discussing her preference in meals, "there are a number of fine charities you could support. Danning gives to the orphan asylum."

And her friend Ruby, now Lady Danning, was building a school in the poorest part of London, Amelia knew. She dared to glance at him. "So you are not opposed to children per se."

He shook his head, hair falling onto his forehead, a swath of black across the sun-tanned skin. "I don't have time or patience to be a husband, much less a father."

"Oh." Why did she keep repeating that insipid word? All her hopes, all her dreams, lay dead at her feet. Didn't they deserve a better eulogy?

Didn't they deserve a fight?

As silence fell once more, the idea Turner had planted took root and started to grow. Why shouldn't she fight for what she wanted? She'd rarely prevailed against her parents, but this was her life, and she was becoming a new woman. She had convictions, as strong as his. Why must she give them up?

She watched this man, her husband, sitting beside her. John's hawklike gaze never faltered. The tension that she had felt now turned on Firenza, intensified. He was as tight as a well-placed thread, so determined to miss no nuance in the mare's condition, so dedicated to keeping her safe.

What if Amelia could turn that attention to her?

The thought sent a shiver through her.

"Here." John must have noticed her movement, for he reached for a blanket draping the stall and tossed it to her. Though it smelled of horse, she pulled it about her shoulders.

As she had suspected, those dark eyes missed nothing. How could she help him see things differently?

Her mother and governess had instructed her how to use her beauty as a weapon. She'd rarely taken advantage of the tactics they'd advised. Flaunting her face and figure was no better than her father flaunting his prestige. In the end, such actions only made the other person feel smaller. She didn't want to do that to anyone else.

But perhaps she needn't go so far. Perhaps she could find more appropriate ways to encourage her husband see her in a new light. She could make his home brighter, his life better. If he saw her dedication, he'd realize she would be a good mother and that the two of them together could deal well with a child.

He might even come to love her.

The last thought took her breath away, and she closed her eyes a moment at the emotions surging through her. She hadn't realized how hungry her heart was until it was offered the chance for something more.

Heavenly Father, would it be too much to ask for someone to love me?

What a dangerous prayer, for how she would hurt if it wasn't answered the way she hoped!

Indeed, from any angle she considered, attempting to help John would be risky. He might never notice her actions. Worse, he might resent what could be seen as interference in the life he had carefully planned for himself.

But, oh, wasn't the risk worth the potential reward?

She opened her eyes and raised her head. She would do it. She would start a campaign to win her husband's heart, for her sake and his.

John thought surely Amelia would either fall asleep on his shoulder or decamp for the house partway through the night. Instead, she stayed beside him, the orange-blossom scent of her hair drifting on the air. She was as watchful as he was, pointing out when the mare's breathing became labored again, stroking the horse's coat when Firenza grew restless. She helped the mare to drink when John brought fresh water, evened out the straw when John forked in a fresh batch. And all with a pleasant smile and a kind word.

He'd never met a woman like her.

His mother had always encouraged both her sons to remember their duty and explore their gifts. Like John's father, however, she had not understood her younger son's fascination with horses. From an early age, he'd been enamored with the powerful creatures who could fly around the fields. And when he learned they could soar over fences and across ditches, too, he'd known he'd found his true calling.

His mother had tried to dissuade him when he'd stammered out his intentions.

"A gentleman might own horses, John," she'd said. "He does not start them from scratch."

He'd smiled at the way she'd made it sound as if he was pursuing a career in baking. She had found it difficult to even acknowledge the breeding side of his efforts.

And even Caro hadn't liked the location of the farm.

"So far from London?" she'd said with a wrinkle of

her pert nose when he'd told her about Hollyoak Farm, which he'd purchased three years before meeting her. "What do you do for Society?"

He should have known then that Caro was not the woman for him. Society—the gaiety, the whirl—had ever been her delight. He'd never enjoyed the politics of Society, fueled by gossip and petty intrigues. His horses had more character and were far more loyal than most of the people he'd met in London.

He had to admit, however, that his new bride did not seem to be missing Society overmuch. Nor did she disdain John's efforts. Indeed, she walked with him back to the house when Fletcher came to take his turn, then woke a few hours later to support the unpacking of her things, which had arrived from London.

He did not see her until later in the day, when she came to where he and Fletcher were standing beside the main paddock behind the west stable block. Then she exclaimed with pleasure when she saw the groom leading Firenza around the square.

"You saved her!"

John clapped Fletcher, who was watching the mare's progress, on the back. "We have Dr. Fletcher to thank for that."

"No, indeed," the veterinarian assured him with a smile to Amelia, as well. "It was a joint effort. I understand you helped, too, Lady Hascot."

Amelia demurred, but just then the mare tugged on her lead, jerking it from the groom's hand. Firenza trotted up to the fence in front of Amelia and nickered in greeting.

"Oh, aren't you a darling?" Amelia crooned. She stroked the mare's nose with gentle fingers.

Fletcher elbowed John. "I think you've finally found a rider for your roan."

"Firenza's still not at full strength," John replied, knowing how fractious the mare had been. "I'll not put Lady Hascot on her."

Amelia lowered her hand and turned to the men. Her color was once more high, but he wasn't sure the reason.

"I am a decent rider, my lord," she said.

Did she think he meant to disparage her? "You may well be, madam," he replied. "But Firenza has proved impossible to ride, for anyone but me. I would not see you injured."

She inclined her head. "How kind of you to think of me. Might I tear you away from your work a moment?"

Though the words were as sweet as always, something stronger swam beneath them. Fletcher must have heard it as well, for he hurried to excuse himself, and the groom retrieved the lead and led Firenza away.

Amelia moved closer to John. She wore one of her muslin gowns that he found difficult to tell apart. They all seemed to combine lace and yards of pale material, and she floated about in them as if she was a dainty cloud come to earth. Now, however, by the frown gathering on her golden brow, he thought a storm might be brewing.

"Is there a difficulty?" he asked.

"Perhaps," she acknowledged. "You asked me to manage the entertainment of your guests. Your butler tells me that you rarely entertain. Are you planning something more elaborate than in the past, or is he mistaken?"

John turned for the pasture and motioned her to join him. Together, they started out across the grass.

"We have company often enough," he explained as she lifted her skirts to keep the lace from the grass. "Perhaps once a month, June through September. And nearly every week in May, after most of the horses foal."

Her steps faltered as if she hadn't expected his answer. "How many at a time?" she asked as she caught up to him.

John stopped to watch a group of the horses walk together across the green, the silver-coated Contessa in the lead. "Anywhere from one to a dozen, some with servants in tow."

Now her frown deepened, as if his math did not add up. She pushed back a strand of hair that had blown free in the breeze. "And do you house them, feed them, provide entertainment beyond the horses?"

He had never considered his horses entertainment, but he knew others did. "I have not allowed them to stay, and I do not encourage other pastimes beyond buying. However, we are forced to feed them on occasion. Why the concern?"

She sighed, gaze on the horses, as well. "We have a butler who does not appear to appreciate hard work, a footman who has too much work and a cook who finds his work too difficult. The three of them are utterly insufficient even if we do not intend to entertain."

John shrugged. "Then change things."

She rubbed her hand along the drape of her skirt, his gaze following the movement of her fingers. She had nice fingers—long, supple. He ought to buy a spinet so she could accompany her singing. He'd warrant she played beautifully.

Where had that thought come from?

"I would like to change things," she admitted. Then,

as if expecting him to disagree, she hurried on. "Nothing tremendously noticeable. Just improving efficiencies, perhaps brightening the rooms."

She paused as if seeking his approval, and John nodded for her to continue. Apparently emboldened, she raised her head. Then her frown returned.

"What are they doing?"

John glanced out into the field. Contessa had herded the other mares into formation. As a group, they trotted and turned, weaving about the grass in a complex dance.

"Cavalry drills," John explained. "She was well trained, and the training never left her. We have another mare who also served on the Peninsula, though she came back in better shape. She knows to follow Contessa's lead."

Amelia was quiet for a moment, and he could see she was watching the horses. They gathered, then charged across the field, hooves as loud as thunder, grass flying up behind them. He could almost hear the bugle blowing.

"We all march to the drum," she murmured. "However we are raised, however we are trained, it never seems to leave us. Do you think we can break free?"

John frowned, glancing at her. Her gaze never left the horses, but her hands were clasped in front of her so tightly her knuckles showed white.

"I have done everything to make Contessa comfortable," he assured her. "For all intents and purposes, she is a hunter again."

"And yet she remembers. I wonder if the same could be said of people."

Was that her worry? Did she think herself too used

to London Society to deal well in the country? She seemed to have acclimated well, if he was any judge.

"We can all learn," he answered. "All grow and change. That choice is ours to make."

She unclasped her hands and turned to him, taking a deep breath as if his words had given her hope.

"And so we must choose," she said. "Thank you for being willing to consider my changes in the household, my lord. Unfortunately, your butler insists that we have no funds to support additional staff. I thought perhaps my dowry…"

John held up his hand to stop her. "There's no need to touch your dowry."

She took another breath as if trying to come up with a way to counter his refusal. "If there isn't any other budget…"

There wasn't a dowry, either. He might never have married before, but he knew about the arrangements that were generally made when people of their class wed. A wealthy man might agree to settle a father's debts, take care of an aging mother or younger siblings. A bride from a wealthy family, such as Amelia's, might expect monies to be set aside for her use in buying clothing or accoutrements, for her children's future and her own should she become a widow. Certainly James had provided for Caro, though he hadn't thought she'd need that money quite so soon.

The solicitor for Amelia's family had made sure the marriage settlements included the language about Lord Wesworth's colt. John had added in the words about setting aside money from Hollyoak Farm for Amelia should he pass away prematurely. Her father had offered nothing for her dowry. Marrying someone related to the

Wesworth title seemed to be sufficient contribution to the marriage in his mind.

"I can find the monies," John told her now. "I'm not a skinflint, Amelia. I've refused some of the staff's suggestions because I don't believe in spending money on fripperies. But I will own that I find the house un-inviting. If you have the patience to deal with that, I commend you. Draw up a plan, and I will provide the funds to complete it."

He would have thought he'd offered her the moon by the way she smiled. More, moisture glistened in her blue eyes as if she was truly touched. This time, he could not stop himself from leaning closer. Lips curving, she leaned closer, as well.

"Watch out!"

John jerked back at his groom's cry, but not before a black shadow flew past. Magnum thundered to a stop in front of Amelia and blew a breath of challenge in her face.

Most people would have cried out, backed away. Amelia held her ground, calm, cool.

"Good afternoon, Magnum," she said as if meeting the vicar in Hyde Park. "Have you forgotten your manners, sir?"

Apparently so, for the black reared up and pawed the air, bugling his protest. From across the field, Contessa answered, whirling to race toward them.

John dodged in front of Amelia. "Down!" he commanded the black.

Magnum's hooves hit the ground with a thud. He shook his massive head, hard.

"Go on," John told him with a wave of his hand. "Fight with someone your own size."

The black wheeled and took off across the field. When John was sure the stallion was running with Contessa, he turned to Amelia.

Her face was crumpled, her lower lip trembling.

John didn't know what to do. Had she been a horse, he would have used calming words, perhaps stroked her face. Both seemed impertinent in the extreme. How was a man to soothe the fears of his own wife?

"I don't know what got into him," he said.

"Perhaps he, too, dislikes change," Amelia murmured. "Excuse me, my lord. I have work inside, where I belong."

She turned and hurried for the house. Magnum's reaction had clearly hurt her. She took such things seriously, it seemed.

So did John. He'd always found horses to be excellent judges of character.

What was it about Amelia that Magnum should so dislike her?

Chapter Nine

His horse hated her! Amelia hurried back across the field for the safety of the house. She was still shaking from the way the black had reared over her. Her father's master of horse had always advised her never to show a horse that she was afraid. Even though she'd tried to remain calm, she was fairly certain Magnum knew he terrified her. But by remaining calm, at least she hadn't disgraced herself in John's eyes!

She took a deep breath and forced her steps to slow to a ladylike tread. She should focus on her campaign.

Her governess had provided an overview of history, and Amelia had been fascinated enough to read some of the treatises in her father's library about the lives and plans of various military men of renown. They studied their opponents, revised their tactics, looked beyond individual battles to winning the war itself. Magnum's attitude was a skirmish. She had bigger battles to fight.

She had nearly reached the house when she noticed a movement on the road leading to the farm. Shading her eyes with her hand, she peered across the pasture.

A man sat on a swaybacked brown horse. She could

not make out its features or his, but something flashed in the sunlight. The reflection of a spy glass? Was someone watching the farm?

A groom called out just then, and she turned to find that one of the yearlings had slipped his lead. He trotted into the yard, rear end higher than his shoulders, so ungainly yet, and so curious about everything, sniffing at a water pail, hopping past a weed growing up through the gravel. Amelia smiled as the groom came running and the horse darted away, clearly intent on being chased.

When she looked back at the road, the man was riding off, the reins held wide. Far too wide.

No! It couldn't be the same man they'd seen on the way north. What would he be doing in Derby and spying on John? There had to be another explanation. And she had more important things to attend to in any regard. The most important was to develop the proposal John had asked for. She smiled as she let herself into the house. He acted as if he had the utmost confidence in her abilities. How refreshing! She would not let him, or herself, down.

Accordingly, she spent the rest of the afternoon at the secretary in the withdrawing room, writing out her plan. Turner puttered about the room, straightening books on the shelves, rearranging the porcelain figurines Amelia had brought with her and placed on the side tables. She seemed to take any excuse to wander by and glance over Amelia's shoulder.

"You will see," Amelia finally said, offering Turner a smile as she paused beside the secretary, "that I've included a spot for a lady's maid."

Turner dipped a curtsy, spreading her gray skirts wide. "I can't read, your ladyship, so I didn't know." She offered a smile back. "But I can recognize my name, and I was curious if it might appear on your paper. Is that a list of servants you're laying out, then?"

"A list of positions and responsibilities," Amelia confirmed. "I'd like to include wages as well as uniform and food costs, but I'm not sure what those would entail. I never had to deal with such things in London, and I imagine the cost here is different in any regard."

"Oh, very likely," Turner agreed. "I can help you there. Mrs. Dunworthy was forever going on about the cost of things. And I know how the other houses run on account of the Conclave."

"The Conclave?" Amelia asked with a frown, lifting her quill from the page.

Turner nodded eagerly. "It's a group of servants who meet at the village inn every Sunday afternoon for fellowship." She sidled closer. "If you have need of other servants, I can tell you who's looking."

Amelia would hardly be welcomed in the dale if she went around poaching other people's staff. "I wouldn't want to encourage a servant to leave his master," Amelia warned her.

"Oh, certainly not!" Turner's protest was at odds with the fervent light in her eyes. "But there are any number of reasons a serving person might wish to change places." She went on to name a few.

Mr. Hennessy at Lord Danning's lodge felt his talents wasted at the retreat that saw no more than a month's activity a year. Amelia had been impressed with his orderly way of managing things when she'd stayed at the lodge earlier. A footman and maid at Bellweather Hall, the home of the Duke of Bellington, were about to be discharged before his mother, the duchess, returned from London because their mistress felt they weren't "grand" enough for a ducal estate.

And because Turner's mistress had left the area, the maid would have to return to cleaning and polishing if she wished to stay on at the Grange.

"So we could solve most of our servant problems right here in Dovecote Dale," Amelia explained to John that night over a much-improved supper.

"Excellent plan," John said as he reviewed the papers she'd handed him. He took a bite of the salmon with dill sauce and nodded. "Carry on."

Indeed, he never argued, never complained as she set about making changes in the house. She donated the heavy, dark drapes that eclipsed the windows to the Poor House to make shrouds for coffins. She retired the butler and brought in Mr. Hennessy, who promptly set to work instructing the two footmen, new maid and Turner on what he expected of them.

Out went the dark furnishings, to be replaced by lighter woods and paler colors still in keeping with the country estate. Dusty navy bed hangings were traded for flowered chintz. Carpets were beaten, upholstery brushed and every wooden surface polished. She put flowers in each room, mirrors wherever feasible. The only two rooms she didn't touch were John's library and his bedchamber.

If John noticed the changes, however, he did not comment. He ate dinner with her along with Dr. Fletcher, listened to her and offered insights when necessary. If she asked after his horses, she was likely to receive a quarter hour's discourse on such things as dealing with colic, replacing a thrown shoe and replanting the south pasture. It was all too easy to be disappointed.

Yet she could not doubt that what she'd done was an improvement. The staff worked efficiently and effectively; the rooms were far brighter and more comfortable; meals were pleasing to the taste as well as the sight, and they generally arrived when expected.

The same, unfortunately, could not be said of John's visitors. The first set arrived less than a week after Amelia had come to the farm. She'd been discussing options for the proper storage of the silver with Mr. Hennessy when the new footman, Reams, came to find her. While the butler was a strapping fellow with a commanding presence as well suited to the battlefield as household management, Reams still needed to add a few pounds before he grew into his height.

"Begging your pardon, your ladyship, Mr. Hennessy," he said, bobbing his head so hard he lost the center part on his brown hair. "But his lordship has visitors." He lowered his voice. "He called them Amble Bys."

Amelia had heard Dr. Fletcher use the phrase. It seemed to apply to people who came to exclaim over John's horses but not to buy. She'd been one the first time she'd come to Hollyoak Farm with Lord Danning. Now it was her turn to entertain them.

"Tell Mr. Shanter to have lemonade, pastries, cheese and fruit ready," Amelia told her new butler. "Reams, ask Turner to bring me my white parasol with the tassels."

Suitably armed with her parasol over her head, Amelia ventured out into the stable yard. Standing beside a travel carriage were a white-haired gentleman whose stomach nearly popped the silver buttons off his embroidered waistcoat and two young ladies with an excessive amount of brown curls and a tendency to giggle behind their gloved hands.

John's glower was particularly pronounced as he waited next to them, hands clasped behind his tweed coat. His head came up as Amelia approached, and his hair fell across his brow as if it, too, longed to escape.

"My wife, Lady Hascot," he said without preamble. "Mr. Gideon Pettibone and granddaughters."

Mr. Pettibone took her hand and pressed it fervently. "Lady Hascot, a pleasure. I was just telling my girls how Hollyoak Farm must have changed with a lady in residence. Count on it, I said. She'll have knocked the rough edges off the fellow. Eh?" He laughed at his own wit and set his granddaughters to giggling anew.

"I have no more time for pleasantries," John said, displaying all his rough edges. "Good day." He stalked back to the nearest stable.

Amelia drew a breath. He'd said she was to look after these sorts of visitors, but she hadn't expected him to disappear. She'd never been particularly good with strangers. Certainly her mother had been better at discouraging acquaintance rather than encouraging it. But now three sets of eyes looked to her for understanding and entertainment.

"Welcome to Hollyoak Farm," she said. "I take it you like horses."

As opening gambits went, it was not especially witty or endearing. But Mr. Pettibone and his granddaughters brightened, and they told her all about their admiration of shire-bred horses, the best of the hunting class, as she led them along the fence edging the pasture closest to the house.

"See there, girls," Mr. Pettibone said with a nod out

to the obstacles John had erected on the field. "That's where he teaches them to jump."

One of the grooms was working with a two-year-old named Falling Star for the bordered star that ran down her nose. As Amelia watched, he urged the dark bay horse to take a low fence. The Pettibone granddaughters applauded when the mare sailed over.

"My friend Squire Welton brings his hunting dogs by every September," Mr. Pettibone confided to Amelia. "To help accustom the horses to working with the hounds."

That must be an interesting week at Hollyoak Farm. "I understand from Dr. Fletcher, our veterinarian, that all our horses are thoroughly trained before their first hunt," Amelia explained to her interested listeners. "They must be able to control their speed, walk backward and wait should other horses need to pass." She went on to point out the various horses currently visible. Dr. Fletcher had told her their names over dinner a few evenings ago.

"What about that one?" one of the girls asked, pointing to where Contessa had nipped at the shoulder of the mare Providence, who had leaned too close. "She looks mean."

Amelia smiled. "She is more stern than mean, like a good governess. She leads the herd and must make sure every horse is safe. She's very disciplined, having served on the Peninsula carrying a valiant officer into battle."

The youngest girl was instantly enamored, her brown eyes shining, and Amelia couldn't help thinking that John had made a great mistake by depriving himself of their company.

"Charming," Mr. Pettibone assured Amelia after he and his granddaughters had consumed excessive amounts of food and Amelia had returned them to their waiting coach. "I must say, it isn't at all what I expected."

"What did you expect, sir?" Amelia asked, curious.

He made sure his granddaughters were safely in the coach before lowering his voice and leaning closer to Amelia.

"You must know, my dear, that your husband has a reputation for incivility. A few in the capital have taken offense at his refusal to sell to them. You would do well to watch yourself." He patted her hand, then climbed in after his girls.

Amelia waved at them until they left the yard. She knew John had earned his reputation for gruffness, and certainly he was allowed to sell to whomever he pleased. She simply didn't understand how that would affect her. It wasn't as if she was going to be spending any time in Society soon.

She scarcely spent time in her husband's society. She was to tend to the interior of the house; his province was outside.

But perhaps she could change that. Campaigning generals did not hesitate to advance into enemy territory if it served their purposes. Perhaps instead of waiting for John to come to her, it was time she took her efforts to John.

His home was no longer his own. John couldn't help the thought as he rode Magnum in from inspecting the south planting. Hollyoak Farm still crouched upon the fields, squat and square, but inside she sparkled. Nay, she demanded a smile, a cheerful attitude, a pleasant word. Though his library and bedchamber remained untouched islands, he found it all a bit uncomfortable.

Yet he could not deny that Amelia had made a difference. He had never eaten better. No longer did his footman have to apologize for the dust on his seldom-used coats. And listening to Amelia over dinner was a highly satisfying way to end the day.

He rode into the paddock, turned Magnum to help quiet him. No groom came running to take the reins. John slipped from the saddle and grabbed them up himself. Still no one came to lead the big horse to its stall.

Had something happened?

He strode into the stable, pulling Magnum with him. It appeared the farrier had arrived, for John could see the man on one knee at the end of a stall. Every one of his stable staff who was not out with horses was clustered around the same stall, some hanging over the walls on either side, others crowding behind the farrier.

"So you see no difficulty with her going for a ride?" Amelia was asking.

She was standing beside Firenza in her plum-colored riding habit, a tall-crowned hat on her head and lace trailing down behind her. Most of her hair was up under the hat, but a long curl bounced on either side of her face as she talked, like moonlight winding through a forest.

The farrier put down Firenza's rear foot carefully. He knew what the mare could get up to, even if Amelia did not. "Her shoes are in good condition, your ladyship. She's ready."

Magnum bumped John's shoulder, shoving forward, and John pulled the reins tighter. The horse stomped his dish-size hooves and bellowed a challenge. The mares still in the stable shifted anxiously.

So did John's staff. They all looked up, spotted him and found reasons to be elsewhere. The farrier, Mr. Jones, rose.

"Your lordship. I was just starting my inspections."

"Go on your way, then," John told him. A groom hurried up but stopped just short of reaching for Magnum's reins. The black was still stiff beside John. He blew out a snort and shook his head, whipping his mane about.

Amelia stood in the stall. While John applauded her composure, he couldn't help worrying about the roan. The mare was cured of her affliction, but Firenza had been known to turn her head and nip at those closest to her. When saddled, she would refuse to move. He wasn't sure how she'd react when caught between Amelia and Magnum.

"Take him," John said to the groom, who accepted the reins with an ill-concealed grimace. The black kept an eye on Amelia as they passed. The roan shifted her body across the entrance to the stall.

Interesting. Was she shielding Amelia or trying to show off for the stallion?

"Good girl," he heard Amelia murmur. One gloved hand came up, and she stroked Firenza's back.

"What are you doing here, Amelia?" John asked.

Her hand hesitated, but she peered over Firenza with her usual pleasant smile. Did nothing ever anger her, or was she simply too well brought up to show it? He knew he routinely missed the nuances of human behavior. Look at how he'd misinterpreted Caro's response to his suit. Now he couldn't be sure what was going on in that pretty, platinum-haired head.

"I wanted to see how my girl was doing," she told him with a smile to the roan. "Mr. Jones says she is ready for a ride."

"Mr. Jones was commenting on the state of her shoes," John replied. "That doesn't mean you can ride her."

Amelia continued to smile at the horse. "Why ever not?" she cooed. "Firenza and I have become good friends."

The roan turned her head to look at John as if to disavow all knowledge.

"She's kicked Danning and two grooms," John told Amelia. "Bitten three others who weren't quick enough to avoid her. When she runs, she's easily the fastest horse in the stables, besides Magnum. You couldn't handle her."

Her gaze turned to him at last. "You made that judgment on remarkably little evidence, my lord."

He inclined his head. "Forgive me, but I've seen the nags you ride."

"Belle is no nag!" Her voice was rising, and Firenza shifted in the stall. John supposed Amelia must still be smarting over the fact that her father had refused to send her dainty white mare north with her. "And even if she was less impressive than a Hascot horse," she continued, "you must remember that I did not choose my mounts. My father did."

He could not argue that her father knew more about horses than she did. Lord Wesworth was an avid collector of fine horse flesh. But that was his problem. He saw horses as nothing more than another item to be acquired. And after the way he had treated Amelia, John was fairly certain he hadn't taken great pains to find his daughter a fiery mount.

"I know your father chose your horses," John told her. "And I have nothing against your Belle. But Firenza is a different animal."

"Then she will be a challenge." She removed her hand from the horse's back and came around in front. Firenza nipped at the veil as it passed, but Amelia did not appear to notice. She approached him, blue eyes solemn, and laid her hand on his arm.

"Please, John," she murmured. "Let me try."

It was one of the few times she had used his given name, and he was surprised to hear how sweetly it sat on her lips. Her face was turned up to his, her look imploring. Even her touch spoke of how much she wanted to ride that horse.

He knew those feelings. They blossomed every time he saw a colt mature. It was an honor and a thrill to be the first one to ride his horses, to teach them to carry the most precious cargo of their lives, another human being. To sit upon their backs and soar.

"Very well," he said.

Her hand fell off his arm as her eyes widened in obvious surprise. "Oh, John, thank you."

She looked as if she was about to throw her arms around him to express her thanks. John turned hurriedly away. "Let me try her first. Just to be certain she's ready." He beckoned to a groom, who brought up a leather saddle.

"Very kind of you," Amelia said, "but, no."

The groom hesitated, glancing between the two of them. John hesitated, as well. "I will keep my promise, Amelia. You may ride her, under certain conditions."

She tapped her finger to her lips. "You did not mention conditions, my lord." She turned to the groom. "I'll require a sidesaddle, if you please. If mine has not been brought down to the stables, ask Turner where it was stored."

He glanced at John, then back at her. "It's here, your ladyship. I'll bring it right over." He scampered off.

"Amelia," John started, but now she put her finger to his lips to seal them.

"No, John," she said, gaze on his, touch soft. "This is important to me, and I cannot help thinking it is important to our marriage. If you cannot trust me with your horses, any horse, you cannot trust me at all."

He wanted to argue, but he feared she was right. Already Magnum's animosity was making him wonder about her. Perhaps she saw the truth of it in his eyes, for she pulled back her hand as the groom hurried up with her saddle.

Amelia stepped aside so the groom could place the sidesaddle on the mare's back. Firenza shoved him up against the wall of the stall, head whipping back.

"No!" Amelia ordered, marching forward.

John stiffened. Amelia kept her gaze on Firenza. He didn't dare make a sound for fear of breaking her concentration.

"Come now, my girl," she told the roan, "behave yourself. What will the gentlemen think of a lady with no manners?"

The mare shifted away from the wall, and the groom escaped with a grateful gasp of breath.

Amelia moved in front of Firenza and stroked her nose. "That's my fine girl. Now we're going for a walk, then we'll cinch you all up so we can ride. You want to get out of this stable, don't you?"

As if she suddenly remembered that John and the groom were watching, she glanced his way. "I think they like when we talk to them," she said, and he could hear the defiance in her tone.

"I know they do," he said.

Her smile brightened the stable. Taking hold of the headstall herself, she led the mare out of the box.

Everyone stopped. The grooms stood with hands on pitchforks or harness, Mr. Jones lowered a horse's leg so he could focus. Even the other animals turned in their stalls to watch.

Head high, Amelia floated down the aisle, Firenza walking beside her, groom and John trailing her like the train of a ball gown. The sunlight set her curls to gleaming.

Fletcher came running from the house as John followed her into the paddock.

"Is it true?" he called to John. "You're going to let her ride Firenza?"

John could only snap a nod. He couldn't seem to take his eyes from Amelia. Every movement spoke of confidence, determination. She directed the groom to lay on the saddle, but she held the headstall to prevent Firenza from nipping at him and praised the roan when the mare allowed the leather on her back. But when he started to tighten things in place, Amelia stopped him.

"Hold her, if you will," she said. "I think I should learn how to do this myself. My lord? Would you teach me?"

John's feet felt rooted to the ground. "You want to learn how to saddle a horse?"

She smiled at him. "I do. Shouldn't every horseman or woman know how to do so?"

"Yes." His own convictions thrust him forward. "Yes, they should. Allow me, my lady."

He came to stand behind her and pointed around her at the saddle. "You want the saddle to sit near the highest point of the horse."

"And Peters has done a very fine job of that," Amelia said with a nod to the groom, who grinned.

"These pieces of leather hanging down are the girths," John continued, stemming the wish that her look was directed at him. "One forward, one back. Buckle the right one first, making sure the strap is snug but not tight."

Her supple fingers worked the brass buckle into place. She glanced back at him. "Like that?"

Her face was inches from his. He could have dived into the expansive blue of her eyes and forgotten himself entirely. He took a step back. "Just like that. Now the other."

She turned to accomplish the task, but still he found it hard to breathe. "It won't buckle," she complained.

John peered around her. "We'll need to oil that when you return. For now, allow me." He reached around her.

Her body was enclosed in his arms, and the scent of orange blossoms brushed him even as a tremor ran through her. His hands were shaking enough that buckling was difficult. It didn't help that Firenza kept shifting away from him. She knew John's emotions even if Amelia wasn't yet certain.

At last the prong slipped into place, and John checked the girth straps. "Well done," he pronounced. He pulled back, then bent to cup his hands. "Your ride awaits, my lady."

Amelia put her foot into his grip. He helped her into the saddle, then stepped back to watch. If the mare so much as turned its head toward her, John was prepared to act.

Firenza stood perfectly still as Amelia arranged the skirts of her riding habit. Reins in one hand, crop in the other, she directed the mare around the paddock. Firenza walked slowly, carefully, as if well aware of the woman she carried on her back. John took a deep breath. Amelia shot him a grin.

John hadn't even returned her smile before the mare broke into a gallop, leaped the gate and took off across the fields with Amelia on her back.

Chapter Ten

"Fetch Magnum!" John roared, racing to the edge of the paddock. Already Amelia and the roan were disappearing into the field. Why hadn't he heeded his misgivings? Amelia was inexperienced; she couldn't handle a fiery-tempered horse. Now she was on a runaway, and it was all his fault.

The groom returned in a rush, Magnum trotting beside him. John leaped into the saddle even as another groom ran to release the gate. The black reached top speed the moment he cleared the opening.

Across the fields they flew. Some of the other horses attempted to pace them and soon fell behind. Contessa tried to follow but couldn't keep up. John urged the black faster.

He knew the danger of an unruly horse and had tried to break Firenza's bad habits without bruising her wonderful spirit. Perhaps that was why he hadn't refused Amelia. He'd seen her confidence building with each task she accomplished. He wanted her to succeed.

But he wanted more to keep her safe.

He spotted the mare heading for the grade toward

the Rotherford mine and pushed Magnum after her. The slope forced the roan to slow, and the black easily closed the distance.

"Amelia!" John called as they drew abreast.

She had been intent on directing Firenza. Now she flung him a smile. "Oh, hello, my lord," she called. "So glad you could join us. Isn't she magnificent?"

He was so surprised he actually reined Magnum in.

Firenza climbed to the top of the slope, paused on the crest and stood, head high, mane blowing back to brush her rider like flames. Yet it wasn't the roan but his wife that held John captive. Amelia sat, poised, calm, in complete control. Her back was straight in her plum riding habit, her gloved hands graceful on the reins. The smile she cast him was all pleasure and pride, and he felt similar emotions rising up inside him.

He rode to join her, and they walked along the ridge, side by side.

Amelia patted the roan's shoulder. "That's what she needed, a good run and a little sunshine." She took a big breath of the fresh summer air. "Lovely."

She was lovely. Her cheeks were pink from the rushing air; her eyes sparkled from the exhilarating ride. Yet every movement was collected.

"She's yours," John said. "You earned her trust."

The pink deepened. "And she earned mine. She won't disappoint me or hurt me. Not ever."

Neither would he. She might not know that yet, but it was becoming increasingly clear to John. Lady Amelia would challenge every belief he held, about his horses, about his future and about his stance on love.

Amelia wanted to burst into song. She would never forget the way the concern on John's face had melted into admiration. He was beginning to see that she could stand beside him, helpmate, partner. Now she just had to encourage him to see her as the mother of his children.

What she had not expected was to see him as the father of hers.

They had ridden into the stable yard when John urged Magnum forward. A moment later, he was out of the saddle and striding to the paddock, where Peters, one of the younger grooms, was attempting to bridle a two-year-old, a liver chestnut named Diamond in the Rough, with black ears, mane and tail. Seeing his master approaching, the groom dropped the tack, and the horse capered away to the opposite side of the fenced area.

Other grooms came for Firenza and Magnum, and Amelia stepped down on a mounting block as her husband entered the paddock.

"You hit his teeth," John said, gruff voice stating a fact rather than an accusation.

Peters flushed nonetheless. "Aye, my lord. Diamond isn't used to the bridle yet."

"And not likely to become accustomed unless you help him." John nodded to him to retrieve the tack, then clucked to the young stallion. Diamond raised his head, ears flicking.

Amelia ventured closer to the paddock as Peters moved back toward the fence.

"What is he doing?" she murmured to the groom.

Diamond was trotting about, weaving this way and that. John paced him, smile on his face, as if they were dancing. Then he stood still, hand raised, and the chestnut walked up to him.

"Teaching him, your ladyship," Peters murmured

back. "There's none with a lighter touch than the master."

John positioned himself to Diamond's left, one hand on the halter around the horse's nose. He rested his other hand just behind the alert black ears. John stroked the spot, murmuring, as if he was whispering instructions. Diamond lowered his head.

"Good lad," John praised him, patting the two-year-old's lean neck.

As Amelia watched, he went through the cycle twice more. How patient he was, gentle in touch, yet firm in his expectations. She could see by the way Diamond stood—muscles relaxed, tail still—that the chestnut was willing to be led by him. His faith was unquestioning.

Oh, Father, to have such faith!

"Peters," John called, and the groom hurried forward with the bridle. Diamond started, but a word from John calmed him again.

"See how his head is down," John told the groom. "It puts his mouth at the proper angle. Then if you slide in the bit—" he suited word to action "—it's easier to avoid the teeth, and he's less likely to balk." He stepped back to let the groom fasten the tack into place. The look in his dark eyes was kind, tender; the lines of his face soft. That was how a father would gaze at his children, with pride and love. That was how she'd wanted her father to look at her.

And as for how a husband should look at his wife, she could only wish for such sweet devotion.

Her face warmed, and she had to turn away.

But she could not forget the scene as the day went by. It intruded on her thoughts when she set up her embroidery frame in the withdrawing room along with new fabric for a seat cushion of crimson roses. It colored her view of him as they sat with Dr. Fletcher over dinner, making her appreciate the intent way he always listened. And that night, when she said her prayers, asking for health and prosperity for her parents, the king and prince and the nation, she found another thought slipping in.

Father, help me to be worthy of such love.

She was still considering the next move in her campaign to win her husband's heart the next day when Turner came to find her. Amelia had been reviewing Mr. Hennessy's inventory of the linen when the maid approached.

"Begging your pardon, your ladyship, Mr. Hennessy," she said with a bare dip of her knees below a gown in the jade-green color Amelia had chosen for her staff. "But a carriage just pulled up at the door from Bellweather Hall."

Mr. Hennessy snapped to attention, stretching the shoulders of his black coat and his own jade-colored waistcoat. "Check that the withdrawing room is ready to receive guests, Turner," he ordered. "Tell Morton to let down the steps for them on your way. I'll greet her Grace at the door." He turned to Amelia. "How much time will you need to prepare yourself, your ladyship?"

She understood the flurry. Bellweather Hall, which stood at the entrance to the dale, was the ancestral home of the Duke of Bellington. A carriage from there must be transporting a member of his family, and by the sound of it, Mr. Hennessy was certain it was the duchess. The ranking member of the local aristocracy and one of the highest ladies in the empire, she would be a power to court.

"Give me five minutes," Amelia told her butler. "Discover her preferences for refreshments, and tell Mr. Shanter to have them ready."

"Right away, your ladyship."

She had put on a blue-striped morning gown earlier; it ought to be suitable for callers, even one as exalted as the Duchess of Bellington. Amelia took only enough time to make sure her hair was sleeked back in the bun at the nape of her neck and draped a cashmere shawl of sunflower yellow about her shoulders. Then she went to meet her guest.

Instead of merely the duchess, however, she found two women waiting for her in the withdrawing room. One reminded her of her mother—sturdy, silver-haired, with double chins pressing against the white ruff at her throat and ample curves filling her gray lustring gown. That must be the duchess.

Her companion, however, was more slender. She had a pinched nose and sallow skin made worse by the saffron-colored embroidered muslin dress she wore.

"Your Grace," Amelia said, coming forward and dropping her best curtsy, "we are honored to have you with us."

Lady Bellington waved a plump beringed hand as if to grant Amelia the right to sit in her own home. "As the senior lady in the district, I see it as my duty to welcome the new brides." She hitched her own shawl closer as Amelia sat on a spindle-legged chair nearby. "Of course, neither Rotherford nor Danning waited upon my visit before taking their wives elsewhere. This is my daughter, Lady Prudence."

Lady Prudence sniffed, and it took Amelia a moment to realize it wasn't in distaste. "A pleasure to meet you," she said, her voice coming out high and cracked. "Please, forgive me. I always seem to develop a corpulent inflammation of the sinusoidal membrane when we return home."

"It's all in your head," her mother insisted, then she turned to Amelia. "It's all in her head. I'm convinced she proves no danger of contagion, for I spend a great deal of time with her, and I never take ill. Do I, Prudence?"

"No, indeed, Mother," Lady Prudence replied before coughing into her glove.

Lady Bellington was watching Amelia. "Now, tell me," the duchess demanded. "Have you met Rotherford's wife?"

"I haven't had the pleasure," Amelia admitted.

Lady Prudence snorted into a lace-edged handkerchief, a phlegmy rattle in her throat, but her mother brightened.

"She was his governess!" she declared in ringing tones.

"I believe," Lady Prudence put in, "that she was his daughter's nanny, and a gentlewoman fallen on hard times."

"Yes, yes," Lady Bellington said with another wave. "And what about Danning? I hear he enticed two ladies of good family to join him at his lodge and then chose a cit!"

Amelia knew she was blushing and hoped the duchess would put it down to embarrassment over the gossip. She wasn't about to admit she had been one of the two ladies of the *ton*.

"Lord Danning is not the sort to make empty promises," Amelia said instead. "And his new wife, though of common birth, does him great credit."

Lady Bellington perked up. "Ah, so you know her! What does her father do? Barkeep? Hangman?"

"He's a jeweler!" Amelia protested.

"Oh." Her Grace looked positively disappointed.

"Have you seen much of Dovecote Dale, Lady Hascot?" Lady Prudence asked as if oblivious to the fact that she was changing the subject.

"Only a little," Amelia confessed. "I've been busy setting the house to rights."

Lady Bellington leaned forward. "Why? What was wrong with it? A madwoman in the attics?"

"No, certainly not." If she stayed in this room another moment she might end up the madwoman in the attics! She rose. "Goodness, where are my manners? May I offer you refreshments?"

Lady Bellington relaxed back in her chair with a sigh. "If you must."

"Not for me," Lady Prudence said with another sniff. "My physician has me on a diet of watercress and sugar cubes."

"Oh, I'm sure we can find a sugar cube somewhere," Amelia promised her. After all, John had to reward his horses! "If you'll excuse me for a moment."

Out in the corridor, she took a deep breath. She could simply have rung for Mr. Hennessy or one of the footmen, but she needed a moment to collect her composure. Like the duchess, her mother had had a way of making pronouncements that required all of Amelia's skill to deflect. Either Amelia had grown rusty or the ladies from Bellweather Hall were more demanding, because she felt the need for reinforcements.

"Bring the refreshments," she instructed the butler, who had been waiting just down the corridor for her call. "And send someone for Lord Hascot."

In the act of obeying her first command, Mr. Hennessy froze. "Lord Hascot, your ladyship? Are you certain that's advisable?"

"It may not be advisable," Amelia said, "but it is necessary." With a nod of conviction and a prayer John would be amenable for once, she returned to her guests.

Somehow, she kept the conversation going until the footman brought in a laden tea cart. She met Mr. Hennessy's gaze where he stood in the doorway, and he shook his head. Was John out in the pastures or too busy to heed her call for help?

"So how did the Dowager Lady Hascot take the news of your wedding?" Lady Bellington asked as she accepted tea in a delicate floral cup from Amelia.

Amelia didn't know who she meant. She was certain John had said his mother had passed away.

"Oh, look, Mother," Lady Prudence said with a nod to the tea cart. "Here are those apricot tarts you so adore. A shame they give me a petrified dyspepsia."

Lady Bellington ignored her, eyes glittering as if she'd found something much more savory to enjoy. "Lady Hascot, his brother's widow," she informed Amelia. "She very nearly married him before switching her allegiance to the older twin brother."

"Twins," Lady Prudence said rapturously. "I hear they feel the same things, even when they're ill."

Amelia's bewilderment must have been showing, for Lady Bellington positively chortled. "He hasn't told you! Very likely he still can't bear to talk of it. They say it broke his heart. He never courted again, never so much as looked at another woman. How did you entice him to offer?"

Merely by falling asleep in his stable. And only because he was a gentleman had he done the right thing to spare her scandal. Small wonder he refused her attempts to grow closer. He had given his heart to another. Her company, her care, would never be preferable.

"Mother," Lady Prudence scolded. "You have only to look at Lady Hascot to know her husband must dote on her. She is sweet tempered, kindhearted and lovely, everything a gentleman might want." She sighed as if she wished for such attributes.

Amelia raised her head. "You forgot one mark of character some gentlemen prize over all others—loyalty."

Lady Prudence beamed as if she thought herself capable of that, at least.

Her mother, however, frowned. "You had better pray he values loyalty, my dear, for Lady Hascot is a widow. I had heard it said she regretted her marriage and wished she'd made another choice. There is nothing to stop her from staking her claim once more."

Nothing but a band of gold. John had always struck her as an honorable man. Yet how could he be true to his vows when he loved elsewhere?

John heard about Amelia's summons the moment he came in from the fields. Something must be wrong that she wished *his* company to entertain visitors. He left Magnum with a groom and started for the door of the stable only to find Marcus Fletcher blocking his way.

"By your leave," the veterinarian said, laying a hand

against John's navy coat, "you may want to reconsider. Her ladyship has visitors from Bellweather Hall."

"The Terrors," one of the grooms murmured with a shudder as he passed.

John had heard the unkind name the locals had given the Duchess of Bellington and her daughter. It was all too easy to understand the reason. The mother collected every bit of gossip like a dragon hoarding treasure, and the daughter had never found an illness she couldn't like. At times he pitied the duke.

"I can't leave Amelia to them," he told Fletcher.

His friend shook his curly head. "She's likely to fare better than either of us," he insisted. "You may not have noticed, but your wife is quite clever."

She was more clever than he had a right to expect. "I don't doubt her intelligence," he said. "I merely dislike seeing her put upon. Excuse me."

He knew he had to go carefully as he drew up to the rear door. He'd given Amelia charge of the house after all. But she had felt comfortable joining him in his domain, and with her help, he thought he might be able to stand on his own in hers. And surely if he could find a way to converse with the Terrors, he could converse with anyone.

Unfortunately, he reached the front of the house in time to see her Grace and Lady Prudence being draped with their wraps by the door. Lady Prudence, in fact, was frowning at the footman.

"He looks a great deal like a fellow who works for us," John heard her tell Amelia as John approached from the back of the house. "Is he a twin?"

Her mother peered closer. "He doesn't look familiar to me. I wouldn't have such a common fellow on staff."

"What a blessing each house has its own character," Amelia said as the red-faced footman backed away respectfully.

"And what a blessing a wife is to this house," John said, seizing the opening. He came up beside Amelia and nodded. "Forgive me for not joining you sooner, my dear. I didn't realize we had company."

And not too welcome company by the pallor of Amelia's face. "Her Grace and Lady Prudence were just leaving." She stepped forward as if to usher them out the door herself.

"You have a lovely wife, my lord," the duchess pronounced. "Tell me, do you intend to keep her with you out here in the wilderness?"

Amelia stiffened. So much for polite conversation. John could think of only one way to answer the woman.

He leaned forward and met the duchess's bright gaze. "Until my dying day, madam."

She sagged as if he'd destroyed a dream, then jerked upright again. "And how close is that? Your brother passed away only last year. How are you feeling?"

"Never better." He strode to the door and held it open himself. "Do not allow me to detain you. I'm sure you have others to regale with what you've learned here."

She scowled at him. "I haven't learned anything of merit. Your wife, my lord, is remarkably closemouthed."

And thank You, Lord, for that!

Amelia lowered her gaze, but Lady Prudence ambled toward the door. "Come along, Mother," she said. "Lord and Lady Hascot are on their honeymoon, if you recall. We may well impose."

The duchess pounced on the idea. "Oh, the honeymoon. Of course! Wait until I tell Bell. If Hascot can

set up a nursery, he certainly should be able to, as well."
She turned to Amelia and shook her gloved finger. "I
expect to be the first to hear when you are increasing."

John waited for the pink to spring into Amelia's
cheeks, but if anything, she turned even paler as the
ladies exited the house.

"We should see them to the carriage," Amelia murmured.

"We should not," John replied, and he shut the door
on them.

He thought Amelia might argue, but she stood
hunched over, as if she was in pain. The way she kept
blinking made him wonder if she were fighting tears.

Why was she treated so shabbily? Couldn't they see
her character, her kindness? He could.

John strode to her side, touched her chin and raised
her gaze to his. The hurt behind those blue eyes stabbed
at him.

"She's an old harridan, Amelia," he told her. "You
cannot allow her thoughtless words to hurt you."

"They were rather thought-provoking words, actually," she replied. She pulled away from his touch, drew
her shawl more tightly around her shoulders. "She informed me of something I wish I'd known sooner."

Had she been a horse, he would have thought her
spooked, ready to leap away and fly from the thing
that distressed her. But even as he was coming to know
her as well as one of his horses, he could not imagine
what sort of gossip the old woman had dragged out that
could have brought about such a reaction. He'd never
done anything the least scandalous.

"Oh?" John prompted, watching her.

She gazed up at him, and sorrow was etched on every feature. "You were not free to marry me, John. You're in love with another woman."

Chapter Eleven

Amelia wanted John to deny that he loved another. Oh, how she wanted him to deny it! For if he had truly placed his heart in someone else's keeping, she did not like her chances of retrieving it.

"If you are referring to my brother's wife," he said, face so still it might have been carved from marble, "it would be inappropriate to feel more than familial affection."

Inappropriate, perhaps, but not impossible, especially given the circumstances Lady Bellington had related. Amelia was coming to know her husband— he was nothing if not committed. Look at his dedication to his horses. His love, once lit, would not easily be snuffed out.

Perhaps that was why she craved it.

And she did crave it, she realized with a pang. She wanted more than his admiration and respect; she wanted him to love her. When he was troubled, she wanted to be the first one he turned to for counsel and comfort. When he laughed, she wanted to share the joy. That was what a true marriage meant.

She had started her campaign from Turner's suggestion. She had had a setback, a terrible setback. But surely retreating was not the answer.

Mindful of the footman hovering beside her, she stepped closer to John. "Might we discuss the matter, just the two of us?"

He glanced at the footman as well, then offered her his arm. "Come to the library with me."

The library was one of the two rooms she hadn't redecorated. For one, the massive floor-to-ceiling dark walnut bookcases were firmly anchored to the walls. For another, it seemed to be John's favorite room, and changing anything felt like a sacrilege. Now the solemn colors and the dark wood furnishings seemed to crowd against her, press the very air from her lungs. She broke from him to go open the drapes and let in the light.

Turning, she saw that John was standing by a set of black leather-upholstered chairs near the fire, hair once more fallen onto his brow. One of these days she was going to put it back herself, if only to feel the warmth of those dark tresses. Had the Dowager Lady Hascot touched him so?

He waited for her to take a seat before sitting opposite her. "What would you have of me?" he asked.

Everything. How he felt about the other Lady Hascot, how he felt about her. Yet did she really want to hear him say aloud how little affection he bore her?

"Lady Bellington claimed you were in love with your brother's wife before they wed," she said. "Is that true?"

He leaned back from her. "I thought myself in love, yes. She chose my brother instead."

How calmly he stated the matter, as if Lady Caroline

had merely decided upon a different dress that morning. "Were you not hurt by her defection?"

Now his gaze avoided hers, as well. "She was wise to choose the security of the title. Isn't that what all young ladies are taught?"

Certainly her mother and governess had drummed it into her. "I suppose so," Amelia allowed. "At the very least, we are schooled to try for the best marriage possible. Still, she is free now. Why did you marry me?"

As if he, too, sought more air, he rose and went to the window. The light etched the planes of his face in sharp relief. "The church frowns upon a marriage between a man and his brother's wife. I am to look on Lady Hascot as a sister."

His tone remained dispassionate, removed. It was as if the other Lady Hascot was nothing to him. Why didn't that give Amelia comfort?

"I'd forgotten that," she admitted. "So of course you could not marry." She licked her lips, steeling herself to address the next issue. "That doesn't mean you didn't wish it otherwise."

His answer came immediately. "My wishes are immaterial." He turned to look at Amelia, and now the light behind him caused his face to disappear in shadow. "I married you, Amelia. I will honor our vows."

How could she help him understand? Amelia stood and approached him. "And if you cannot? 'Forsaking all others' the rector said. Your wife is to have all your love and devotion."

"And a husband should have all his wife's," he replied. "Do you tell me you've held nothing back?"

She stiffened. "No, nothing! I've never loved another."

"And do you claim to love me?"

Amelia swallowed, gaze falling to the black-and-green carpet even as she halted a few feet from him. "Perhaps not yet." Her voice sounded so small. "But I'm trying."

He moved to close the distance between them and touched her cheek, drawing her attention back to his face. Standing so close, she could see that gold flecks danced in the dark eyes, as if some part of him still clung to light, to hope.

"I know you are trying, Amelia," he murmured. "You've turned this mausoleum into a home. You may well have saved Firenza's life. I admire your efforts."

A tear slid down her cheek. "Admiration is not love."

"No," he agreed, wiping the tear away with the pad of his thumb. "But it can serve as a foundation."

His touch made her tremble. "So I have heard," she murmured. "Yet love is not always the result. How can you know what the future holds?"

He released her. "No one knows the future, Amelia. I can only tell you this—I feel more strongly for you than I ever thought possible. Those feelings can only grow."

She wanted to believe that, yet her parents had known her all her life, had been given every opportunity to love, and hadn't managed it. And she'd always feared that the fault must lie with her. If she could not earn the love of her parents, a love most would say was her due, how was she to earn his?

"I pray you are right," she murmured, dropping her gaze once more.

His fingers moved to her chin, lifted her countenance to his once more. His look was fierce.

"Any man who cannot love you," he said, "is the most flint-hearted person on earth."

As if to prove it, he lowered his head and kissed her.

She'd never been kissed on the lips before. No fellow would have dared risk her father's wrath. The sweet pressure, the rising emotion, made her weak at the knees. John's arms stole around her, fitted her against him. It was as if they were becoming one heart, one spirit. No more loneliness, no more loss. She wanted to stay like this, protected, cherished, forever.

Slowly, he raised his head, and she gazed up at him. His dark brows were down, his eyes narrowed, as if he had found something quite unexpected in his arms. Was he as shaken by the kiss as she was?

"If you doubt me after that, madam," he said, voice gruffer than usual, "I have nothing more to say."

"You were quite persuasive, my lord," Amelia answered. "Let us see how we might make more of this marriage."

John stared down at the woman in his arms, his wife. He'd been gazing upon her for a week now, at the breakfast table, across the stable. Always he'd thought her beautiful, but as she met his gaze, pink lips parted and warm from his kiss, skin radiant, she nearly took his breath away.

The kiss had done more than that. He felt as if he'd opened some part of himself, a part no one had ever touched. That part whispered more was waiting, if he dared open himself just a little further.

But he knew exactly what could happen when he allowed anyone too close—betrayal and pain. Amelia seemed to be different—he was surprised how much he wanted her to be different, but only time would tell if his fledgling feelings were justified.

He released her from his embrace, and the room felt somehow colder as she stepped back.

"We'll take our own time," he promised her. "Very likely we'll be fine so long as we ignore the well-meaning advice of our friends and neighbors. This matter is between the two of us. We must be the ones to determine the outcome."

She curtsied. "Yes, my lord."

He hated when she was subservient. He always felt as if he'd kicked a puppy. "I like you better when you fight me."

Her head came up, brow furrowed. "You want me to be unpleasant?"

"I don't think you know how," John replied. "You are always kind, always considerate. But if you have an opinion on a matter, madam, state it. I may be the king of my castle, but I am not a despot."

She nodded. "Very well." She put her hands on her hips and raised her head. He was in for it now. He waited for her to demand another increase in the household allowance, to order him to let her ride Magnum.

"This is the ugliest room in the house," she said. "And I wish you'd give me leave to redecorate."

John blinked, then glanced around. He hadn't really looked at his library for a long time. He used the room to update his breeding book, to draft correspondence, to review matters with Fletcher or another member of his staff. The space was a bit on the dark side, and he'd never been particularly fond of those leather armchairs by the fire. No matter how many times he had sat in them, they had never conformed to his shape.

Returning his gaze to hers, he spread his hands. "There is nothing sacred here. Do what you wish with it."

By the light in her eyes, he knew she would. He managed to make his escape to the stables before she suggested other things that needed to be altered in his life.

"Why do women always want to change a fellow?" he complained to Fletcher later that day as they examined a mare that had come up lame.

"My mother had a theory," Fletcher said, running his large hands up the injured leg, checking for lumps or bruises. "She said Adam was imperfect. That's why God made Eve."

John grimaced. "To remind him of his shortcomings."

"I believe it was actually to help him," Fletcher said with a smile, light flashing in his spectacles. "Ah, there's the culprit—damaged tendon, not too bad right now, but we want to nip it in the bud. Hand me the liniment, if you will."

John reached into the carpet bag the veterinarian had brought with him to the stables and pulled out the jar of cream. Opening it, he wrinkled his nose. "Rue?" he asked as he handed the jar to his friend.

"To reduce swelling," Fletcher said. "There's also arnica for pain and other ingredients, too. My father swore by it."

His father, John knew, had raised sturdy highland ponies, the type that worked for their supper. "And what did he advise in matters of the heart?"

Fletcher grinned. "That a gentleman should merely nod and say yes."

John chuckled. "I wish it was that easy."

"Why do you make it difficult?" Fletcher asked, rubbing the cream into the mare's fetlock. "I cannot imagine our sweet Lady Hascot is so demanding."

"She wants to redecorate the library," John said.

Fletcher's hand stilled. "The library? Oh, that is cutting close to the bone." He glanced at John. "What did you say?"

"I nodded and said yes."

Fletcher shook his head as he returned to his work, red curls brushing the mare's belly. "See? You're doing splendidly." He leaned back, wiped his hands on a rag and patted the mare. "And so is this little lady."

John reached into the bag and pulled out the roll of bandages. "You'll want these next."

Fletcher accepted the cloth with a nod of thanks. "I'd say," he ventured as he unwound a length, "that you are remarkably fortunate in your choice of brides. Your lady doesn't pick at a fellow, as I've seen some do, questioning his choices."

"Lady Caroline did that," John remembered. "Subtly, mind you. She had a way of looking at my cravat or boots that told me they weren't up to snuff."

"Thank the Lord your wife is not so inclined." He busied himself wrapping the mare's leg. "And if she has a larger complaint, it's likely justified."

"Whose side are you on?" John demanded.

"Yours," Fletcher assured him. He tore off the end of the bandage and tied it in place. "But I'd be no kind of friend if I didn't want the best for you, and it seems to me your wife feels the same way."

Did she? John thought about it more that day and the next morning as the footman helped him dress for Sunday services. He had told Amelia to state her opinions, her needs, and she was beginning to take his advice. Why, then, couldn't he bring himself to give his heart? She'd improved the house, in looks and operation, just as he'd hoped. She was good with the horses, with the possible exception of Magnum. She was relentlessly kind. Surely he could trust her.

Together, could they make a family?

The matter was so much on his mind that he found himself unable to attend to the readings as he sat beside Amelia in the Hascot pew that day at St. Andrew's in the village of Dovecote. He had always liked the church. Though it was merely a country chapel, all the landowners in the area had donated to make it the finest, from the new pipe organ to the stained glass windows beaming down on the congregation. And it was an orderly church, with the tombstones in the churchyard sitting as straight as the boxed pews. The Reverend Mr. Battersea would have had it no other way.

Usually John searched the words in the reading and the rector's lecture, looking for something from the Lord. Ever since his brother and Caro had betrayed him he'd felt as if God had distanced himself, as well. Certainly John's prayers never seemed to go higher than the vaulted ceiling.

Did You put Amelia in my life for a reason, Lord? Am I to learn something from all this?

"And thus," the rector concluded, peering at his alert congregation through his silver-rimmed spectacles, "we are reminded that all things work to the good for those who love the Lord and are called according to His purposes. Join me in singing."

John rose with Amelia, and she held the songbook

so he could see the words. But he didn't need it. Her perfect voice was written on his heart.

"Gracious Spirit! Love divine!
Let Thy light within me shine;
All my guilty fears remove;
Fill me with Thy heavenly love."

Love. Was that what the Lord wanted of him? That he should drop his guard and let Amelia in? Yet why would God put such a strong emotion as love before John once more? The last time had nearly been John's undoing. Was he any stronger now?

Chapter Twelve

Amelia could not remember a finer service. No one looked down on her that her gown, a favorite muslin with lace at the cuffs and hem, was last year's fashion. Indeed, with John in a navy coat and fawn trousers the footman had found at the back of his wardrobe, a tall-crowned hat on his dark head, hair finally in place, the two of them made a handsome pair.

Then, too, no one complained as her mother often did that the rector spoke too long or on too personal a subject. And Amelia could not fault John's attendance to the service. It had been a comfort to have him beside her, hearing his deep voice joining with hers as they responded to the rector, feeling his fingers brush hers as they shared the *Book of Common Prayer*.

Yet she could not help sensing that the service had been more to John than a chance to gather with others of the faith to worship. That intensity she sometimes noticed had seemed to gather around him like a thundercloud building on the horizon, and his sharp gaze had devoured the rector as if hungry for every word. She had found herself listening more closely than usual as a result, trying to sense what he sensed. But instead of gaining insights, she had felt a welcome peace.

Thank You, Lord, for bringing me to a very good place!

"And this must be the Lady Hascot of whom I've heard so much," the rector called out as John passed him at the end of service. Amelia stopped, forcing John to pause, as well. The Reverend Mr. Battersea was an older man with flyaway white hair and a manner of looking over his spectacles that made it seem as if he was sharing a particularly good joke. Now his gray eyes positively twinkled at her.

"My wife, Amelia, Lady Hascot," John said in his gruff voice. "May I present our rector, Mr. Horatio Battersea."

His wife. Something inside her fluttered when she heard John say those words. She smiled and offered the rector her hand, and he took it in both of his.

"Delighted, your ladyship," he said, voice as friendly as his look. "I only wish I might have had the privilege of conducting the marriage ceremony, but perhaps we will have cause for other celebrations in the future." He released her hand to beam at John. "Say, perhaps, a christening?"

"You have other parishioners waiting, I see," John replied with a nod to the people who clustered around them as if to hear his answer to the rector's question. "Forgive us for keeping you." He tugged Amelia onto the flagstone path that led through the graveyard toward where their carriage was waiting. Though she was glad not to have to answer the question, she knew they could not keep dodging it forever.

Nor could she dodge the duchess and her daughter.

The Bellington coach was waiting right behind theirs, and Lady Bellington and Lady Prudence were standing next to it as if expecting conversation with their neighbors. Had they been in London, Amelia was certain many would have rushed to curry favor with so highly placed a family. Now, however, the other members of the congregation seemed to be going out of their way to avoid the two.

"We should say good morning," she murmured to John.

She heard him sigh. "Yes, we probably should." Still, he kept walking toward their own carriage.

Amelia gave his arm a squeeze. "A big strong fellow like you can't fear two little ladies."

He shuddered. "With every fiber of my being, I assure you, madam." But he allowed her to lead him from the path and over to them.

"Lady Bellington, Lady Prudence," Amelia greeted the pair, "how nice to see you."

Lady Prudence sneezed. "Pollen," she explained and proceeded to blow her nose loudly and at length. "My Castleton physician says it can cause a scurrilous coruscation of the bowel."

"Luckily," Amelia said, aware of John shifting uncomfortably beside her, "it also results from the most beautiful flowers." She nodded to the daisies growing along the edge of the yard. "How wonderful we can share them with you."

"And I have something to share!" the duchess crowed, leaning forward, her taffeta gown rustling against the grass. "Bell is finally to marry!"

That was good news. "How marvelous," Amelia said

with a smile. "May I know the name of the bride so that I can send our congratulations?"

"I don't know her name," the duchess confessed. "He couldn't come out and say it, you understand. It was all in the subtext of his note to me." She lifted her reticule with one hand and began digging through it with the other. "Ah, yes, here it is."

Would she read the entire thing to Amelia now? Had they been sitting in the withdrawing room, it might have been fine, but Amelia knew John would have a hard time being so patient.

"How kind of you to offer the information," she tried, "but surely such correspondence must be between a mother and son."

"Not at all, not at all," Lady Bellington insisted. She opened the parchment and held it far out in front of her, peering at the bold black lines. "Oh, I cannot read it in this light. Here, Lady Hascot, your voice is better for this sort of thing. See, what he writes there?"

She thrust the note at Amelia, who took it with some trepidation. It was mercifully short.

"Am bringing friends with me next week," she read aloud.

"There, you see?" the duchess declared, snatching it back from her as if it was a treasured heirloom. She folded it carefully away, chortling the entire time. "Oh, I can hardly wait! Grandchildren to dandle on my knee."

"I'm not sure Dr. Willingston-Pratchard would allow me to dandle," Lady Prudence said with a frown.

John's grip on Amelia's arm tightened. "I believe the horses have stood long enough," he said. "Good day, ladies."

"We should have encouraged her," Amelia protested

as he all but dragged her to their coach. "She says so many dismal things that surely we can celebrate when she says something positive for a change."

"We'd do better to encourage the truth," John said, opening the door and helping her climb in. "Bellington may be a duke with funds to spare, but he's had a difficult time convincing the right lady to marry into his family. And none can blame him for that fact." He shuddered again.

"I think you are too hard on them," Amelia insisted as he took his seat beside her. "No one is perfect."

"See that you remember that," he replied, then thumped on the roof to signal their coachman to set out for home.

Did he think she expected perfection? The idea refused to leave Amelia the rest of the day. As usual, John changed his clothes the moment they reached the farm and spent the afternoon out with the horses. Amelia tried to read an uplifting book, returning to her copy of *Waverly,* but the story of adventure on the Scottish highlands did not sweep her away as it usually did.

She had spent her life avoiding unpleasantness, ignoring slights and slurs. Perhaps it was time she took them on directly.

Accordingly, when John joined her for dinner, she broached the topic straightaway.

"I do not expect you to be perfect, my lord," she said.

John paused, lamb raised halfway to his mouth. "I am very pleased to hear that."

He said it so cautiously, as if preparing to fend off whatever Amelia was going to say next. Amelia set down her own fork.

"You don't like to fight either, do you?"

As if to deny it, he shoved the lamb into his mouth and chewed furiously a moment before answering. "A gentleman knows when to say his piece and when to hold his tongue."

"So does a lady," Amelia agreed. "But I am beginning to realize those rules are different between a husband and a wife."

He frowned. "Why?"

Amelia wiggled her lips, trying to find a way to explain the certainty that was growing. "A husband and wife are closer. Partners, if you will. They must know each other's thoughts, anticipate needs."

He shook his head and returned to his food. "You ask the impossible."

"No, I don't think I do." Amelia leaned closer to him. His strong hands never stopped moving; the glower never left his face. "You, for instance, require a certain amount of solitude to be happy."

His look softened, and he chuckled. "You didn't need to be my wife to discover that. I'm not exactly social."

"Indeed. But only someone close to you would understand. I am not attempting to change you, my lord."

He cocked his head, dark eyes watchful. "Aren't you? Can you truly say you accept me just as I am, Amelia? That you have no regrets in marrying me?"

"My regrets," Amelia said, "are not with the past, my lord. My regrets have to do with the future."

"There is no sense worrying about the future," he countered. "What will be, will be. It's up to us to make the best of it."

She was to remember those words the next day. She'd thought hard and prayed harder about how to win her husband over. She felt as if she was missing some piece of the puzzle that was John, some aspect of his character that would unlock his heart. A campaigning general, after all, required reconnaissance. Perhaps a consultation with the veterinarian was in order. He clearly saw more of John than she did. Accordingly, she asked Marcus Fletcher to attend her when he had a moment.

"Dr. Fletcher," she said when he made his bow where she sat at the little secretary that afternoon, "I would like your advice."

He glanced around the room as if looking for a place to hide. Fortunately for Amelia, it was no longer the shadowed cave it had been when she'd arrived at Hollyoak Farm. Bright paintings of country landscapes graced the walls, and filmy curtains let in the light from the two windows. As if he realized that he could not escape her question, the veterinarian ventured closer.

"How might I be of assistance, your ladyship?" he asked, tugging down on his paisley waistcoat.

"You have worked for my husband for quite a while, have you not?" Amelia returned.

"Since he purchased Hollyoak Farm," he confirmed. He cocked his head, gaze going to the parchment in front of her. Like Turner, he seemed inordinately interested in what she had written, but she knew the veterinarian could read.

"I would imagine you've spent a great deal of time together," Amelia continued with a smile. "He must greatly admire your efforts."

He stood a little taller. "I like to think so. And I admire his, your ladyship. He has a way with the animals, an understanding, if you will. I've never seen its like."

That yearning was rising up inside her again. Why

should even horses know affection when it had been denied her?

"He has a gift," she agreed. She faced the veterinarian fully. "I have come to greatly admire him, as well, Dr. Fletcher. I've tried to make things pleasant for him."

"Oh, you have, your ladyship," he assured her. "You've only to look at this room to see that."

"But is he happy?" Amelia protested. "Do you see him smile more often?"

Fletcher ran a hand back through his hair, fingers sticking in the red curls. "By your leave, your ladyship, he isn't a man to smile all that much to begin with."

"I know."

Her sorrow must have been evident, for he hurried forward and knelt beside her, putting his face on a level with hers.

"Now, you mustn't blame yourself, your ladyship," he said, gray eyes earnest. "That's just his nature. I've read it's even in a man's spleen, whether he's happy or melancholy."

He was a doctor, but she found his theory difficult to believe. "I've always thought that happiness is more of a choice, sir," she said. "We are born with a temperament, to be sure, and our surroundings shape it. But we can choose to be content in our circumstances. Didn't the Apostle Paul say so?"

"He did," he acknowledged. "But he'd never met Lord Hascot."

Amelia couldn't help laughing. "That I cannot argue. But I wish I knew what more I could do to please him."

He sighed. "I'm hard-pressed to say, your ladyship. Except, perhaps..."

Amelia leaned forward. "Yes?"

"Give him a little time?" He ducked his head as if he knew she wouldn't like the suggestion. "He's a proud man, a determined man. He doesn't change easily, even when he knows it's for the best."

Amelia nodded, leaning back. "So I have noticed. It's just so hard to wait!"

He patted her hand on the desk. "I know." He climbed to his feet. "But you've made a big difference already. Just keep at it, and I promise you won't be disappointed."

She wished she could believe that. She was about to thank him for his time when Reams rushed into the room.

"Begging your pardon, your ladyship, Dr. Fletcher," he managed, body trembling and coat askew. "But we have visitors."

Amelia rose. "Her Grace and Lady Prudence?"

"No, your ladyship." He visibly swallowed. "Mr. Hennessy says it's a Hascot coach and a big wagon."

"A Hascot coach?" Amelia frowned. "But my things have already arrived."

"Only one other person's allowed to use a coach marked with the Hascot insignia," Dr. Fletcher said. He met Amelia's gaze, and dread washed over her.

"You mean…" She couldn't bring herself to say the name aloud.

He nodded, color fleeing. "That's right, your ladyship. The Dowager Lady Hascot is here, and by the sound of it, she intends to stay awhile."

John sighted the cavalcade from the field. He'd been out with Magnum, making sure Contessa was behaving for once, and he'd taken the opportunity to check the creek for any more of the water hemlock that had sickened Firenza. As they rode back toward the stables, Magnum had bugled in warning.

"Buyers," he told the black with a pat on the horse's muscular neck. "Never you fear. You're not for sale."

Still, he knew his duty, so he urged the stallion across the grass, jumping this ditch and that wall. It was a show, an exhibition. Gentlemen saw Magnum's abilities and hungered for a horse of his caliber. He had several hunters ready to take to the field. Perhaps one of these people would be a good match.

But as he drew nearer, he saw the baggage wagon, piled with trunks and boxes. A maid in a black gown was riding next to the driver, which meant there was a lady in the group. And the gentleman dismounting his charger at the front of the procession was dressed in the blue-and-gold uniform of the 10th Royal Hussars, the Prince's own cavalry unit.

John felt his shoulders tightening. Then he caught sight of the carriage.

His family carriage.

Caro.

He felt as if someone had rammed a fist into his gut. Magnum must have sensed the change in him, for the black's gait stuttered. John reined him in, stroked his neck.

"I don't like it," he murmured. "But we can't abandon Amelia."

Magnum tossed his head as if to argue. The black had never warmed to Amelia, and John still wasn't sure why. But he had to agree with the stallion that this visit would only mean trouble.

The cavalcade reached the house the same time he

and Magnum did. Amelia and Fletcher had come out onto the steps. She stood tall and proud. Her pleasant smile was so firmly fixed to her lips it might have been drawn on with oil. Her posture only stiffened further as the footman lowered the step and helped Caroline, Lady Hascot, to alight.

She was as lovely as ever, golden curls tickling the sides of her creamy face below a tiny hat nearly eclipsed by a profusion of feathers and satiny bows. Her rosy lips widened in a smile of welcome as John handed Magnum's reins to the footman and came forward to greet her.

"John, dearest!" The musky scent of roses engulfed him as she held out her hand and angled her chin to present him equal opportunity to kiss either location. He refused.

"Lady Hascot," he said. "We weren't expecting you."

She trilled a laugh as the cavalry officer attending her stepped to her side. "Well, you always said I was welcome at Hollyoak Farm any time," she reminded John. "And you didn't give me a chance to meet your charming bride in town." She leaned around John and wiggled her gloved fingers at Amelia. "Oh, but she's lovely, John. I can see why you offered for her."

Before he could respond, she reached for the officer's arm and drew him closer. "Allow me to present Major David Kensington of the 10th Royal Hussars."

Major Kensington extended his hand. "Lord Hascot, an honor. My commanding officer rode one of your beasts into the battle of Waterloo. A magnificent creature."

"I'll be more impressed if you tell me the horse survived the battle," John said without shaking his hand.

"Oh, of course. With great distinction, I promise you." Kensington pulled back his hand and rubbed it along the gold stripe of his trouser as if that had been his intention all along. "I was very glad Lady Hascot suggested this trip, for I've long wanted to learn more about your program." He eyed Magnum over John's shoulder. "I see you continue to breed the best."

"I merely appreciate the Lord's work," John replied. He would have liked nothing better than to send the two to the inn in the village, but he suspected Amelia would want him to at least attempt the social niceties. "Come, meet my wife," he told them.

John led them toward the house even as grooms took away Magnum and the major's horse, a spirited chestnut gelding.

Amelia inclined her head as they approached the stairs. "Welcome to Hollyoak Farm," she said, graciousness itself for all that her color had fled.

John stepped between her and Caro. "Amelia, Dr. Fletcher, may I present my brother's wife, Lady Hascot, and Major Kensington."

Fletcher nodded to both. Amelia inclined her head to Caro and allowed the major to kiss her hand, retrieving it quickly.

Caro laughed again. "I can see this Lady Hascot business is going to grow tiresome. There is only one thing for it. You must be Amelia, and I must be Caro. We are sisters now after all." She pushed past John and linked arms with Amelia. "I just know we'll be the best of friends, as well. You must tell me all about how John courted you. We can compare notes."

John moved to intercept, but Kensington blocked his way.

"Women," he said with an easy grin as Caro all but dragged Amelia into the house on a rose-scented cloud. "I say, allow me to change out of my travel dirt, and I'd be delighted to see more of your stock."

John opened his mouth to refuse, but Fletcher stepped forward. "Allow me to show you around, Major. I am the veterinarian at Hollyoak Farm, so you might say I've know each horse from before it was foaled."

"Capital!" Major Kensington clapped him on the shoulder. "I'll just be a moment, if you could point out my room."

"Lady Hascot will have one waiting for you," Fletcher assured him, bowing him ahead into the house. As soon as the major was out of earshot, Fletcher turned to John. "This has all the makings of a disaster."

"Or a farce," John replied. "You needn't trouble yourself. I'll see to the major after I've made sure Caro and Amelia are getting on. Just inform the others that I don't intend to sell another horse to the military, not after seeing how Contessa was treated."

"If I may, that was one misguided cavalryman," the veterinarian protested. "I'm sure many valiant officers treat their horses better than their friends."

"Then they are free to approach me. In the meantime, keep your eyes on Kensington when we dine tonight. I want to know what you think of his character."

Fletcher nodded. "And I would counsel you to keep a very close eye on the ladies. Your wife has only begun to feel as if Hollyoak Farm is her home. She won't appreciate having to share it, or you."

Chapter Thirteen

Did the other Lady Hascot have to be so perfect?

Amelia managed a smile as Major Kensington and Dr. Fletcher laughed at one of the woman's jokes. Caro sat at the dinner table, head cocked so that her golden curls brushed her cheek, lips curved in delight. She was witty, clever, a born flirt. Amelia felt like a great lump.

They were taking an early dinner, but that hadn't stopped Caro and Major Kensington from dressing for the evening. Caro's gown of russet satin gleamed in the candlelight and was rivaled only by the sparkle of the gold braid on the major's uniform.

Amelia was thankful she'd had rooms made up a while ago just in case some of John's buyers would need to stay overnight. As it was, she had only murmured the locations to Mr. Hennessy, and the butler had directed the various servants where to go. A word to Mr. Shanter had brought out the best salmon for dinner. She could confidently say she'd been a credit to her husband. Somehow, that fact wasn't as satisfying as she'd hoped.

"How long do you plan to stay?" John put in from the head of the table. Mr. Hennessy had placed Caro on his right and Major Kensington on his left, with Dr. Fletcher between Caro and Amelia at the foot. She knew it was protocol, but she couldn't help wishing she was the one sitting next to her husband.

Now Caro laughed. Everything seemed a happy circumstance to her. A shame Amelia couldn't see the visit that way.

"Now, don't you worry about how you'll entertain us, John," Caro said. "Major Kensington is ever so eager to learn more about what you do, and you might even convince me to get into the saddle." She leaned around Dr. Fletcher to smile at Amelia. "I never was much of a rider. I'm sure you understand."

"Amelia is an excellent rider," John said. "She managed one of my most difficult horses with her voice alone."

Amelia's face warmed with his praise. So, she felt, did her heart.

Major Kensington raised his glass in toast. "Well done, Lady Hascot. I appreciate a woman who knows how to tame a savage beast."

"Particularly when he is her husband," Caro teased before taking a sip from her own glass.

John glowered.

"I would have no need to tame such a considerate husband," Amelia put in smoothly. "And as for the horse, Major Kensington, Firenza is not nearly a savage."

"Firenza?" Caro shook her finger at John. "Another fanciful name, I see." She turned to Major Kensington. "Do you know he named that black brute he was riding Magnum Opus, as if he was a great composition?"

"What would you have me name him?" John challenged, eyes narrowing. "Blacky? Save me from such a lack of inspiration."

"I do believe," Dr. Fletcher put in, "that Weatherby's *General Stud Book* encourages original names for its registry."

Caro bowed over her silver-rimmed plate as if paying homage. "And all hail Weatherby's. Heaven forbid that we do anything to displease the masters of horse."

"You haven't answered my question," John said.

Amelia dropped her gaze to her salmon before her guests could see her smile. Bless John for his constancy! It was becoming very clear, at least to her, that he found their guests far from amusing. She should not take such pleasure in that.

"I haven't decided," Caro told him breezily. "Everyone who is anyone has left London for the Season, in any event."

True. Most of London's elite found country houses to visit during sweltering August. Amelia would never have thought Hollyoak Farm to be among the more sought-after invitations.

"Will your friends not miss your company?" she tried, earning her a fierce nod of approval from John.

Caro waved a hand. "I am certain they will survive my absence. Besides, I like being beholden to no one. I come and go as it pleases me."

"And the best you could do was Hollyoak?" John demanded.

She dimpled at him. "Right now, it pleases me to become better acquainted with your charming bride."

Amelia wished she could return the compliment. Part of her was curious about the woman John had once considered marrying. Another part warned her that she would not like what she found.

John had never been good at the sparkling conversation that brightened London Society. He didn't care about the facile comments and empty praise, could never think of a witty response until the topic had moved on. Quips and jests flew back and forth between Caro and the major, with Amelia occasionally joining in. He found he much preferred a quiet dinner with his wife.

Yet he had to admit to a curiosity. Why had Caro come calling? She'd said she wanted to meet Amelia, but one-hundred-and-eighty-some miles of dusty roads, a travel carriage, a luggage wagon and an entourage seemed a great deal of effort merely to make an acquaintance. Couldn't she have waited until John and Amelia went up to London next spring?

Had Caro been a mare in his stable, insisting on joining another pasture when she had perfectly good grass where she was, he would have said it had something to do with the horses in the other pasture. Was it possible the same motivations applied in this case? It would lend credence to Caro's claim that she wanted to know Amelia better.

He watched his sister-in-law that evening after Fletcher excused himself and the others adjourned to the withdrawing room. Amelia suggested whist, and their guests happily agreed. The partners should have been obvious, John with Amelia and Major Kensington with Caro. But before John could reach his seat, Caro linked arms with him.

"Do partner me, dearest," she said, lashes fluttering. "You know I haven't a head for numbers, and I'd hate to make a poor showing in front of your darling Amelia."

John glanced at Amelia. That pleasant smile he was coming to dread sat upon her pretty lips, but she seemed to be standing taller than usual, as if her spine had stiffened.

"Nonsense," John tried, attempting to remove Caro's hand from his arm.

Major Kensington stepped to Amelia's side and held out his arm. "I'd be delighted to partner our charming hostess."

Amelia cast John a look but kindly agreed.

John resigned himself to play opposite Caro. At least she would be across the table and not at his side. As it was, Kensington sat on his left and Amelia his right at the round parquet table. His bride had her hands set one atop the other, head high as she waited. She was a perfect contrast to Caro, who nearly squirmed in her seat with anticipation.

Kensington led, dealing the cards as if from long practice. His look was cool, assessing, as it moved from John, to Amelia, to Caro. John laid down a king of hearts to start. Amelia followed with a queen, setting it carefully on top of his. Caro threw down a lower heart with a wink to John that he ignored. Kensington chuckled.

"I can see we have our work cut out for us, Lady Hascot," he said to Amelia as he set down a lower heart, as well. "It seems our opponents have agreed upon a set of signals. I saw that wink, Caro."

Caro tossed her head as John took in the trick. "And

may a lady not acknowledge the handsome gentleman who is partnering her, sir?"

Kensington winked broadly at Amelia. "Indeed. And the gentleman can acknowledge his charming partner, as well."

Amelia colored, dropping her gaze to her cards and keeping it there for the rest of the hand.

The audacity of the man! John wanted nothing more than to tell the major to take his eye-winking face out of the house and never return. Amelia was a married woman. Kensington had no right to flirt with her.

The right to flirt with her was all John's.

He grimaced and nearly misplayed his hand. Him, flirting? Amelia would likely laugh in his face. Certainly Caro had done so more than once when they'd been courting, though always with such charm that he couldn't hold it against her. If the major was offering Amelia such fulsome compliments and attentions, shouldn't John follow suit?

"Your hair is very fetching tonight, Amelia," he said aloud as the play progressed to her.

She glanced up at him, blinking. "My hair?"

Perhaps it wasn't any different than the way she'd worn it before, up at the back with one long curl brushing her shoulder. But with the candlelight gleaming down on the platinum strands, he had the oddest urge to stroke his hand along the silk.

"You remind me of the statue of Diana in Lady Brompton's garden," Major Kensington put in with a smile to Amelia as he played on Caro's spade. "Such stirring lines, such an elegant countenance."

Amelia immediately dropped her gaze again. "You are too kind, sir."

John wanted to thump the fellow over his own elegant head with the remaining cards in his hand.

"Oh, Major Kensington is such a tease," Caro proclaimed as the major drew in the trick. "You must watch yourself around him, Amelia. More than one lady has had her heart broken."

"Alas, if only that were true," Kensington lamented, setting down the king of clubs. "I fear I am more likely to have my own heart broken by the fickle fancy of the finest."

Caro tittered at his wit. John could think of any number of body parts he would have liked to see broken on the major. He threw out a two of clubs and sat back in his seat, disgusted with himself.

"I'm certain Amelia would never break a heart," Caro said as Amelia played a four. "She is too kind." She laid down the ace of clubs and swept in the trick.

She made it sound as if kindness was a flaw. "Amelia's kindness is one of her most sterling qualities," John said as Caro threw out the queen of diamonds.

"Hear, hear," Kensington said, playing the seven.

Caro's smile seemed to be pasted to her face. "Do you hear them, Amelia? One moment you are elegance defined, and now you are merely kind. How is one to counter such faint praise?"

"I don't find it faint," Amelia said as John played on the trick. "I'm honored if my efforts are seen as kind."

"Pshaw," Caro replied with a wave of her cards that was not lost on the savvy Kensington. "I would far rather be known for my dash and daring."

"I fear dash and daring are not my long suit," Amelia said, but she set the king of diamonds down on top of the trick and gently pulled it in.

John smiled to himself. His Amelia might never be known for her daring, but he could only be thankful. A more daring miss would never have been willing to marry him.

They continued playing for another hour. If he had been a man set on winning, he might have been pleased with his partner. Despite her protests, Caro played brilliantly. She seemed to know which cards to lay down and which to save for greatest impact. And her steady stream of conversation probably masked her concentration to people who did not know her well.

Amelia, on the other hand, was more obvious in her efforts, studying her cards, biting her soft pink lips when she was unsure which to play. If she was pleased with her hand, her lovely face brightened. If dismayed, she frowned and scrunched her nose. Major Kensington did his best to make up for her gaffes and pronounced her the perfect partner even when they lost by a rubber.

Still, John could not go up to bed without having a word with his wife first. He managed to pull Amelia aside as Caro and the major made their excuses and headed upstairs.

"Thank you for managing things today," he started. "Especially when this entire visit must be distressing to you."

She glanced up the stairs as if to make sure their guests were out of earshot, then returned her clear gaze to his. "Do I appear distressed?"

Her face was flushed a pleasing pink, and she stood perfectly poised beside him. "Not in the slightest," John assured her. "But you'd have reason to be. I did not invite her, Amelia, but as she is my sister-in-law, I can hardly deny her access to a family property."

"Of course," Amelia said. "Society decrees her family, and we should treat her as such. You need not concern yourself. I am quite capable of dealing with a fortnight's house party."

John grimaced. "Hardly a house party."

Amelia spread her hands. "It appears to be why they came. I know she teased you that you would not have to entertain her, but that is generally what is expected of such a visit."

"Heaven help us," John murmured, feeling as if someone had forced a stone down his throat.

Amelia smiled at him. "Prayer would not be remiss, sir. However, I think we can keep them sufficiently busy. Tomorrow morning, we can show them the farm, perhaps take a ride afterward. I'll write to Lady Bellington and see if we can arrange a visit for the next day."

"That should frighten Caro out of the area," John predicted.

Amelia shook her head, smile turning wry. "Such was not my intent. And we can tour the Rotherford mine, attempt fishing on the Bell, perhaps climb Calder Edge. There are many ways to keep them occupied, my lord. I shall try not to interrupt your routine overly much."

John had every confidence in Amelia, but as it turned out, his normal routine was interrupted the very next morning. He'd thought he'd have a few moments alone when he came down to breakfast just after dawn. However, Major Kensington was waiting for him in the dining room, cup of tea in one large hand.

"Ah, another early riser," he exclaimed as John poured himself a cup.

John cast him a glance. He had changed out of his dress uniform for the uniform of a London gentleman—navy coat and buff trousers. The more casual dress made him no less a figure of legend. Small wonder Caro claimed the ladies swooned over him.

"And had you a purpose for getting up so early?" John asked as he sat across the table from the man. "I thought this was a social visit."

"Oh, it is," Kensington assured him. "But I was in the habit of rising early on campaign. I never accustomed myself otherwise. Don't allow me to inconvenience you."

"Wouldn't dream of it," John replied.

They sipped in silence for a time.

"I did mean to say," the major put in, "that I admire the way you supported Lady Hascot in her time of need."

John frowned at him. Was he talking about Amelia? Had Amelia's father broken his promise and shared the reason they had wed? Why?

"What do you mean?" he asked cautiously.

"A widow of a previous titleholder can have a rough time of it," Kensington replied. "Your support allows her to maintain her place in Society."

That Lady Hascot. Why had John forgotten that title was forever Caro's?

"You are mistaken," John told him. "No extra support was necessary. My brother had funds at his disposal, and he left his wife well provided for."

The major lowered his gaze. "I'm sure that was a great comfort to Lady Hascot."

By the smile John caught before the fellow lifted the cup to his lips, it seemed to be a great comfort to the major, as well. Had he been trying to determine the state of Caro's finances? Was he a fortune hunter? It wasn't unknown for a handsome man with empty pockets to prey upon a helpless widow.

John nearly snorted aloud. Caro? Helpless? If the major thought to hoodwink her, John pitied the man. Caro was perfectly capable of looking out for her own best interests. She'd proved that by choosing James over him.

Fletcher came in just then, and Major Kensington excused himself. The veterinarian watched him go, then sat beside John and leaned closer.

"I don't like him," he confided.

That was a strong statement for the soft-spoken veterinarian. "Why?" John challenged. "He seems to be going out of his way to be friendly."

"Perhaps too friendly, by your leave." Fletcher hitched himself closer to the table and reached for the pot of tea to pour himself a cup. "I do not approve of the way he treats your Lady Hascot."

John shook his head. "Neither do I. But I understand some women appreciate compliments."

"There's nothing wrong with praising beauty or accomplishment," Fletcher agreed. "Unless it is for the sole purpose of gaining favor. You asked for my opinion on his character, my lord, and I would say both your guests are here for some purpose other than making your wife's acquaintance."

John could not argue with him there. But he didn't like his chances of ferreting out the true reason for their visit simply by watching them further. His best approach to surviving the next few days was to keep his attentions focused on his responsibilities: Amelia and his horses.

And he was a little surprised to realize it truly was in that order.

Chapter Fourteen

Amelia had plenty of time that morning to send a note to Lady Bellington and make other arrangements for their guests' entertainment, for John and Major Kensington were already out in the stables when she came down to breakfast, and Caro was still abed.

"Fashionable ladies sleep late," Turner advised Amelia as she tidied the bedchamber. "And Lady Hascot is terribly fashionable. She has an entire gown made from gold muslin. I saw it."

Amelia had never purchased anything even trimmed with the costly material. "She goes about far more in Society than I do," she told the maid.

"Doesn't mean you can't dress as well," Turner countered. She peered at Amelia through the corners of her eyes as if unsure of her mistress's reaction. "His lordship might like a bit more dash."

"Then his lordship shouldn't have married me," Amelia replied.

Apparently her maid realized she'd spoken out of turn, for she said no more on the subject.

Amelia knew she should remain available for her

guest, so she kept herself busy that morning, checking on Firenza, making suggestions on a change in training and debating with Dr. Fletcher if the mare might not be eating properly. Caro did not venture downstairs until noon. Amelia was certain that she personally would be pale and cross for having slept so late. Caro, of course, was all sparkling joy as she took tea with Amelia in the withdrawing room.

"However do you do it?" she asked Amelia, glancing about the room with a wrinkle of her nose as if she found the space lacking. "I think I would perish so far from London Society."

"I like it here," Amelia confessed, rearranging her muslin skirts on the polished wood chair. "John's horses are surprisingly good company."

Caro laughed. "Oh, you are perfect for him! I have never heard anyone but him speak so fondly about their animals."

Amelia decided to take that as a compliment. "He has reason to be proud of them. He raises them from birth, watches them from the moment they take their first halting steps until they clear every obstacle in the field at a gallop."

Caro raised her tea cup. "May he show as great an interest in your two-footed children."

Amelia tried to hide her blush behind her cup, but Caro lowered hers and leaned closer. "My dear Amelia, have I discomposed you? It cannot be that you are increasing so soon. I know there was scandal when you wed John, but I never dreamed…"

"No!" Amelia's head jerked up. "You are mistaken. John and I never, that is, we didn't… What do you mean by scandal?"

Caro leaned back, brows arched. "Why, everyone in London knows you spent the night with him in his stable."

Amelia felt ill. How had the story spread? She certainly had never told a soul about that night. It didn't seem to matter that she was innocent, that John had been a gentleman. Everyone assumed the worst.

You know the truth, Father. That should be all that matters.

Her concerns must have been evident, however, for Caro set down her cup and reached out to pat Amelia's hand.

"There now," she said, face and voice commiserating. "You mustn't mind the gossip. Why, I've grown quite used to such things by now. It is simply the way London works." She trilled a laugh that Amelia could not find in the least comforting. "And when the heir arrives a good eleven months after the wedding, all rumors will be silenced."

Amelia had always believed in facing adversity with a smile, but she could not force her lips to curve upward. Caro's smile faded.

"Unless you meant… No, it cannot be." She dropped her voice. "Amelia, haven't you consummated the marriage?"

Amelia could not meet her gaze. "Forgive me, Lady Hascot, but I am unaccustomed to such frank conversation."

She heard the rustle of Caro's muslin gown as she must have straightened. "No, forgive me. Our friendship is much too new for me to so presume upon it. And what a sweet way to remind me of my manners. I've met your mother on occasion, and I'm sure she'd have told me to mind my own affairs and made the lecture an object lesson at the same time."

At last her smile fought through. "Yes, she is quite good at that."

"I imagine it must have been challenging growing up in such an environment," Caro said, sobering. "I can understand. My own family life was not happy. My father drank a great deal, and we never seemed to have the funds to cover what was needed to maintain our places in Society. Happily, you will have no such problems with John."

Indeed. Amelia could not imagine John losing control enough to allow himself to become inebriated. And despite their former butler's allegations, her husband had been quite accommodating when it came to funding anything she suggested.

"I don't expect to mix much in Society," Amelia admitted. "My place is here, with my husband."

Caro puffed out a sigh. "I fear your post will be a lonely one. You must know that when it comes to affection, John is not demonstrative. You may have to look elsewhere, in a friend, for example." She smiled at Amelia. "I'd be happy to be your friend."

She had never turned down an offer of friendship, rare as they were, yet she struggled to accept this one.

You say to love, Lord, but I cannot find it in me to trust this woman. Something is off, and I fear it's my own worries.

"You are too kind," she said aloud, taking up her cup once more.

"Well, of course." Caro took up her cup as well, as if the two of them were discussing the weather at Gunter's sweet shop in London. "We are both Lady Hascot after

all. What would be more natural for us than to band together like the sisters the law has made us?"

Amelia had always wanted siblings—a brother to
satisfy her father and a sister to satisfy her heart. She
and Caro had both been raised to the expectations of
Society, at least; yet she could not see her as a sister.

For when Caro had guessed Amelia and John had not
consummated the marriage, Amelia had caught a look
in her eyes before the woman had dropped her gaze.
Their lack of closeness pleased Caro. True sisters, and
friends, did not take pleasure from a loved one's pain.

So Amelia merely offered to fill Caro's cup again.
Tea was such a helpful beverage that way. If her hands
trembled a bit on the silver pot, it might be because of
the weight and not that she was embarrassed beyond
belief that Caro suspected Amelia and John's marriage
was not all it should be. And fussing with the sugar bowl
and tongs gave her a moment to compose her face before carefully changing the subject.

She hoped John and the major might make an
appearance—surely Caro would not be so frank in front
of them! But Reams reported that they had ridden out
to the far pasture. It took surprisingly little to convince
Caro to go out after them, for all that she had said she
wasn't much of a rider.

The two women went to change into their riding
habits, Amelia in her comfortable plum wool and Caro
in a tailored black ensemble with a top hat wrapped
in tulle. They then ventured out to the stables. Two of
the grooms came running at the sight of Amelia in the
doorway, and she requested that they saddle a horse
for each of them.

"Why not ride Firenza?" Dr. Fletcher asked, coming out of a stall to greet them. Straw stuck to his wool coat, and she was not at all sure of the oily substance sticking to one of his red curls. Caro took one look at him and turned her smile on Amelia.

"Yes, dear," she said with a dimple. "I'd love to see this creature you tamed. Perhaps I should give her a try."

"I'd like to see that," Dr. Fletcher said.

Amelia frowned at him. Caro was very good at wrapping the gentlemen around her little finger—that much was evident by the fawning attitude of Major Kensington. But surely the veterinarian could not have succumbed so far as to suggest the roan. He knew the danger Firenza represented. John had barely allowed Amelia to ride her. The mare would be unlikely to allow a stranger onto her back.

"I'm afraid Firenza isn't up to company," Amelia told Caro. "She's still recovering from an illness. But here's a lovely mare that quite complements your habit."

Caro brightened as the groom led forward a silver-coated mare named Argentia. Amelia stepped back to allow Caro to mount the horse, and Dr. Fletcher moved in closer.

"You should have let me put her up on the roan," he murmured. "That would have shown John the lady's true colors."

Amelia's brows shot up, but the groom led the dun mare Precious Gem up beside her.

"Allow me," Dr. Fletcher said, bending with cupped hands.

Amelia put her foot in his fingers and pushed herself up into the saddle. As she settled her skirts around her, he put a hand on the girth as if to check it.

"Watch out for her," he murmured, gaze on Amelia's. "From what I've heard, she thinks only of her own needs."

He stepped back before she could question him, and saluted them both. "Enjoy your ride, ladies."

They rode out of the stable and east across the closest pasture. The emerald hills rose all around them. To their left, the gray stone ridge of Calder Edge braced the blue of the summer sky. The cool air, the sound of birds calling, soothed Amelia's spirit, and she drank in a deep breath.

"How many horses does he have on the property?" Caro asked as they approached the gate between this pasture and the next.

"Twenty," Amelia replied. "Three still need their mothers, six are yearlings and two-year-olds too young to ride, one is too old, and of course, Firenza and Magnum are not for sale."

"So there are five available."

She sounded disappointed. Had she hoped for a set of six for a carriage? Didn't she realize the type of horses John raised?

"They are mostly hunters, you know," Amelia explained, reaching out with the handle of her crop to open the gate for them. "Or, failing that, riding horses."

"Oh, assuredly," Caro agreed, following her through the gate. "Great brutes like his Magnum. Every gentleman on the *ton* is keen to have his like. I won't be surprised if Major Kensington leaves with a purchase."

"Oh, has he mustered out?" Amelia asked, careful to close the gate behind them. John would never forgive her if one of his darlings strayed because she had been careless.

"He is currently on half pay, awaiting his next assign-

ment. He was a hero at Waterloo, did you know that?"
She waited for Amelia to come abreast again. Ahead,
the pasture rose toward the hillside that hid the Rotherford mine from view. "He went from captain to major
for his bravery. I expect he'll run for Parliament, if he
can impress the right people. Ah, here they come now."

Amelia spotted them, as well. John and Major Kensington were riding down the hillside. Though the major
looked dapper in his navy coat, the sight of her husband
on horseback sent a thrill through her. He and Magnum
moved as one. Confidence and power flowed with each
fluid stride. Amelia drew in a breath as he and the major
reined in beside them.

"Good afternoon, Amelia, Caro," Major Kensington
said with a tip of his tall-crowned hat.

John merely eyed them. "Can you handle Argentia, Caro?"

She laughed. "And a good afternoon to you, too,
John. Yes, I'm getting on tolerably well. Though I was
momentarily crushed when Amelia refused to allow me
to ride her Firenza."

John snapped a nod to Amelia. "Sensible of you. I
concur."

"Villain!" Caro rapped his arm lightly with her free
hand. "You'll darken my reputation."

"I will defend you," Major Kensington promised.
"You look like an Amazon on the horse, my dear Caro."

"Ha!" Now she leveled her crop at him. "You, sir,
may ride beside me." With a toss of her head that didn't
even unseat her top hat, she turned her mount, and
Kensington fell in beside her as they ambled back toward the stables.

Amelia moved to follow, but John reached out to

catch Precious Gem's bridle. "Let them go. I prefer to ride with you."

Pleasure shot through her. "Very well, my lord."

Magnum shook his head as if he had other ideas, but John turned the horse to parallel Amelia's. They walked along in silence a moment, and Amelia was quite in charity with him until he said, "How have you and Caro been getting along?"

In such a situation, her governess would have advised her to dissemble. Her mother would have thrown the question back at him, demanding to know how he and the major were getting along. But John had encouraged her to state her opinions openly, so she did.

"I find her distressingly bold, my lord," she said. "She wanted to discuss our inability to consummate the marriage."

John reined in so fast Magnum nearly pitched him from the saddle. "You told her?"

Amelia reined in, as well. "I didn't have to. She guessed."

He gazed off over the fields, jaw tight. Was he embarrassed his first love knew his marriage was less than happy? Angry Amelia wasn't better at dissembling?

"Forgive me," he said. "That must have been difficult for you."

Tears were starting again. "A little. I just wish..."

He turned to her. "What?"

The words fell past her lips. "That I'd met you first."

John stared at his gentle, quiet beauty of a wife. The telltale pink was already rising in her cheeks. She simply couldn't be so forthright without blushing.

"It's all right, Amelia," he said. "You are my wife. That is what matters."

She nodded, but he didn't think he had convinced her. Words alone never convinced his horses. He was coming to realize how much people had the same responses.

He threw his leg over the saddle and slid to the ground.

"What are you doing?" she asked with a frown.

"Showing my wife the courtesy she is due." He went down on one knee on the damp ground. Magnum lowered his head and butted John's shoulder. He pushed the horse back.

"Amelia, Lady Hascot," he said, "do you remember the vows we made each other?"

She nodded, blue eyes centered on him as if he was everything to her.

"For better, for worse, for richer, for poorer," John reminded her.

"To love, cherish and obey," she agreed. "Till death us do part."

John spread his hands. "Before this company, I vow that I have lived up to these promises, and I always will."

Her mouth twitched. "This company, my lord? I see only the two of us and our horses."

"Of course." He climbed to his feet. "Do you think I would lie to Magnum?"

Another woman would likely have laughed at him, but she shook her head. "In front of your trusted friend? Never. But you will recall he doesn't think much of me. What if he should counsel restraint?"

"I would argue him down," John vowed. He caught

the saddle and swung himself back into it. "Horses can learn, people can change. I am living proof of that, Amelia."

She smiled as they set off toward the stables.

John thought his gesture had reassured her, for instead of retreating to the house, she stayed at his side while he took Major Kensington and Caro on a walking tour of the stables. He'd already gone over the finer points with Kensington earlier. Now he completed the tour by directing Caro's attention to the foals, which she cooed over.

"You know, old man," Kensington said, leading John aside as Amelia attempted to introduce Caro to Royal Filigree, a fine strawberry roan, "I am acquainted with a few officers who'd love to take these mares off your hands when the foals are weaned. I could even find a fellow interested in breaking your Firenza. What do you say?"

He could not know the insult he'd offered. Did he think John incapable of taking care of his own horses?

"I don't sell to the cavalry," John replied, keeping his gaze on Amelia, who was feeding a foal an apple. "When your friends retire, I'd be happy to hear from them."

Kensington's face darkened, as if he meant to argue, but John turned his back on the man and went to rejoin the women. When the foals had exhausted their appeal for Caro, she excused herself to change for dinner. Kensington also made his excuses and followed, leaving John and Amelia to bring up the rear.

"Day one nearly over," John said as the footman opened the rear door to the house for them.

"Cause for celebration," Amelia agreed with a smile to him. She reached up and swept his hair off his forehead.

The touch was intimate, but it also spoke of expectations. Did his hair trouble her? He'd never been able to keep it in place. Neither had the footman, and it wasn't easy finding another barber out in the wilds of Derby.

"Would you mind terribly changing for dinner?" she asked as they started down the corridor.

Apparently he was deficient in that area, as well. Something inside him balked, like a horse led to a wall for the first time. "I'll change my boots," he said, then strode ahead of her before she could ask for more.

But Amelia wasn't the only one wanting something from him. Caro was loitering in the corridor just beyond his bedchamber when he left a while later, evening pumps on his feet.

"There you are," she said, leaving no doubt in his mind that she had been waiting for him. She threaded her arm through his. "Let's have a chat. We've so much to discuss."

John removed her arm from his. "I'll wait for Amelia."

She made a face. "Can't I have you to myself just once?"

"No," John said.

She started laughing. Years ago he'd found it the most charming sound on the planet. Now it annoyed him.

"You really are the most predictable fellow, John," she complained. "I wasn't intent on an assignation. I'm trying for once to be circumspect." She lowered her voice and gazed up at him, brown eyes troubled. "I must speak to you about my portion. I think I may be in a pickle."

John sighed. Caro's financial situation was the one topic he had no right to share with Amelia. "Very well," he said and motioned her to follow him.

He led her down the stairs to the library but left the door open. Drawing her to the hearth, he nodded. "What happened? And why can't your solicitor deal with it?"

She rubbed her hands over each other as if stirring the emotions inside her. "To tell the truth, I'm not sure what happened. James told me that I would be provided for should anything happen to him. You told me nothing had changed. My solicitor, Mr. Carstairs, said I could go on as I always had. So I did. Now he advises me to economize."

She stilled, regarding him. "I do not economize well, John."

He imagined she did not. "What James left you should be adequate."

She made a face. "Well, there is adequate and there is adequate. I had to rent the town house for the summer to make ends meet."

John shook his head. "Is that why you decided to move in? You'd be better off at the Hascot country house in Devon."

"I understand repairs are needed," she said, dropping her gaze. "I didn't want to trouble you."

John sighed. "It is the family seat, for all I prefer Hollyoak. I'll write to the solicitor and see what can be done."

She sagged. "Oh, thank you, John! I knew I could count on you." Tears glimmered in her eyes as she put a hand on his arm as if to steady herself. "You have always stood by me. I want you to know how grateful I am."

She tilted up her face as if to offer him her lips. John took a step back, forcing her to release him.

"Think nothing of it," he said. "It is all part of the responsibilities of the title."

"Oh, but I think a great deal of it," she protested. "In fact, I think about you all the time. I'm so, so sorry for the misunderstanding between us. You see, I loved you from the first."

John reared back, feeling as if the world had tilted again. "What?"

She closed the distance between them, face once more tilted up. "It's true. I've always loved you, but when you took so long to propose, I thought you didn't love me. Naturally, I accepted your brother's offer. I'm so sorry. I thought you'd want to know."

Two years ago, before she'd wed his brother, he'd have given anything to know, for then he might have fought for her. A year ago, when his brother had died, he might have wanted to know, at least as a salve to his consequence.

Now? Now he wanted nothing to do with the matter, for he was married, and his heart was already turning toward Amelia.

But hearing Caro's confession could only make him wonder. If he had lost the first woman he'd loved through his inability to express himself, what made him think he'd have any better luck with Amelia?

Chapter Fifteen

Amelia went to bed that night quite satisfied with herself. She'd not only survived a full day with her unwanted guests, but John had gone out of his way that evening to stay by her side. He'd partnered her in whist, and even though they'd lost the rubber, a small grimace was the most he'd shown of any disappointment. And he'd held her hand a moment, in full view of the others, when she bid him good-night. After his gesture in the pasture, kneeling before her and reciting their wedding vows again, she could not help feeling encouraged.

Perhaps this visit would prove a blessing after all.

But what she felt that night she very much doubted by the afternoon of the next day. They woke to misty rain she was beginning to realize was all too common in the peaks even in summer. Riding would be unthinkable for anyone but John, and even if they had been willing to travel by carriage, there was no one else to visit. Neither the Rotherfords nor Lord and Lady Danning were in residence. Lady Bellington had appointed the following day for their time at Bellweather Hall. Amelia knew she would have her work cut out for her to keep the major and Caro entertained indoors.

She dressed in one of her favorite morning gowns striped in sunny yellow with lace at the throat and cuffs, and marshaled her forces outside the dining room.

"Her ladyship won't rise until noon, most likely," Turner explained.

"Whatever time," Mr. Shanter promised with a twirl of his mustache, "I'll have sustenance ready." He nodded in respect to Amelia, and she smiled her appreciation.

"I'll lay out the ebony and ivory chess set, your ladyship," Mr. Hennessy offered. "That might amuse the major."

"And there's paper and pencil for silhouettes," Amelia remembered. "Reams, set up a station in the library, just in case."

"Right away, your ladyship," the footman agreed.

Armed with her plans, Amelia retreated only to her secretary in the corner of the withdrawing room, thinking perhaps she should attempt a letter to her mother while she waited for Caro to wake. Yet the words refused to come. She knew what her mother expected of her—to write that all was well even if it was not and to ask after family and friends she hadn't seen in years. But that life seemed very far away, and she could not muster sufficient regret. She still hadn't managed more than a sentence before Major Kensington found her, Turner having gone upstairs to finish airing Amelia's bedchamber.

"I wonder, dear Amelia," the cavalry officer said, coming to her side and offering her a bow in his navy coat, "if I might impose on you for some writing paper and a fresh quill. I have correspondence I must complete."

She would not have taken him for an avid correspondent. "Certainly, sir," she said, pulling together the materials in front of her.

"You needn't look so surprised," he said with a chuckle as Amelia handed him a sheaf of vellum. "Even we military types write on occasion."

Amelia blushed. "Forgive me, sir. Of course you must write, orders and battle plans and such."

"Yes, I'm learning even civilian life requires a battle plan from time to time," he replied with a smile. "For the moment I thought to write to an old friend who needs cheering." He patted his thigh. "Lost a leg at Talavera."

"Oh, I'm so sorry!" Amelia handed him the quill, as well. "Please thank him for his valiant sacrifice."

He brightened. "Why don't you help me compose the letter? I vow it would do the old fellow a world of good to know someone else cared."

"I'd be honored," Amelia said.

He went to fetch one of the wood-wrapped armchairs and positioned it next to her. "Perhaps you should start," he suggested, nodding to the paper on her desk.

Amelia picked up a quill and dipped it in ink. Major Kensington leaned closer, stretching his arm to rest along the back of her chair.

"What is his name?" Amelia asked, intent on the letter before her.

"Hmm?" Major Kensington seemed to be having trouble concentrating. "Oh, his name is Thomas."

"Baptismal name or surname?" Amelia asked, glancing up.

The major seemed even closer than he had been a moment ago. She had the distinct impression he was trying to gauge the scent of her hair. And his arm behind her was entirely too much like an embrace. Amelia attempted to edge away from him, but the desk hampered her efforts.

"Both," he said with a charming smile. "Thomas Thomas. We used to call him old Tom Tom for short."

She wasn't about to address a gentleman so familiarly. "And his rank?" she asked, forcing herself to focus on the letter.

"He isn't titled." He shifted closer, and his trouser pressed against her skirts.

Amelia hitched her chair to the side until she bumped against the silk-papered wall. "I meant his military rank," she said, repositioning the paper. "I believe it is customary to address an officer by his rank even when he is retired."

"Oh, assuredly. I believe he made captain before his unfortunate accident." He edged his chair up against hers. His smile was far too knowing. "Are you running away from me, Lady Hascot?"

She did not wish to give him the impression that his actions concerned her; that gave him too much power. "Merely seeking the light," she said, motioning with her quill to the nearby window. "Now, then, let us begin. 'Dear Captain Thomas, I am writing for your friend, Major Kensington.'"

"Davy," he said.

She looked up to find his face mere inches from her own. "He always called me Davy," he murmured. "You could, too, you know. I'd like to think we've become good friends."

"You are too kind, Major," Amelia said. She handed him the quill and pushed back her chair, forcing his arm to fall away from her. "Perhaps you should write this letter after all, if he is such a dear friend. Excuse me while I see what's keeping my husband."

She hurried from the room before he could protest.

In the corridor, she paused and took a deep breath. What behavior! No doubt he was simply so used to flirting that he forgot himself around a married woman, but she refused to allow him such familiarities. From now on, she'd make certain she was never alone with the fellow. That ought to keep his attentions on the proper plane.

She instructed a footman to wait upon the major's needs and retired to the lap desk in her room to write to her mother. But even in the quiet that was broken only by the whisper of Turner's skirts as she put away some clothes in the wardrobe, Amelia could not decide how to continue. Her mother had always overseen all of Amelia's activities. Which part of their situation could Amelia relate without expecting a scold in return?

Turner had headed for the corridor with a bundle of soiled linens, but as soon as she opened the door, she slid it part of the way shut again. She shifted this way and that, peering through the gap.

"What are you doing?" Amelia couldn't help asking, putting away her unused quill.

"Shh," the maid cautioned.

Amelia shook her head as she rose. "Turner, there's no need to spy on the other servants. I'm persuaded we have a good group in place now."

The maid glanced at Amelia over her shoulder. "It's

not the servants that worry me, your ladyship. It's the other Lady Hascot."

"Turner," Amelia scolded, coming to the door. "She is our guest."

"Mighty funny guest if you ask me," Turner said. "You look out there and tell me what you see."

Something in her manner warned Amelia she would not like the picture in the corridor. Dread gathered at her throat. Could she have been wrong about John? Was he even now telling the other Lady Hascot how much he still admired her? She could not keep herself from peering out the crack.

But instead of her husband beside Caro, Major Kensington stood close and familiar, one hand on the shoulder of Caro's lavender evening dress.

"You're taking your sweet time," he said to her.

Amelia thought he must be talking about the lady's habit of sleeping late, but Caro waved a hand. "I told you he would not be rushed. John is nothing if not methodical. If you wish his cooperation, you must earn his trust."

John's cooperation? Why did the major require his cooperation? Amelia knew she should close the door to avoid overhearing a private conversation, but she couldn't seem to move.

"And how am I to earn his trust when he spends all his time with his cattle?" Major Kensington complained. He pulled back his hand to adjust his stock. "I prefer to expend my efforts on the wife. She might be useful, and she's far more entertaining."

Amelia stiffened, but Caro rapped him on the arm. "Stop that! She has no influence on him. If she had, she'd have convinced him to consummate the marriage by now."

If Amelia had ever considered a friendship with the woman, the hope died right then. How could Caro tell another person, especially a gentleman, about the secret she only suspected? It was as if she had tossed Amelia's shame into the air for all to see.

"I wouldn't blame that on her," Major Kensington answered. "Any man who could resist such a beauty is obviously touched in the head, which doesn't bode well for our chances of success."

Caro patted her golden curls. "Doesn't bode well for your chances. If you give me time, I'll bring him around."

Amelia felt cold all over, but Major Kensington bent his head. "I'd estimate that you have at most two days before our mutual acquaintance loses patience and comes to Hollyoak Farm himself. Is that what you want?"

She jerked back. "I'm not afraid of him."

"Indeed. Then why are you doing his bidding?"

She shrugged, but Amelia thought the gesture too contrived. "I've already spent his money, and there will be no more unless I make good on my promises."

His money? Was Caro short on funds? Had John taken money from the estate to support the changes Amelia had requested at Hollyoak Farm? If so, the woman's need to find alternative funding was at least partly Amelia's fault.

"Hascot seems to think you were left well-off," the major informed her.

As Amelia frowned, Caro put a hand on his cheek.

"Well-off for one is insufficient for two, my sweet. I would prefer to be able to keep you in style."

He bent his head then, and Amelia started to close her door.

Caro jerked. "Is someone there?"

Major Kensington whirled, and for a moment the charming smile slipped to be replaced by a fury that made Amelia suck in a breath.

Turner pushed past her. "Pardon me, ma'am. Just going out with the dirty linen. Didn't wish to disturb you." She bent to tuck up some of the hanging pieces. Only Amelia could see her face. "Carry on as usual," she advised in a whisper. "I'll fetch the master. I warrant he'll have something to say about the two of them being thick as thieves."

Amelia allowed her to shut the door, then leaned against the panel. It was clear Major Kensington and Caro wanted something from John, and it sounded like money. For some reason they felt they had to trick it out of him. And who was this other acquaintance, the one Major Kensington seemed to think Caro should fear?

She could only hope Turner could prevail upon John to join them, for she wasn't sure even her highly trained hostess skills were up to this sort of thing, and she couldn't hide in her room for long.

"You're hiding," Fletcher said.

John drew himself up from where he'd been examining Magnum's right fore pastern at the back of the stable. It seemed to him the black had favored the leg on their ride through the rain, but he'd found no sign of a stone in the shoe.

"I have work to do," he told his veterinarian, reaching for the cloth he used to rub down the stallion.

"Your staff has work to do," Fletcher countered. "And by your leave, they are very good at doing it. You are likely needed inside."

John grimaced as he rubbed Magnum's coat, and the stallion's muscles relaxed. He knew he was avoiding his guests. He doubted his refusal to sell his horses to the military had gone over well with Major Kensington. He wasn't about to change his mind, but he didn't think Amelia would be pleased if he started an argument in her lovely new withdrawing room.

Then there was Caro's confession the previous evening that she still loved him. Why had she bothered to tell him? Surely she knew him well enough to realize he would never be unfaithful to Amelia. Why stir things up now?

"Is Amelia having trouble?" he asked the veterinarian, hanging the cloth on the stall to dry.

"Your bride is a lady through and through," Fletcher assured him. "She would never complain. But I'm certain your aid would be greatly appreciated."

John puffed out a sigh. "I cannot like it, Fletcher. I feel like one of my foals in training, forced to go this way or that simply to please another."

Fletcher shrugged. "And yet we both know that training improves the horse, fits it for its intended duty."

"And we both know some horses fight to the bitter end," John countered with a nod down the stable to where Firenza had kicked over the box of grooming implements about to be used on her.

"By your leave," Fletcher said, "you are not a horse, my lord."

John chuckled. "Don't tell Magnum."

Just then, John spotted Turner coming along the center aisle of the stable. Standing on her toes to see over the boxes, the maid glanced this way and that, and John knew by the way her face hardened when she'd spotted him.

"Begging your pardon, your lordship, Dr. Fletcher," she said as she hurried up, "but her ladyship requires your assistance inside."

The veterinarian raised a brow at John as if to say *I told you so.* "I'll be right in," John promised her.

He took the time to push his hair off his forehead, then ventured indoors. The footman directed him to the withdrawing room, where Amelia, Caro and Major Kensington were taking tea.

John paused in the doorway and realized the tableau was everything he hated about Society. Major Kensington sat so stiffly he might have been posing for his portrait. Caro refused to look at him, and the swing of her skirts as she sat on one of the chairs told John that her toe was tapping, most likely in vexation, against the carpet.

Amelia was as serene as always, dispensing the brew, commenting consolingly on the weather, offering cakes and delicate biscuits.

"I imagine today has been too staid for you," John said, coming into the room. "But, take heart. The skies should clear by evening."

Caro brightened, and she patted the seat of the chair beside her. "John, darling! Come sit by me and have a cup."

John went to Amelia, who hurriedly poured for him. He could see the tremor in the cinnamon-colored liquid as she handed him the cup. He put his hand on her shoulder and remained standing beside her as he took a sip.

"I've been wanting to speak with you," Amelia said.

He would have thought she'd fired a pistol for how quickly Caro and the major reacted.

"Yes, Hascot, so have I," Kensington said, setting aside his cup. "I see you have a very fine chessboard here. What about a game?"

"Don't be silly," Caro said, rising in a rush of silk. "John would much prefer a ride. Allow me to accompany you, my lord. It will only take me a few moments to change."

How had he become so popular? "Amelia?" he asked, glancing down at her.

To his surprise, there was a decided twinkle in her blue eyes. "You see how your guests have missed you, sir? You know what people can get up to when left to their own devices."

Kensington's laugh reminded John of a frightened neigh. "Indeed. If not chess, old man, what about giving me a look at your breeding book? I imagine it's a fascinating read."

John wasn't about to fuel that fire. "In my experience," he returned, "such books are fascinating only to the breeder."

Major Kensington held up a hand. "Say no more. I'll simply have to console myself with your wife's company."

Amelia's blush appeared, a deeper red this time, and the twinkle in her eyes vanished.

"You do that," Caro all but purred, strolling toward

John and bringing the scent of roses with her. "I'm sure John and I can find some other way to pass the time."

"I would never be so rude as to abandon my own wife," John returned. He purposely reached for Amelia's hand and clasped it in his own. Her fingers were stiff.

"Certainly not," Major Kensington agreed. "Why, if I had such a treasure, I'd never let her out of my sight."

"What gallant gentlemen," Caro proclaimed, an edge to her voice. "But I'm afraid I simply cannot sit around like a hothouse palm. Who's for a ride in the rain?"

John shook his head. "I prefer to remain indoors. Kensington?"

The major stretched his legs across the carpet. "Give me a warm hearth and a kind hostess any day."

John had never seen Caro's face so tight. "Very well. I'm sure I can find a groom to attend me. Excuse me while I change into my riding habit." She swept from the room.

"Do you play chess, Amelia?" Major Kensington asked.

"Not well enough," Amelia admitted, busying herself with putting away the tea things. "I'm sure John would give you a better game." Her glance up to him all but begged him to trounce the fellow.

"I'll take white," John said, going to the table where the pieces had been laid out. But as Kensington moved to join him on the dark side of the board, John couldn't help wondering what game Caro and the major were really playing and how they had managed to involve Amelia.

Chapter Sixteen

Something was very wrong. Amelia sat quietly in the withdrawing room, her embroidery frame before her and a needle and floss in her hand. She was very glad John and Major Kensington were absorbed in their chess game, or they would surely have noticed that she hadn't taken a single stitch. Instead, her mind was busy determining how she might manage a private word with her husband.

When she'd ventured from her room to serve her guests tea, she had hoped to learn that the major and Caro had an innocent reason for their conversation in the corridor earlier. Unfortunately, their subsequent actions seemed to prove otherwise. They had gone out of their way to be pleasant to her, Caro even offering to share a set of gloves that would perfectly complement Amelia's gown. Amelia could not help thinking it was a bribe to ensure her silence. They did not know how much Turner had heard in the corridor, and they could not be certain the maid had not gone carrying tales to her mistress.

Their behavior with John had only confirmed the

fact. Neither wanted her to speak with him, which only made her more determined to do just that.

She waited until the clock on the mantel chimed the hour, then rose. "I suppose we should change for dinner."

John frowned at her. He hadn't done more than swap his boots for evening pumps the previous afternoon. Major Kensington looked just as surprised, even though he had effected an entire change in clothing the other nights.

"I think I'll remain in civilian clothes," he said. "Hollyoak Farm has spoiled me that way."

Of course he found an excuse! "My lord," Amelia tried again, "a word about the menu."

John's frown deepened. "Whatever you prefer is fine."

"Indeed it is," Major Kensington assured him. "Your wife is an uncommonly fine hostess."

And an entirely frustrated one. Was there nothing she could do for a moment alone with her husband?

Father, how can I attract his attention without swishing my tail like a horse!

Inspiration struck. "John," she said, "I'm worried about Firenza. She seems off her feed."

John rose. "Why didn't you tell me sooner? Where's Fletcher?" He started from the table.

"Check!" Major Kensington proclaimed, leaning back in his chair as if from triumph. He was too much the soldier to show his panic, but Amelia thought his face had paled. "I have you now, my lord."

John, dear John, waved a hand. "I'll finish the game another time. Come with me, Amelia, and tell Fletcher exactly what behavior you've seen. I won't lose that horse."

"Of course, my lord," Amelia said, hiding her smile.

Major Kensington jumped to his feet. "I'd be happy to be of assistance."

"No," John flung back over his shoulder as he moved to the doorway. "Firenza won't abide strangers. We'll see you at dinner."

The major slumped back into his seat as Amelia followed her husband.

John's stride ate up the corridor to the back of the house, and Amelia could barely keep pace. But she waited until they had reached the stable yard before calling his name. He jerked to a stop and stood until she had reached his side.

Amelia put a hand on his arm. "I've already spoken with Dr. Fletcher. He feels she is merely expressing her displeasure at our recent training."

"I'd prefer to check on her all the same," John said.

Amelia glanced back at the house in time to see a curtain twitch in the library. Was a servant cleaning, or were she and John being watched? She took her husband's arm. "What a very good idea, my lord. I'll join you."

The stable was its usual busy place, with grooms preparing the horses for evening. Firenza stood in her box, head already buried in her feed trough. John watched her from the side, his face still, as if every sense was tuned to look for problems. Amelia knew she shouldn't interrupt, but she was finding patience more difficult by the moment.

Finally, he stepped back to Amelia's side. "She's fine, but it's best to be watchful."

"I quite agree," Amelia said. "And the same might be said for our guests."

Now he turned that intent gaze on her. "Why? Surely they can see to their own needs."

Amelia took his arm and drew him back a little ways from the grooms. "That is entirely the problem, my lord. I'm concerned they are seeing to their own needs, to the detriment of yours." She took a deep breath and plunged in. "I overheard Caro and Major Kensington talking about finances."

He cocked his head. "Was he pressuring her?"

"No," Amelia replied with a frown. "At least, not about money. Why would you assume him to be at fault?"

He straightened. "Forgive me. I should not make assumptions about people's behavior. I have a history of misunderstanding. But it seemed to me that Kensington was short of funds and hopes Caro will make up the difference."

His theory aligned with what she'd heard. "You may be right, my lord. However, it seemed to me that Caro is also short of funds and hopes *you* will make up the difference."

He shrugged. "I'm willing to listen to reason."

Perhaps too willing, where Caro was concerned. "I'm not sure she intends to use words to persuade you."

Now John frowned as if he didn't understand. Would he make her say it aloud? "She is pretty, John."

"She is lovely," John agreed, and she wanted to yank a horseshoe off the mare that was passing and throw the iron at him. "That isn't the point. Either she has a reason for her request, or she doesn't. Neither a pretty face nor winsome words will sway me."

"Of course," Amelia murmured, dropping her hold on him.

Still, she could feel him watching her. "What troubles you, Amelia?"

This was the perfect time to do as he had encouraged and state her opinion. "I cannot understand why she is here at all," she admitted. "She complains we have no Society, lives by town hours and doesn't care a jot about the horses."

He stepped aside to allow a groom past with another of the mares, drawing Amelia with him. "She is here because she has nowhere else to go at the moment. She's rented the town house, and the Hascot seat isn't habitable."

Amelia threw up her hands. "And doesn't that strike you as convenient?"

"No," John said. "It strikes me as remarkably inconvenient, for us."

Amelia sighed. "I wish I could believe it merely inconvenient, John. I feel as if we're being manipulated."

The familiar glower settled over his features. "That I will not countenance. I'll keep a closer eye on them, Amelia. Together, we will manage."

Amelia could only hope he was right.

Dinner was a quieter affair, as if both Caro and Major Kensington expected to be evicted at any moment. When they all adjourned to the withdrawing room with no pronouncement from John, the two relaxed sufficiently to play another game of whist. But both found reasons to make it an early night. Amelia was almost loath to see them go, for more time alone meant more time for them to plot further ways to hurt John or her.

* * *

She was relieved to find the next day bright. At least now she could move her guests out of the house. She felt a little guilty for hoping John's prediction would prove true, and their scheduled visit to Bellweather Hall that day would convince Caro and the major that they much preferred London Society.

The distance down the dale was far enough and the occasion formal enough that they took John's carriage. Caro attempted to seat herself next to him, but he shifted across to Amelia's side. How could Amelia doubt him when he went out of his way to show her his preference?

Yet the more John drew away, the more Caro seemed intent on capturing his attentions. She fluttered her lashes, nudged his boot with her slipper. Amelia had to fight the urge to stomp on her instep.

Even worse, with John seated beside her, Amelia was left looking at Major Kensington, who smirked and winked his way through the trip. He claimed she looked like a ray of sunlight in her butter-yellow spencer and told her he had rarely seen a woman sit so serenely through every bump in the country road. She refused to acknowledge him with more than an indifferent smile.

But smiling at all became much more difficult when they reached Bellweather Hall. Amelia had seen the magnificent country house at a distance when she'd visited the Earl of Danning's fishing lodge nearby. Up close, the hall was even more splendid, with a fountain shooting as high as the white marble colonnaded portico in front of the sweeping wings.

Her mother had assured her the hall boasted more than two hundred rooms, each lavishly appointed. Certainly the entry hall, floored in marble inlaid with gold, lived up to Amelia's expectations. However, while her father's London house was as well decorated, Bellweather Hall was more welcoming, with bright clusters of arranged flowers and portraits of smiling ancestors.

A footman in a powdered wig and gold braid across his shoulders led them down a long corridor lined with alabaster statues and suits of armor to a withdrawing room laid out in shades of jade. The duchess and her daughter were seated on gilded chairs next to a hearth carved from serpentine marble. Each wore frilly muslin gowns that dripped lace, and Lady Prudence had confined her mousy curls inside a white satin turban with a pearl-studded band that seemed too ornate for an afternoon visit.

Both ladies smiled as John introduced his guests, but the duchess positively beamed as she met Caro.

"Ah, the Dowager Lady Hascot," she declared. "I warrant you have some interesting tales to tell. Come, sit by me."

"Yes, do," Lady Prudence insisted with a sniff. "I seem to have come down with distemperate anemia, but I don't believe it's contagious." She blinked rapidly, and Amelia realized she was attempting to flutter her lashes at the major. Though his smile remained charming, he adjusted the stock at his neck as if feeling the noose tightening. Already she could feel a similar tension in John. Surely she could think of some better way to pass the time than sitting around being uncomfortable with each other.

"I wonder," Amelia said before anyone could position for seating. "It is a lovely day today, and I understand you have beautiful gardens, Your Grace. The turning paths might be quite conducive to conversation."

Lady Bellington and Major Kensington both looked intrigued by the idea, and soon everyone had followed the duchess out the double doors at the end of the room. Caro linked arms with John and made sure to walk beside him. Amelia shook her head. Would the woman never leave off?

Her frustration made it hard to pay attention to the blooms along the graveled path. Unlike the boxed-in formal garden at her father's estate in London, the gardens at Bellweather Hall were a riot of colors and shapes, with curving paths wandering past flowering shrubs and into grottos with pools of water.

Amelia was more concerned about their guests. Lady Bellington commandeered Caro, and their heads were soon close together as if they whispered secrets. Major Kensington anchored himself beside John as if requiring reinforcements. Amelia found herself walking beside Lady Prudence and resigned herself to commiserate on a host of complaints.

"You cannot allow her to win," Lady Prudence said, dabbing at her nose with a lace-edged handkerchief.

Amelia blinked. "Forgive me, but I'm not sure what you mean."

Lady Prudence nodded toward the front of the column where Caro's laughter floated on the breeze. "Lady Hascot. She is far too bold."

Amelia managed a smile. "I'm sure she seems so to many."

"You will think me quite forward," Lady Prudence confessed, pausing to blow her nose, "but you have been kind to me, and I would not see you ill used. That woman is attempting to eclipse you."

Amelia stared at her. "Do you sense the competition, as well?"

"It is not obvious," Lady Prudence assured her. "You are far too gentle natured and far too well-bred to let your frustration show. But I have been in your position, you know. My brother Bell is widely sought after, and not always with the best of intentions."

Amelia glanced at her. Though the lady's face remained pale under the parasol she had brought with her, there was nothing infirm in her step. Indeed, she marched down the path as if intending to claim it for her own.

"And how does your brother deal with such difficulties?" Amelia asked her.

Lady Prudence tucked away her handkerchief. "Bell is generally good about seeing intentions. But he tends to give the ladies the benefit of the doubt. I'm afraid I'm much more cynical. I refuse to smile while danger creeps up on family."

Amelia stared at Caro, who had paused to admire a rose climbing up the lacework of a trellis. "Do you think Lady Hascot to be dangerous?"

"To you physically? Perhaps not. But to your marriage, definitely. You must use all your wiles to protect your husband. You must show her that *you* are Lady Hascot."

Her wiles. Over her two Seasons, she'd only resorted to such measures twice, batting her lashes and murmuring sweet words to convince a gentleman to see things her way. The first time had been to sway a Parliamentarian to support something her father wanted, earning her a rare compliment from him. The second time had been to help Ruby Hollingsford in her campaign to win the earl. Both times Amelia had felt dirty, deceitful afterward. It was one thing to be her best self in a situation. It was another to use her beauty to influence a man's actions.

"I fear that isn't in my nature," she confessed.

Lady Prudence sighed. "A shame. I fear it would be entirely too much in my nature, only I haven't the arsenal you do." She sniffed. "Perhaps that was the Lord's plan. He knew I would be too controlling to be a beauty."

"I did not consider you controlling," Amelia assured her.

"Ah, but I am." She took out her handkerchief again. "I like attention. If you cannot use your beauty, I advise you to find a reliable disease or two. The device has worked wonders for me." She raised her voice. "Mother, I think all this light is affecting a bilious extrusion upon my chin. Would you come look for me?"

The duchess immediately turned from Caro and trotted back to her daughter with a long-suffering sigh. "Oh, let me see. No, no, dear girl, you are fine. Come up with Lady Hascot and me. She was just relating a most interesting story about the Count of Kurion and a certain Russian princess."

With an arched look to Amelia, Lady Prudence moved to the front of the cavalcade with her mother.

Amelia shook her head. Pretending to fictitious diseases might serve to win Lady Prudence a moment of attention, but it had helped alienate the pair from the rest of society. It was also manipulative, a fault she quite agreed with John to be abhorrent. And what if one of

Lady Prudence's physicians actually attempted to cure a fancied ill? The treatment might kill the woman!

Yet Amelia could not fault Lady Prudence's skill. Within short order, the young lady had switched places with John, putting herself at the major's side. Whatever conversation she initiated soon had Major Kensington's handsome face turning red. Amelia detoured around a bush to avoid intervention.

Unfortunately, she found herself requiring intervention instead.

John had stopped, Caro and the duchess before him. He positively scowled, hands fisted at his sides, while Caro's perky smile faded into concern and Lady Bellington glowed with delight.

And Amelia knew something was very wrong, indeed.

It had been a miserable morning. First, John had had to endure a quarter hour of Kensington's egregious flirting with Amelia while John had tried to discourage Caro. Then he'd had to pretend civility with two women who, in his opinion, should be locked in their rooms until they could behave sensibly. The garden was lovely, but he would far have preferred to visit the stables.

Especially now that Lady Bellington knew his secret.

"Well?" the duchess demanded. "What have you to say for yourself, sir? Surely you know that every gentleman owes it to his name to sire an heir."

"The situation between a wife and husband is not for common conversation, madam," he managed.

"Indeed." Amelia glided around a flowering bush to join them. "How kind of you to take an interest in us, Your Grace. And when might we wish your son happy?"

How well she did things like that, turning the conversation from difficulty to pleasantness. He could only admire her skill, for it was one he utterly lacked.

Now Lady Bellington turned her bright eyes on Amelia. "He is to return within the week. You can be sure you'll be invited to tea, Lady Hascot. And you as well, Lady Hascot," she said to Caro. "If you are still in the area."

"I have no plans to leave anytime soon, Your Grace," Caro said with a smile to John. "I'm enjoying myself far too much."

"How gratifying," Amelia said. "Perhaps you should spread some of that enjoyment to Lady Prudence. She seems to be having trouble with Major Kensington."

"Oh, perhaps he has trifled with her!" Lady Bellington seized Caro's arm with a grin that suggested she'd be pleased to have her suspicions confirmed. "We must find out."

Either Caro was as interested in the answer or she couldn't protest fast enough, for the duchess bore her off.

Amelia immediately turned to John. "I said nothing, John, I promise you. I don't know how people keep surmising the issue!"

John thought he knew. Caro was in such a mood to attract attention that she could well have told the duchess her theory. He simply couldn't understand how Caro had guessed. Oh, he'd seen couples who smelled of April and May, hands clasped, gazes locked so tightly it was a wonder they didn't trip over each other. However, plenty of lords and ladies wed without such obvious devotion, and they managed an heir within a year.

Why didn't people assume he and Amelia would be among their number?

"Lady Bellington could find scandal in a nursery," John replied. "Do not encourage her, and it will all blow over."

She bit her lip a moment before answering. "I wish I could believe that. But I fear the only way to stop the rumors is for me to produce an heir, and we both know that isn't likely unless something changes."

Something, she said, as if she was the one at fault. He knew what had to change. It wasn't Amelia's temperament or her character. Both, he was committed to believing, were exemplary. Nor were her attempts to fix his clothing or hair a solution. What needed to change was his heart.

The realization had been coming on slowly, but he knew it for the truth. The day his brother had betrayed him, he'd considered violence, and the blackness inside him had disturbed and disgusted him. He never wanted to feel that strongly again. Certainly he didn't dare expose a child to such feelings. Since then, he had blamed God for abandoning him, but John had been the one to flee, away from the light that showed his inner darkness.

He wasn't sure he was ready to let another see his true self, even Amelia.

Still, he tried to do his duty the rest of the visit. He stayed at Amelia's side, nodded when appropriate, answered questions put to him. He escorted his wife to the carriage and sat next to Kensington across from her so she could meet his gaze instead of the major's. He had as little to do with Caro as his role of host allowed, which seemed to annoy the Dowager Lady Hascot, if her barbed comments were any indication.

He was congratulating himself on getting through another afternoon when they pulled into the stable yard behind the house, and Amelia turned white.

"Oh, look," Caro said, glancing out the window. "You have more company."

John twisted to see out the window, as well. A massive travel coach sat on the gravel, with a set of white horses at the front, each exactly fifteen hands high by his estimation. They had good lines and were likely prime goers, but he'd never seen them before. "I don't recognize the team."

"I do." Amelia's voice was as faint as an echo.

John turned to her in surprise. In the shadows of the coach, her face was a beacon of white, her eyes huge. Caro and Major Kensington were both staring at her, as well.

"It's my father," she said.

Chapter Seventeen

Oh, could this day get any worse? First, Lady Bellington had complained about their marriage, and Amelia was fairly certain the comment had grown out of the duchess's conversation with Caro and would likely feature largely in any future discussions with Amelia. Now her father had come. Who would blame her for refusing to climb from the carriage?

Oh, everyone.

So Amelia allowed John to help her down and walked with him toward the waiting coach, with Major Kensington and Caro behind them. Each step felt as if she was drawing closer to the gallows. John's arm under her hand was as stiff as a stair rail and as unyielding.

Her father had deigned to alight and stood beside the door of his carriage. Though he had to have traveled far that day, his top hat, dove-gray coat and black pantaloons were crisp, as if giving no quarter even to inconvenience.

"Amelia," he said with an inclination of his head. "Hascot. I expected to find you home."

"I would have been waiting," Amelia assured him,

"had I known you were coming." She glanced inside the carriage, only to find it empty. "Isn't Mother with you?"

"She insisted on remaining in London," he said.

She found it difficult to believe her mother preferred the miasma that hugged the capital in August, but she supposed the marchioness might have been hoping for a better invitation than to Hollyoak Farm.

"A shame," she said. "I believe you know one of our other guests, Lady Hascot."

Caro and the major stepped forward. "My lord," she said with a curtsy.

"Lady Hascot," he greeted her. "Kensington."

So he knew the major, too. Amelia glanced at the cavalry officer to find that he had paled. Apparently he also had few good memories of her father.

"And what brings you to our door?" John asked her father.

The quirk of his mouth was the closest Amelia had seen of a smile. "Does a father require a reason to visit his daughter?"

Hers did. He had rarely bothered to climb the extra flight of stairs from the chamber story to the schoolroom to check on her progress when she was a girl, had only occasionally accompanied her and her mother on their social rounds after she had been presented. She would have guessed he'd come for his colt, only she knew John had no young ones ready to leave.

"You are welcome in our home, regardless," John said. "I will leave the arrangements to Amelia. She manages the house exceedingly well."

Though John meant it as praise, he made it sound as if she was no more than his housekeeper. She could only pray that she would not blush for once and confirm the matter.

"Of course," Amelia said aloud. "This way, Father."

She managed to settle him in the withdrawing room with Caro and Major Kensington, then retreated to the corridor for a hurried conversation with Mr. Hennessy.

"There's only one bedchamber left, your ladyship," he explained as if she hadn't taken inventory herself, "and it's by far the smallest and on the schoolroom story. I'll have to double up the beds in the attics for all the servants as it is."

"Give my father my room," Amelia instructed. "Have Turner move my clothing and personal items to the smaller room."

"Yes, your ladyship," the butler said, but the look on his long face told Amelia he wasn't pleased with the arrangements.

Neither was she, but she knew her duty. She returned to the withdrawing room with a smile for all her guests, only to find that John had disappeared. Indeed, Major Kensington and her father were in close conversation, the major's face flushed, and Caro was rubbing her hands over each other as she watched. Amelia slipped out before anyone noticed her.

This was the outside of enough! She understood the house was her domain according to the agreement John had proposed. She could sympathize with his discomfort dealing with people. But he'd promised her he'd keep a closer eye on Caro and the major, and she simply couldn't manage her father and them, too.

As she had expected, she found John in the stable, discussing something with a groom before Magnum's stall. As usual, the stallion stepped forward at the sight of Amelia, lowering his head and baring his teeth.

Amelia narrowed her eyes at him. "Listen, you. I am in no mood for your posturing. You back up and behave, or I shall move *you* to a smaller stall!"

Magnum shuffled back and sank his head into his water trough as if she didn't exist. One look from Amelia, and the groom excused himself, as well.

John raised a brow. "Is something wrong?"

"Wrong?" Amelia put her hands on her hips. "Shall I enumerate? My father, who has never had a kind word for me, has come to visit. Major Kensington will not leave off pestering me. Dear Caro seems bent on re-establishing herself in your affections, and you run away. I quite understand why, John. I'd like nothing better myself. However, neither of us has the luxury."

"Why not?" He leaned against the wall of the stall. "I'm ready to pay for rooms at the inn, just to be shed of Caro and her major. If you wish it, I'll send them all packing."

Amelia dropped her arms. "Really?"

He straightened. "Say the word."

Could she be so bold? Major Kensington would be no social loss, and she had no wish to pursue a friendship. Nothing Caro could say would affect Amelia's true friends in London. But to evict her own father?

"No," Amelia said. "That isn't the sort of person I wish to be. Caro is family, and so is my father. I should be pleased he is determined to visit. However, I will need your help to entertain him."

"Nonsense," he said, reaching for a pitchfork to add straw to Magnum's stall, even though he had staff aplenty to see to the work. "You'll do fine."

Amelia threw up her hands. "How can I reach you, sir? Shall I leap ditches in the pasture? Beg for a pail of oats? Would you then pay attention to my needs instead of your horses!"

Magnum's head came up, ears pricking, tail stiffening. In the other stalls, other heads came up, from both horses and grooms.

"Lower your voice," John said quietly, straightening slowly.

"Why?" Amelia challenged, fighting for calm. "Everyone already knows how little use you have for me."

John stepped up to her, gaze drilling into hers. "Lower your voice. By your posture and your tone, you are telling the horses there is danger here. And you are putting yourself at risk from their reactions."

She felt it, as well. It was as if a thundercloud had shadowed the stable, threatening lightning. Heavy bodies shifted, muttered fear. She took a deep breath, forced her shoulders to relax, calmed her face. But though she might no longer look frustrated, she felt it nonetheless. She turned and walked slowly from the building, out toward the pasture, away from the house. As the sun bathed her face, she drew to a stop and closed her eyes.

Forgive me, Father. I don't know who I am. I don't know what John wants of me. I don't know what You want of me.

"Amelia."

She opened her eyes to find John standing in front of her. The planes of his face had tightened, his dark brows drawn down.

"What have I done to make you think I have no use for you?" he asked. "How could anyone so much as dislike you?"

She sucked in a breath. "I don't know. I try, John, I truly try to be kind and accommodating."

He met her gaze, intent. "I have never met anyone kinder than you. Always you find the good in the situation. Kensington was right—you are a ray of sunlight."

"But still you care more for your horses than your wife." Oh, why had she been given this gentle voice, this quiet heart? She wanted to rail, to shake her fists, to shout at someone. To change the world.

He took a breath, as well. "I can understand why you would think that. I spend a great deal of time with the horses."

"You spend all your time with the horses," Amelia corrected him. "Admit it. You wanted to bolt for the stables even when we visited Bellweather Hall today."

"I will not deny the attraction," he admitted. "But I will deny that it has anything to do with you. I am comfortable with my horses, Amelia. I understand what they're thinking."

Amelia shook her head. "How can a person possibly understand the mind of a horse?"

"Here, I'll show you." He took her hand and led her back to the door of the stable. Inside, her rivals for his affections were being brushed, given water and boxed in for the night.

"There," he said, nodding to Argentia. "You see how she's bobbing her head to the groom? Very likely she's done something to offend him and is letting him know she's sorry."

"Really?" Amelia watched as the groom stroked the horse's neck.

"It's all right, Argentia," she heard him say. "I know you didn't mean to step on my foot."

"And there," John said, turning her attention to the mare Providence. "Listen, and you'll hear her nicker. She's anticipating her dinner."

A low rumbling sound came from the mare, her nostrils twitching along in time as a groom approached with hay. John drew Amelia back out into the sunlight.

"I have learned to understand how horses think," he said. "But no matter how hard I try, I cannot understand people in the same way. They smile and say kind words, then lie and cheat. What kind of father mistreats his only daughter? Why would a man steal the woman his brother loved?"

She felt as if her heart was breaking anew, and this time for him. "Oh, John, I don't know. I've asked myself the same sorts of questions. Is it something I've said, something I've done, something I lack?"

He caught her face in both hands. "There is nothing, nothing lacking in you, Amelia. The fault lies entirely with your father, I am certain of it." He let his hands fall. "I only wish I could say the same of myself. I could not find the words to tell Caro how I felt once. Those feelings have gone. Now I have others, and still I struggle to say them aloud."

He had feelings? For her? Her heart seemed to fly up into the blue of the sky and dance from sheer joy. "I am listening."

"And here I stand, tongue-tied, staring at you like a horse at his oats. That is why I hide in the stables, Amelia. If I cannot speak my thoughts to you, how can I communicate with people far more complicated, like your father and our guests? Believe me when I say that you are better off without me. I would only shame you."

His head was bowed, his tone subdued. Even though

they stood in the sunlight, the shadows crept upon him. Had he been one of his horses, she would have thought him sickening.

This was wrong. He was a fine man, an honorable man, for all it had taken time and proximity for her to appreciate that. Amelia felt her spine stiffening, her head coming up.

"John," she said, "you could never shame me. You are honest, loyal, dedicated to those you care for. If our guests cannot appreciate that, they are the ones who should be ashamed, and I am very tempted to tell them that this very instant!"

John had rarely seen Amelia so sure of herself. Her head was up, her eyes shining with righteous indignation. She might have been leading a charge across a field of battle, so firm were her convictions. He only wished he shared them.

"And are you certain you won't care if one of my blunt sayings insults your father?" he challenged.

Those petal-pink lips curved. "If you insult my father, most likely it will be because he deserved it."

He could not deny that. "It still won't reflect well on you."

"On the contrary. He might actually come to respect our strength." She must have noticed she wasn't convincing him, for she put a hand on his arm, the touch soft. "Not everyone will be so sensitive, John. I have seen you be blunt with Dr. Fletcher. Does he take offense?"

"He can't," John said. "He values his position."

"And apparently my father values yours," Amelia replied. "Otherwise he wouldn't have agreed to our marriage."

John snorted. "It wasn't me but the horses he valued, and I think we both know that."

She was turning pink again. "Still, if you hadn't been so insistent, I'm sure he would have refused you."

John regarded her. "Is that what they told you? That I rode up and demanded your hand in marriage? Small wonder you find me a brute. I assure you, Amelia, I came to London to tell your father in no uncertain terms that nothing had happened between us which would require us to wed."

Her golden brows knit. "Didn't he believe you?"

"I don't think he cared," John replied, remembering the cool, assessing conversation. "He was intent on a horse from the first. I think he smarted that I'd refused to sell to him before."

She threw up her hands. "Of course! Even my father prefers horses to my company! Perhaps I should learn to nicker!"

John chuckled. "You have no need to nicker, Amelia. Men are only too happy to draw closer to you."

"If that was true, I wouldn't be living at Hollyoak Farm," she retorted. Immediately she flamed. "Oh, John, I'm so sorry! That sounded as if I'd prefer to be elsewhere." She stomped her foot in a good imitation of Firenza in a pet. "See! This entire business has me so rattled I forget my manners!"

For her, there could be no greater failing. "I understand," John assured her. "We are quite a pair at the moment. You forget your manners, and I had none to begin with."

"Nonsense," she said, and he thought she was recovering herself by the way her chin lifted. "Please, come back to the house with me. The thought of facing my father alone makes me want to jump on Firenza's back and ride until we both collapse."

Which was how they had arrived at their marriage, John realized. Amelia had quarreled with her mother, she'd said, ridden away and cried herself to sleep in his stable. Now she was facing her father the same way. John wasn't sure which was worse, that the man had schemed behind her back, or that he might be unkind to her face.

"Of course I'll come back with you," he replied. "But I can't promise to be civil. If he takes you to task in front of me, he'll find himself sleeping at the village inn."

She slipped her hand into his. "I'd like to see that."

Her touch buoyed him, and they turned for the house together, hands clasped, orange-blossom perfume floating about him. He could feel her determination, drew strength from it. He was so focused on Amelia he nearly missed the fellow leading his horse toward the other stable block. The cob had caved sides and a swayback.

John drew to a halt. "I know that horse," he said, even as Amelia said, "I know that man."

John met her gaze, saw her blue eyes widen. "I saw him on the road north and later on the road to Dovecote. He must work for my father. Oh, John, Father's been spying on us!"

John couldn't fault her logic. But he did wonder why Lord Wesworth felt it necessary to keep an eye on them. Could the marquess have been more concerned for his daughter than he'd originally let on?

"Let's locate your father," John said. "I suddenly find myself eager for conversation."

* * *

Unfortunately, when they returned to the house, they first met Mr. Hennessy, who reported a change in plans.

"His lordship has already donned his riding coat," the butler explained. "I believe he is expecting a tour, my lord. Lady Hascot has agreed to join him. And Major Kensington has gone down to the inn, something about posting a letter."

Once, John would have used just such an excuse to escape. Now he wanted more to confront Lord Wesworth.

"I'll see to your father and Caro," he promised Amelia. "Take the next hour or so for yourself."

"Oh, John," she said, as if he'd given her a priceless jewel. He was surprised to feel rather pleased with himself as he went to find his guests.

They were in the stables, where his lordship was ordering the disposition of the animals he'd brought with him while Caro stood nearby posing prettily. Much as he wanted to speak to the marquess, John interceded on the arrangements first. Most of his more mature horses knew how to get along with newcomers, but the mares and foals would require time apart. He was directing his staff to take the carriage horses to the other stable block when he noticed that Caro had led the marquess closer to Magnum's stall.

"And this is John's pride and joy," she was telling Amelia's father. "I give you Magnum Opus, the magnificent."

Magnum eyed them as if unsure they warranted his time.

"And is not your greatest composition wasted here in Derby, sir?" Lord Wesworth challenged John as he drew up to the pair. "I could more easily see this fellow leading the charge at Waterloo."

"That is something I would not see," John replied. "I understand you wanted a tour, my lord."

"All in good time," Amelia's father said, turning to stroll along the aisle as if he owned the space. He glanced at this horse and that, paused with head cocked as if to estimate size and strength.

Caro nudged John. "An eager buyer, I think."

John didn't answer. He'd originally thought something about the man spoke of cruelty and greed. The marquess's subsequent actions and Amelia's reactions had confirmed the traits. Lord Wesworth had been promised a colt if he could prove himself to John. He owed Amelia's father nothing more.

But now Caro was frowning at him as if she didn't understand his attitude. "Honestly, John," she said. "Do you never intend to sell your darlings? I understand you even refused Major Kensington. The fellow is a hero! I would think that cause for commendation, not reproach."

John shook his head as Lord Wesworth ordered the chestnut mare Providence saddled for his use, despite the fact that the horse had just eaten and was being made ready for the evening.

"Amelia was right," he said to Caro. "You're trying to change my mind about selling to Kensington."

She drew herself up. "She spoke ill of me behind my back? I would not have thought her so devious."

"Devious is not a word I would use to describe Amelia. Dedicated, delicate, perhaps, but not devious." He signaled to a groom to fetch Magnum's saddle, as well.

"And I suppose I am devious?" Her lower lip trembled. "Oh, John, can't you see? She's trying to come between us. She doesn't understand the special bond we share, forged by sorrow and tragedy." She put her hand on his arm and gazed up at him, brown eyes swimming.

The touch should have been sweet, imploring. Instead, he found it controlling, possessive. As if she sensed his feelings, she pulled back.

"I told Lord Wesworth I would accompany you," she said, "but I cannot like your mood, sir. And I believe you are making a great mistake in valuing your wife's opinion over one from a lady who has known you for years. Allow me to prove it to you."

She turned and swept toward Magnum's stall.

John darted in front of her. "Stand back," he ordered. "He's been temperamental lately, particularly around women."

"Around Amelia, you mean," she said. She stood at the stall's entrance and watched as the groom saddled the stallion and led him out for John to mount. To John's surprise, however, she started forward, and the black lowered his neck to nudge her hand.

"There now, big fellow," Caro crooned. "Aren't you a fine figure of a horse? I can see why your master is so fond of you."

Magnum bobbed his head as if he quite agreed.

John raised a brow.

Caro glanced up at him. "I know you respect your horses, John, more than the people around you. Perhaps you should ask yourself why your favorite horse likes me and not another lady of your acquaintance."

Before he could do more than stare at her, she sashayed past him for the house.

Chapter Eighteen

Peace, blessed peace. Amelia let out a sigh as she climbed the stairs. No one to impress, no one to find fault. A few precious moments all to herself.

Thank You, Lord, for Your kindness, and John's.

She didn't like the idea that she was leaving her husband to Caro's questionable graces, but she was beginning to believe that John was proof against the woman's machinations. And with Major Kensington out of the house, Amelia had no one to whom she was beholden, for the next hour, at least.

She nearly entered the room at the top of the stairs, then remembered it was no longer hers. She should continue on to the next story, where her new bedchamber was tucked away near the schoolroom.

But as she made the turn on the landing, another door presented itself, the door to John's room. Though she knew he was in the stables, she felt as if his presence seeped through the paneled wall of the corridor, calling to her. She still hadn't attempted to redecorate the room. She hadn't felt she had the right.

Was it a spacious room? Welcoming? A retreat from

the busyness of life? Or, like her room when she'd first arrived, was it a dark, solemn place more fitted to despair than delight?

Perhaps she should look.

She glanced down the stairs and around the landing, but saw no one in evidence. Still, guilt tugged at her. Recognizing it, she shook her head. What was she doing, sneaking about like a thief? She was the mistress of this house. It was her responsibility to make sure her husband was well cared for, that his room was airy and pleasant. She swept up to the door, put her hand on the latch and swung the portal wide.

Like the other rooms, this one was paneled in long strips of dark wood. The only painting brightening the space was along the wall at her left, two boys standing beside their mother. Wandering closer, she saw that the boys were very alike, dark hair, dark eyes, that hawk-like nose made softer by youth.

But one was decidedly heavier. He stood beside his honey-haired mother, who was seated on a gilded chair, a set of creamy matched pearls at her throat. Though the signet ring on the boy's pudgy finger proclaimed him the heir, his possessive gaze going out into the room left no doubt that he felt himself the owner of all he surveyed.

The other boy's eyes were trained on his mother, and his smile spoke of his love and devotion. So did the hand that rested on hers. It promised care throughout life and into the life beyond. Tears welled up in Amelia's eyes, and she put a hand out to touch the little fingers.

She had no doubt she was looking at John and his brother, and even less doubt which child was which. Was the woman plaguing her now at least partly responsible for the transformation from a sensitive boy to a withdrawn man?

Anger shot through her, and she yanked back her hand and turned from the painting. Shame on Caro for being so inconstant! Shame for building up hopes only to dash them! Amelia had met other women on the *ton* who delighted in winning hearts, only to turn aside this fellow as too unworthy, lacking fortune or face. Such games demeaned them all and left devastation behind.

Wiping away her tears, she approached the box bed. Made from black walnut carved with fanciful shapes and draped with emerald hangings, it dominated the room from where it squatted along the opposite wall. But Amelia was more interested in what lay beside it.

Bracing the bed were floor-to-ceiling bookcases, obviously of a newer date by the lighter wood and plainer construction. She sighted familiar authors and ones she herself loved: Shakespeare, Milton and Everard. The spines were cracked from well use; the books laying on the table beside the bed were dog-eared. The leather cover of one was so well-worn she could no longer make out title or author.

She picked it up and opened to where a black satin ribbon marked a place.

"Then came Peter to him, and said, Lord, how oft shall my brother sin against me, and I forgive him? Till seven times? Jesus saith unto him, I say not unto thee, until seven times: but until seventy times seven."

Amelia closed the Bible and rested her hand on the leather. It seemed she was not the only one having trouble forgetting the past. When was the last time she'd turned to the Bible for comfort?

Forgive me, Lord. Show me how I can reach John.

How can I prove that I will never be like Caro? That his love is something I value?

All at once the room felt too close, too familiar. She set down the Bible, turned and left.

She wanted nothing more than a few moments to herself, time to think, time to pray. But upstairs, she found Turner trying to cram one more gown in the walnut wardrobe that took up a corner of the little room.

"Sorry, your ladyship," she said. "They just won't fit. I put some of the heavier gowns in boxes under the bed."

"A good choice," Amelia told her. "And don't be concerned. I don't expect to stay in this room long."

"Less time than the other Lady Hascot is staying, I warrant," the maid muttered.

Though she feared the same, Amelia tried for a smile. "I thought you found Lady Hascot rather dashing."

Turner sniffed. "That was before she started making eyes at the master." She blushed furiously and bobbed a curtsy. "Begging your pardon, your ladyship. It's none of my affair, even if the whole servants' hall is abuzz with it."

So now they all found Amelia an object of pity. "What passes between a husband and wife is no one's affair but theirs and God's," Amelia said, her voice coming out entirely too sharp.

"Yes, ma'am. Just as you say." Turner closed the wardrobe with considerable force, then turned to Amelia, head cocked. "I could help you, though. Fix your hair just right, find the perfect gown."

"I've had my hair fixed just right since I was six," Amelia told her. "It hasn't made anyone love me."

Turner's face pinched, and Amelia turned away.

"Forgive me, Turner. I seem to be in a maudlin mood this afternoon. That will be all for now."

"Yes, ma'am," she said. Her hand was on the knob when she spun to face Amelia. "But I will just say that if someone like you can't win a fellow's love, there's simply no justice on this earth!" Obviously aware she had overstepped her bounds, she wrenched open the door and fled.

No justice on the earth. That might explain some of the things that had happened to her and John, but Amelia couldn't blame God. Though bad things might happen, she believed fervently that good would triumph in the end. The ebb and tide of human affairs were guided by a powerful hand, and God would set things right. But there were moments when she wished He would move just a little faster.

With a squeak of protest, the wardrobe popped open. Amelia went to shove the dresses a little deeper.

Forgive me, Father, for my impatience. I just want my life different now. I want my father to treat me with respect, John to look at me with love. I want a child to love and teach and watch grow the way John watches his foals. If You are the God of love, why is it so rare?

Her own father came immediately to mind. Love did not appear to be part of his life. He seemed incapable of lavishing his attention on anyone or anything beyond his own ambitions. If he loved, it was only the power of his position. And her mother was equally possessive, if only to defend herself.

But John. Oh, John had a heart. She saw it when he chose to curry a foal himself. She heard it when he spoke about his past. Sometimes she thought she glimpsed it when he looked at her. Why couldn't she reach him?

She managed to squeeze the wardrobe shut once more, then moved to the window, gazing out onto the green pastures, the wall of Calder Edge running along the rim of her world. But if she looked closely, she could also make out her reflection in the glass.

Her hair was like creamy satin, her eyes bluer than the summer skies. She'd had poetry written about both, recited by fervent young men on bended knee, no less. She smoothed her gown over her hips, turned this way and that. Her figure was still accounted quite good. In short, she had lost none of the beauty for which London had once sung her praises.

If she altered her hair, dressed differently, as Turner suggested, would she be manipulating him? Would such changes truly make any difference in how John saw her?

What did she have to lose?

She hurried to the highboy along the opposite wall. She'd dress for dinner tonight, her best gown, her finest jewels. She'd show John she was Caro's equal.

No, her superior.

She'd flirt and laugh and flutter her lashes. She'd be the woman no man could take his eyes from. She'd prove her right to stand by his side.

And when the others had retired for the evening, she would speak to him alone, tell him how she felt, her hopes, her dreams. It would be the boldest thing she'd ever done, and the riskiest. For if he didn't have the heart to accept her, she knew her own heart would break.

John rode Magnum across the pasture, Amelia's father at his side on Providence. The way Lord Wesworth had eyed the colts in the stable, John was sure he was sizing up which one he'd demand next summer. But John had other matters on his mind.

"You had a man watch the farm," he said. "Why?"

The marquess guided the mare around one of the obstacles, a shallow pond that reflected the blue of the sky. "I find it wise to ensure that my agreements bear fruit."

"What did you think?" John challenged. "That I'd mistreat Amelia or fail to supply that colt?"

Lord Wesworth spared him a withering glance. "Strong words, my lord. If you are unable to control your emotions, you cannot blame me for doubting your intentions."

John refused to let him see that he had scored. If the man truly had been trying to ensure Amelia's safety, he understood the necessity even if he did not appreciate the methods.

"I have every intention of honoring our bargain," John said. "It is your intentions that I question."

Lord Wesworth rode along as if his conscience did not trouble him. "I have ever been clear on my intentions." He nodded toward where the last of the horses were being led to the stables. "I see you have several from previous years yet to sell."

The way he stated the matter implied deficiency, either in the horses or in John's ability to attract buyers.

"The right master has yet to approach me," John replied.

"I know a few with sufficient funds to afford one of your mounts," Amelia's father said.

John turned Magnum toward the nearest obstacle, a stone wall. "Sufficient funding is only one of my criteria."

Turning his horse as well, Lord Wesworth glanced at John, pale blue eyes as shallow and cold as the ice John's men chipped from the outdoor water troughs in winter. "If you hope to support my daughter, funding is the only criteria that matters. The Hascot barony is rather land poor, if I recall. And you cannot rely on investment with the war over."

He should have considered whether John was well-off before selling his daughter. "You need have no concerns for Amelia," John told him. "I can provide for her."

"And what of her family?" Wesworth urged Providence to keep pace with Magnum. "It would be good to know that I can count on you if needs require."

Now John eyed him. "Is there a problem, my lord?"

"Not at the moment," he acknowledged, gaze going out toward the hills. "Not financially. But I am concerned about Amelia's social standing. She must have gowns, jewels, the appropriate accoutrements that females require for a good showing on the *ton.* Even if you have the funds to cover all that, you will not do her credit if you refuse men of consequence."

John had made a few enemies by refusing to sell to men with low reputations, but he found it difficult to believe the *ton* would turn on Amelia for such behavior.

"Amelia assures me that my unending ability to be churlish is no reflection on her," he told her father. "Her friends will stand by her."

"Amelia has no friends," he replied. "She was wise enough to keep her distance from sycophants and enviers."

Was that all the man considered other people to be? Surely a woman as sweet as Amelia had managed to garner close friends, true friends, in her time in Society. He thought back to the women who had attended the wedding. Though many had smiled and offered congratulations, only Lord Danning's new wife had begged a private word with Amelia. He'd assumed she'd be surrounded by friends. Was she so very alone?

"I can help you," Lord Wesworth said as if he'd guessed the directions of John's thoughts. "I have any number of acquaintances, men of standing on the *ton,* whose wives can assure Amelia the place she deserves in Society."

They were nearly at the wall. John gave Magnum his head, and the black picked up speed. Hooves churning the sod, the stallion gathered his haunches and launched himself over the stone barrier. For one brief, glorious moment, John was flying.

Amelia's father did not take the jump. Instead, he rode Providence around the wall and met John and Magnum on the other side. Yet there was something in his gaze that suggested he wished it otherwise.

"She will bear you over," John advised.

Lord Wesworth patted Providence on the neck. "Of that I have no doubt. But I stopped leaping obstacles some time ago. My interests lie elsewhere now." He dropped his hand. "I think you should consider my suggestion."

"I have," John replied. "But somehow I can't believe it free of stipulations. What is my part in all this?"

A smile tugged at the marquess's thin lips. "The Duke of York has three officers who covet a Hascot horse. Simply oblige them."

"Officers." The word sounded too much like a curse. "Active campaigners?"

"Oh, the war has ended," Amelia's father insisted. "Your horses will likely do no more than ride in a victory parade or two."

He wished he could believe that. "So you ask me to compromise my principles for my wife's happiness."

"Marriage is compromise, sir," he returned. "Believe no one who says otherwise."

He wanted to argue, to stand his ground. But he could not deny that Amelia seemed lonely. Would having more friends help? If his horses were truly safe, why shouldn't he sell to a military man, especially if it brought her comfort?

"I will take your advice under consideration," he promised Amelia's father, who graciously inclined his head as if knowing he'd won.

Yet how seriously should he take the fellow? John couldn't help thinking about the matter as they rode back to the stables. From what he'd seen of Lord and Lady Wesworth, their marriage was not a happy one, so taking their advice on how to improve his seemed rather foolhardy.

On the other hand, Lord Wesworth counseled compromise, and John could not deny that compromise was inherent in any human endeavor. If he wished for more hay than his fields would produce, he must come to an agreement with another farm in the dale willing to sell its surplus. The greater the need, the more he might be willing to pay.

What was he willing to do to secure Amelia's happiness?

Reams, who now served as valet, was waiting to help him with his boots.

"My black coat tonight," John told him. "And a fancier waistcoat."

"My lord?" Reams ogled him as if John had asked to wear Magnum's bridle down to dinner.

"I own suitable evening clothes, do I not?" John demanded.

"Yes, my lord," Reams assured him. "I'm sure I can find something appropriate. Just give me a moment." He almost ran for the dressing room.

When John went down to dinner a short time later, he fancied he would do credit to his wife. His uncooperative hair was pomaded in place. His black evening coat and trousers were set off by the emerald-striped satin waistcoat Reams had found in his closet. At least he hoped the fellow hadn't borrowed it from the major's trunk. His footman had even tied John's cravat in some fanciful formation dubbed the *Trone d'Amour,* and John found it more than a little difficult to turn his head.

Compromise, indeed.

He heard his guests before he reached the withdrawing room. Someone was laughing, a joyous sound that leaped about the air like one of his foals at play. He didn't think it was Caro. Did they have another guest?

He paused in the doorway, none too sure he wanted to find out. He spotted Caro right away, hanging on the major's arm as if he was everything to her. Yet the look on her face when she gazed up at the officer was nothing short of dismay.

John could see why. The major was entirely absorbed with the woman standing by the hearth. Platinum hair swung in curls beside her face; sapphires glittered in the lace-edged neck of the satin gown, which matched the color of her eyes. He'd always known Amelia was a beauty. Tonight, she outshone the stars.

"Ah, there you are, my lord," she called out. She held out her gloved hand, graceful, polished. "Do lead me in to dinner. I'm positively famished."

Bemused, John came to do as he was bid.

It was like dining with a fountain. Amelia was all movement and joy, sharing stories, encouraging conversation. He couldn't remember taking a bite of the first course before the second was brought in. Major Kensington was clearly enthralled, and even her own father was watching her with that twitch of his lips that suggested approval. John didn't remember Caro's presence until she spoke up as they all walked to the withdrawing room after the meal.

"Allow me to offer some entertainment this evening," she said, moving to the front of the room. "After all, we wouldn't want poor Amelia to have to resort to whist again."

Amelia might have taken offense at the implied slight to her skills as a hostess. Instead, she laughed. "Particularly when I am so very good at losing."

Major Kensington eyed Lord Wesworth. "I wouldn't mind a hand or two, but we are odd numbers for cards."

"That's why I suggest charades," Caro said, taking up a dramatic pose as if prepared to act out her part.

Lord Wesworth raised a brow. "I abhor mindless parlor games."

Caro stilled, one hand raised. Even Amelia dimmed, as if she had been about to suggest such a game, as well.

"I used to sing for my parents," John heard himself say.

They all stared at him. Caro's eyes were wide, as if

she thought he'd gone quite mad. Major Kensington was grinning, as if he thought it a fine joke. But Amelia's look of glowing gratitude propelled John forward.

"It's been a few years," he admitted, taking his place at the front of the room as Caro retired to a chair nearby. "But let's see if I remember." He coughed into his hand to clear his throat.

Major Kensington leaned back in his chair and crossed his arms over his chest. The set of his mouth told John he was ready to critique the piece, and the major fully expected to have a great deal to complain about. There was nothing for it but to dive in.

"Oh, stay, sweet warbling woodlark, stay," John sang, the words coming back to him. His voice had always been deep. Now the notes rolled from inside him and echoed in the otherwise silent room.

"Nor quit for me the trembling spray.
A hapless lover courts thy lay,
Thy soothing, fond complaining.
Again, again that tender part,
That I may catch thy melting art;
For certain that would touch her heart
Who kills me with distaining."

All gazes had turned to his, but the only one he sought was Amelia's. Her lips were parted in wonder, her eyes soft. Did she know he was singing to her?

"Thou tells of never-ending care;
Of speechless grief, and dark despair.
For pity's sake, sweet bird, no more,
Or my poor heart is broken."

He finished and bowed, afraid to see how Amelia had taken it. But when he straightened, he saw an answering smile on her lovely face.

"Well done!" Caro proclaimed, applauding. The others joined in. Even Major Kensington looked impressed.

"Perhaps a duet next," John said, and Caro popped to her feet. John held out his hand to his wife. "Amelia, will you join me? Surely you know 'Return My Heart.'"

She rose slowly, gaze on his. "Yes, I know it. Will you take melody or harmony, my lord?"

John chuckled. "Melody will be difficult enough, I fear."

"Then you lead," she said with a smile, "and I'll follow."

He thought for a moment, hearing the appropriate note in his head. Then he started.

"I prithee send me back my heart,
Since I cannot have thine;
For if from yours you will not part,
Why then should you have mine?"

Amelia joined on the second verse, their voices blending.

"Why should two hearts in one breast lie
And yet not lodge together?
O love! Where is thy sympathy,
If thus our hearts you sever?"

All he could see was her, her blue eyes meeting his, her clear voice sweeping away any other thought but the story of lovers parted and then united. Did she know she'd captured his heart? Destroyed the last of his defenses?

They finished together.

"Then farewell care and farewell woe;
I will no longer pine;
For I'll believe I have her heart,
As much as she hath mine."

The song faded, and John caught his breath. Amelia's lips trembled, and she leaned closer. He met her half-way, touching his lips to hers. And breath and thought became impossible.

Applause reminded him of their audience. John pulled back to find Lord Wesworth on his feet.

"As fine an entertainment as I've ever heard," he pronounced. "You make me proud, daughter."

Amelia burst into tears and ran from the room.

Chapter Nineteen

Well, she'd done it. She'd succeeded in capturing her father's attentions after more than twenty years of striving. And for what? Dressing better than usual and flirting shamelessly.

And John, dear John, had noticed her, as well. Each word of his song echoed in her heart. And when they had sung together, she'd felt perfect for the first time in her life.

She couldn't bear it.

This wasn't her. She wasn't someone to put herself on display, to manipulate people into liking her. Her head was throbbing, her breath was hitching and she just wanted to go upstairs and crawl beneath the covers. What was wrong with her?

John caught her at the foot of the stairs. In truth, she wasn't even sure where she had been going. All she'd known was that she had to escape before she said or did something further to disgrace herself.

"Easy," he said, laying a hand on her arm. His shoulders were down, his breath coming slowly, controlled. She'd seen the response before and knew its purpose.

"Oh, John," she returned, "I'm not one of your horses to be calmed at a word and a deep breath."

He ran his hand up her arm and down again, as if needing to reassure her as much as himself. "I know you aren't a horse, Amelia. But I'm coming to realize that people act a great deal like them."

She didn't want his touch to be so soothing, yet it was. She could feel her own muscles loosening. "Your horses do not dress up and make a spectacle of themselves," she protested.

He shrugged. "I'll leave you to argue that with Magnum. He is inordinately pleased with the purple blanket I gave him last year. But I was actually thinking of the way your father responded to our duet."

"If you tell me a stallion is proud when his colt leads the hunting field, I will not believe you," she warned.

He chuckled. "I think a stallion is more likely to attempt to race his offspring across the hunting field rather than cheer them on. But the same might be said for your father. His behavior reminds me of the way Magnum treats a strange horse in the pasture, baring his teeth and shaking his head."

"The thought that my father might somehow find me a threat would not survive its birth," Amelia insisted. "He is always the one in control. He sent a man to spy on us, John!"

"Apparently to ensure I treated you well," John replied. "But make no mistake, Amelia. You are a threat to Magnum and to him. I should have realized it before. If you ask me, they are both jealous."

Amelia stiffened. "Jealous? Why?"

"Magnum sees you as a rival for my attentions. Horses view all relationships as linear—you are either above or below the horse. I am above Magnum, but only by one notch in his opinion. He thinks you are trying to come between us."

She shook her head. "As if that was possible."

"And your father?" John continued, as if excited to have understood the dynamics at last. "Power and prestige are everything to him. You said so yourself." He touched her chin, drawing her gaze to his. "When you sing, Amelia," he said solemnly, "you are the most important person in the room. That surprised him."

It was rather heady to think that she might have discomposed her ruthless father. But she did not want to be the kind of person who took pleasure from discomforting others.

"Perhaps," she allowed. "But it was not my intention, I assure you."

He lowered his hand, cocking his head. "What was your intention tonight? I will admit you surprised me, as well."

She sucked in a breath and only succeeded in feeling her tears fall faster. "I wanted your attention, sir, but not for being someone else!" She wiped at her eyes, her gloves dampening with each touch. "Oh, forgive me, John. I'm a mess!"

"You could never be a mess," he replied. "Although I have seen you look better."

Amelia felt a smile coming. "Always frank, my lord. I may not have told you before, but I appreciate it. There is no dissembling in you."

He raised his head. "But there is, Amelia. I've done everything to keep you from seeing inside me, but you, your kindness, your dedication, you cracked open my shell. I fear you won't like what you see."

Amelia stared at him. "John, how could I not like what I see? You are a fine man."

His mouth worked, as if he could not decide upon the words. "I could be," he said. "With you beside me."

"Oh, John." She wanted to touch him, but she didn't trust herself. Instead, she motioned down the sapphire-blue gown. "I wanted to be special tonight, to shine for once, to have you want me beside you. But this? This isn't me! I'd rather be wearing my plum riding habit!"

He grinned. Her sober, solemn husband looked as if he'd just won the prize for best horse at the annual show. He reached up his fingers to his throat and tugged down on his cravat, ruining the fold.

"And this isn't me. I will never be perfect, Amelia. But I was willing to dress up like a jackanapes, if it would please you."

Amelia felt her own smile forming. "You did all this for me?"

Down the corridor, Caro poked her head from the withdrawing room. "John?" she called. "Are you returning? We could use a fourth for a hand of whist."

"It appears cards are not quite so boring when *she* suggests them," Amelia said with an exasperated sigh. She waved down the corridor at Caro. "We'll be with you shortly." Lowering her hand and her voice at the same time, she leaned closer to John. "I had another idea for the evening's entertainment. May I ask you to follow my lead?"

"To the battle and beyond, madam," he promised, his usual intensity igniting. Together, they returned to the withdrawing room.

Caro had convinced Amelia's father and the major to take their places around the parquet table for whist.

"How kind of you to see to our guests while I was un-available," Amelia told her, approaching the table. "But allow me to propose a new game, twenty questions."

Her father shoved back from the table. "I told you—I disdain parlor games."

"I think you will enjoy this one," Amelia said, steeling herself to continue despite his disapproval. "For I propose a prize to the winner—your choice of mount tomorrow, any horse in John's stable." She glanced at John, and he inclined his head in agreement, dark eyes watchful.

Caro leaned forward, eyes lighting. *"Any* horse? Even the famed Firenza?"

"Even Firenza," Amelia promised. "Though I reserve the right to try to dissuade you should you choose her."

"I'm in," Major Kensington said, leaning back in his chair and rubbing his hands together before his gold-braid-covered uniform. "I can't wait to ride that black brute, Magnum."

"I also reserve the right to try to dissuade you," John put in. "Though I fear I'll be wasting my breath."

Major Kensington grinned.

They relocated to the sofa and chairs by the fire. All her guests regarded her eagerly now as Amelia took up her place before the hearth. Even her father had a look on his face she'd never seen before. It was as if the fire behind her danced in his eyes.

"Twenty questions," Amelia repeated, catching each gaze in turn. She could feel John watching her as if expecting her to recite the entire New Testament or the Tattersalls breeding book from memory or do something equally marvelous. His faith in her made her breath come easier.

"I am thinking of something," she told her guests. "It is your task to ferret out the answer. You may ask me yes or no questions only, in turn, and no more than twenty in all. Whoever guesses first wins. Caro, please begin."

Caro preened, patting the curls beside her feathered bandeau. "Is it a man?" She fluttered her lashes at John, but he kept his gaze fixed on Amelia.

"No," Amelia replied, turning to the next guest. "Major Kensington?"

"Is it a woman?" he asked, watching her.

Amelia smiled. "No."

"Is it a horse?" her father asked before she could turn his way.

John stiffened, but when Amelia answered, "No," he relaxed again. She would not have dared to attempt to do justice to one of his darlings.

Caro leaned forward, her gown rustling, to take her turn. "It is an object, then," she surmised. "Is it larger than a teapot?"

"Yes," Amelia agreed.

"Larger than a horse?" Major Kensington asked.

Once again, John perked up. What was it with these gentlemen and horses! But she must answer, regardless.

Amelia thought a moment. "Forgive me, but I cannot respond with a yes or no. It would depend on the horse."

Both John and Major Kensington looked thoughtful.

Her father was regarding her with narrowed eyes, as if he had a glimmer of an idea of what went on in her head. That alone would be amazing!

"Is it something a woman would use?" he asked.

"Yes," Amelia admitted, "though men have been known to use it, too."

Caro straightened, eyes brightening. "Is it a hair-brush?" she cried.

"A hairbrush?" Major Kensington stared at her. "It's as big as some horses!" He snorted. "A hairbrush, she asks."

Caro glared at him.

"No, it is not a hairbrush," Amelia said, far more kindly, she hoped. John nodded his encouragement for her to continue.

"Is it a carriage?" Major Kensington asked with a thoughtful frown. "Perhaps a small one, like a gig?"

"A carriage?" Caro sneered. "You think a carriage is the size of a horse? Why does it take a team to pull one?"

Now Major Kensington glared at her.

This was not going the way Amelia had hoped. "Not a carriage," she emphasized. "Allow me to offer a hint. It is something you would find indoors."

Caro and the major glanced about the room as if seeking inspiration. John had narrowed his eyes now, as if he, too, was centering in on an answer, even though he was not one of the players in this game.

"Is it currently in this house?" Amelia's father asked quietly.

"No," Amelia admitted.

Caro and Major Kensington's gazes collided, and they both frowned.

"What color is it?" Caro asked, voice tinged with suspicion. Did she think Amelia had colluded with her father in this?

Major Kensington, however, rolled his eyes. "You have to ask yes or no questions. That's part of the rules."

Caro threw up her hands. "Oh, and you always play by the rules, don't you, *Major?*"

He stiffened. "My battlefield promotion was well gazetted, I'll have you know. You can ask Wellington to his face."

"I shall, the next time I'm in London," Caro threatened.

Amelia raised her brows, trying to think of a way to intervene.

"I believe," John said in the angry silence, "it is Caro's turn for a question."

Caro tossed her head at the major, then turned her attention to Amelia. "Is it pink?"

"Pink?" Major Kensington all but choked.

"No," Amelia hurried to answer. "At least, not that I've ever seen. And you are halfway through your questions."

She could see Major Kensington's lips moving as if he was reviewing the facts so far before asking his question next. Then his face brightened.

"Is it a stove?" he guessed. "One of those great black models the prince insisted on for Brighton?"

Caro looked impressed that he would know about such things.

"No," Amelia replied.

He deflated.

"Nice try," Caro whispered in encouragement.

"Is it a pianoforte?" her father asked.

Amelia couldn't help smiling at him. "Yes, Father, it is. You win."

A smile curved her father's lips. "It wasn't tremendously difficult to guess. You've ever been fond of music."

Although he always spoke with authority, his voice held a timbre she hadn't heard before, as if the memory pleased him. Had he known more about her activities than she'd thought? She felt as if something inside her was warming, melting.

Caro and Major Kensington were less delighted with the result. They both sank back in their seats, and Major Kensington crossed his arms over his braid-draped chest, but neither was willing to gainsay Lord Wesworth.

"As a consolation prize," Amelia said, "perhaps John could choose the perfect mount for each of you."

Everyone brightened at that, and conversation turned to where they might ride the next day and what time everyone could be ready. As if particularly eager, they all agreed on an early night.

"Well done," John murmured as Amelia passed him for the stairs.

"Thank you, my lord." A shiver of anticipation ran through her. All that had happened tonight had almost made her abandon her original plan for the evening. But the next part was the most important.

"Would you be so kind as to follow my lead one more time?" she asked her husband. "Meet me in the library in a quarter hour. There's something I must discuss with you."

He frowned as if he wasn't sure what she was about, but nodded. "As you wish."

Amelia nodded her thanks as well, and watched him head in that direction. She felt as if she and John had reached an understanding tonight, but if the next hour went as she hoped, her marriage would be on much sounder footing by morning.

* * *

John smiled to himself as he sat on an armchair by the fire. Then he paused to settle himself more firmly in the seat. This worn gold-threaded armchair, which had once been exiled to the attics, was far more comfortable than the leather-bound seats that had squatted here before Amelia had redecorated. He would have to compliment her on her choice.

He could find any number of things for which to praise her tonight, most of all her courage. She was no more comfortable in groups than he was, yet she'd found a way to brighten the evening, entertain their guests. And even he looked forward to the morrow.

At a cough, John turned to see Mr. Hennessy standing in the doorway. His butler advanced into the room, head down like a bull about to charge.

"My lord," he said, "this is highly unusual, and I want you to know that I do this under extreme duress."

What on earth? John rose to meet him. "What's wrong, Mr. Hennessy?"

His butler held out a folded note with a gloved hand that shook with indignation even John could not have missed. "I have been instructed to deliver this to you, and I have done so. And if you decide to answer it, I will tender my resignation this very moment."

John's brows shot up, but he accepted the thing from his butler. Even as he opened it, the heady scent of roses drifted upward, and he knew who the author was before he read a single word.

"My dearest John," Caro had written.

I can no longer hide my feelings for you, and I sense you feel the same. I realized you were singing to me tonight, and I want you to know that I have taken your words to heart. I have heard that lack of consummation is no reason to annul a marriage, but perhaps we can think of some way we can be together. Come to me tonight, and we can plan our escape.

Ever yours,

Caro

John crumpled the note in his fist and tossed it toward the fire. "There will be no answer."

Hennessy snapped a nod. "Very good, my lord. Shall I request that her ladyship's maid begin packing?"

"Immediately," John replied.

Hennessy fought a grin, but lost. "Thank you, my lord. It would give me the greatest of pleasure. Will you need anything more tonight?"

"No," John told him. "I'll see that the lights are put out before I go upstairs."

"Very good. Good night, my lord." He bowed himself out.

John shook his head. What had he done to make Caro think he would welcome such a note? After the way he had kissed Amelia, had the woman any doubt on his feelings?

Did Amelia doubt him?

He snorted, turning for the desk. Why even ask the question? Somehow his actions signaled something other than his intentions. He must give off a scent, turn his head to the right instead of the left.

Lord, You must understand me. You made me. I thought I'd disgusted You, but I see now You never left me and You knew just what I needed to be the man You intended. You gave me Amelia.

Thanksgiving rose up inside him at the thought. The feelings were strong, but they were pure, bright, banishing the darkness he'd struggled with for so long. He had to put those feelings into words. He went to the desk, sat behind it, picked up the waiting quill and began writing.

He had filled a half page when a movement caught his eye. Looking up, he saw that Amelia had entered the room. She still wore the blue dress, the satin rippling like a river in the candlelight. But she'd brushed out her hair, and it flowed about her like moonlight as she walked toward him.

His wife. The woman he loved. He couldn't speak for the emotion rising inside him.

"It's all right," she said with a smile, turning toward the chairs by the fire. "I can see you've started something. Finish what you're doing, then join me."

He nodded in thanks. One or two more words, before he lost his courage. Then he'd hand the letter to her, and she would know exactly what she meant to him.

Please, Father, give me the words. She is a greater gift than I will ever deserve. And she deserves to know it.

A sharp intake of breath told him something was wrong. Looking up, a fist twisted in his gut.

Caro's note had apparently missed the hearth, for Amelia was standing, staring down at it in her hand.

John jerked to his feet. "Amelia," he started.

Shaking her head, she turned, dropped the note and fled from the room.

Chapter Twenty

Amelia ran for the stairs, her hands pressed against her lips. What, did some part of her think that would hold in the pain?

He didn't love her. He loved Caro. Amelia had given him a home, helped with his work, tried to be someone else, done things that made her uncomfortable to spare him discomfort and still he preferred another.

Hadn't she learned by now that nothing she did was good enough? She never managed to earn love.

She stumbled on the second flight and clutched the banister with both hands to keep from falling. Her emotions felt like a hive of bees inside her, all so furiously buzzing that it was hard to tell one from the other.

Why did she keep trying? She had done everything to try to make first her parents, and then John love her. Until this moment, she'd never realized how wrong she'd been. Love, true love, wasn't earned. It was a precious gift. A gift she'd hoped to offer John tonight.

"Oh, Heavenly Father," she murmured aloud. "What was I thinking?"

"Amelia!"

She heard John's voice behind her even as his feet pounded on the stairs. But she couldn't face him, not here, not now. She lifted her skirts and dashed up the last flight, then threw herself across the landing to the little bedchamber.

Turner looked up as Amelia slammed the door shut and leaned against it. Then the maid's eyes narrowed, and she advanced on the door, pushing up her sleeves as she came.

"If Major Kensington is behind you," she said, "you just leave him to me."

"Amelia!" John demanded from the other side of the door, and the handle rattled. Amelia stared at Turner. The maid's determination melted into panic.

"Oh, my word, it's the master." She took a step closer and lowered her voice. "Shouldn't we let him in?"

"Amelia, please!" John called. "Let me explain."

Amelia sucked in a breath. She couldn't hide from the truth anymore, or from him. She raised her head and stepped away from the door. Then she turned to face it. "Come in, John."

Turner stood beside her, tugging down her sleeves. And Amelia hoped her own face was less fearful.

She expected John to throw open the door and tell her immediately in his blunt way that he had no more use for her. Yet when he entered, it was slowly, cautiously, as if very unsure of his welcome. His gaze traveled from Amelia to the maid and back again. No one moved.

"You wish to change our arrangement, I understand," Amelia said, in a calm voice that was miles from what she was feeling.

He frowned. "Yes, that is, no. Not the way I think you mean."

"And what do you think I mean?" she replied.

He ran a hand back through his hair, and the locks she was so used to seeing tumbled down onto his forehead. "You read that note from Caro. I can understand why it might upset you. But I did not instigate it, nor will I respond. She will be leaving tomorrow."

Amelia stared at him. "Will you be leaving with her?"

He took a step closer, brows knit, gaze searching hers as if he would see inside her. "Why would I do that? I don't love her."

Her breath was hitching again. "Don't you? You loved her once."

"I thought it love. Fate denied that opportunity."

"And yet she is still part of your life," Amelia pointed out. She wanted to reach out to him and back away at the same time. "What about her rights to the property, your responsibilities to her as the head of the family?"

"I will always bear some responsibility for her as her brother-in-law," he said. "But she forfeited any right to my respect by her behavior." He took another step closer. "I would never break faith with you, Amelia. You are my wife."

"In name only," Amelia reminded him, and Turner shifted as if she did not like hearing it said any more than Amelia liked saying it. "I know that was our agreement," Amelia added. "I should not fault you for keeping it."

"And if I should want to change our arrangement?"

The tone was soft, wistful. After the past few moments she didn't know whether he meant he wanted to deepen the relationship or throw it out entirely.

But she knew what she wanted. Indeed, for once she

had no doubt as to what the right response must be. She might never earn his love, but she could give him hers.

"You must do as you see fit," Amelia said. "But know this—I love you, John. I love the way you treat your horses as if they are people. I love your relentless candor. I've even come to love the way your hair falls into your face despite your best intentions. If my love is not what you want, I can accept that. I merely thought you should know before making your decision."

She waited, afraid to even breathe. If he walked out the door, she thought she would shatter like a porcelain figurine dropped on the hearth. But at least she would know she'd done her Father's will.

Help me, Lord, to survive the consequences!

"Turner," he said, "leave the room."

The maid glanced at Amelia, who nodded. The door snicked shut behind her.

John took a deep breath. "I cannot always find the words to describe what's in my heart," he murmured. "And my actions seem to be easily misconstrued." When still she waited, he leaned closer. "I don't know what to do, Amelia. Show me how to tell you I love you."

Her heart soared. "Oh, John," she said and opened her arms. He rushed into them, pulled her close, kissed her again and again, from her temple to her cheeks to her mouth and back again. And she returned his kisses, trembling in his arms, laughing with the joy of it.

When at last he stopped, leaving her breathless, he pulled back. Those dark eyes were so deep.

"We should get married," he said.

Amelia laughed again. Indeed, she felt as if she would burst if her happiness didn't find expression.

"What, have you compromised your own wife, my lord?"

His smile was soft. "No, I mean really married."

Amelia cocked her head. "And what, sir, does being really married mean? I fear I will have those words from you yet."

He sighed. "And I fear they will not please you." He took another deep breath. "I would like to be the husband and father you and our children deserve, Amelia. I don't know if I have it in me, but I'd like to try."

Amelia laid her head against his. "Me, too."

His embrace tightened, as if even now he was afraid of losing her. "We'll clear these people out of our house," he promised against her temple. "Tomorrow. Then we can determine the best way forward."

Lips trembling too much for her to speak, Amelia nodded.

He kissed her on the forehead in a seal of promise and stepped back. Then he frowned.

"Why are you in this tiny room?"

Now he noticed? Amelia shook her head. "Because I gave my father the larger room."

"The rules of being a hostess are ridiculous," John pronounced. "Next time, put him up here." With that happy thought, he left her.

Amelia hugged herself, joy overflowing. He loved her! He wanted to make their marriage a true marriage, with all the blessings that entailed. She threw up her hands and a prayer of thanks at the same time. She had a real chance for a future, at last.

Turner poked her head in the room. "Do you need me, madam?"

"Yes, Turner," Amelia said, lowering her arms with a

smile. "I know I must change for bed, but I don't think I shall sleep a wink."

The maid must have seen the happiness on Amelia's face, for she, too, smiled as she came forward to do her duty.

"I told you a new hairstyle would help," she said as she assisted Amelia with her dress. And that made Amelia laugh all over again.

She wasn't sure how she slept that night, but she managed to be up and downstairs earlier than usual the next morning, hoping for a moment alone with her husband. Funny how that had gone from an effort to a delight, all in one night. She could imagine many mornings, taking tea together, planning their days, sharing their lives.

John, however, had beaten her to it. Indeed, it appeared her husband had been busy, for when Amelia glanced out into the stable yard, she saw that Caro's carriage and wagon were already being loaded. John and her father were just coming in from their ride, her father on the back of Magnum. The big stallion pranced as if he knew he was carrying someone of importance. That must have pleased her father a great deal.

She waited for them by the door, knowing her smile was probably brighter than the rising sun. John's smile was grimmer with determination.

"One down, two to go," he murmured as he approached. His lips brushed her temple as he passed, and her stomach fluttered. She knew it had nothing to do with hunger pangs.

"A cup of tea would be appreciated," her father greeted her, as if she was the maid.

Though she heard the censure behind the words—

she was obviously inconsiderate for not thinking of the matter herself—she refused to let it hurt her. John was right. Her father was fixated on position. She did not have to aid or encourage him.

"Of course, Father," she said, going ahead of him down the corridor and into the dining room, where Mr. Shanter had warm bread, freshly churned butter and apricot preserves waiting along with the tea. Reams, the footman, stood ready to pour, but Amelia didn't mind doing that little service for her father. She poured him and herself cups of the steaming brew and brought them to the table while the footman prepared her a plate.

"Did you enjoy your ride?" she asked from beside her father after he had taken his first sip.

"Very much, as I suspect you know," he replied. "Your husband raises fine horses, Amelia. A shame he doesn't know how to use them to advantage."

Amelia smiled. "John prefers the company of his horses more than the admiration of the *ton.* I do not fault him for it."

"You should." Her father set down his cup and leaned forward. "He has raised the expectations of the breed, Amelia. Some men will not rest until they have acquired a Hascot horse."

"Then they would do well to look to their own characters, sir," Amelia replied. "If they are worthy, they will not be refused."

"Worthy." He sneered the word. "A man's worth in the eyes of the *ton* involves the breadth of his fortune and the height of his position. You make such men your enemies at your peril."

"And they make John an enemy at theirs," Amelia countered.

He shook his head. "You have become enamored with this wild man. I did not raise you to embrace sentimentality, girl."

Amelia raised her cup. "You did not raise me at all, sir. You left that entirely to others. So take heart. You bear no responsibility for the woman I have become."

He stared at her as she took a sip of her tea. She could see the calculation behind his eyes, trying to determine how he could make her see things his way. "You have changed," he said at last.

She smiled as she lowered the cup. "Why, Father, I believe that's the nicest thing you've ever said to me." She thanked the footman as he set a slice of bread with butter and preserves before her. Her father watched her as she calmly took a bite.

"You have a choice, Amelia," he said, waving away the plate Reams offered him. "You can honor my wishes and convince your husband to sell to my acquaintances, or you can follow Hascot to your social ruin. Do not expect me to protect you from the consequences."

Expectations. Yes, he had a great many, and she had tried to fulfill every one. No more. She had her own expectations, for herself and her future, and his bullying had no place in them.

"Thank you for your concern, Father," Amelia said. "But I agree with my husband's stance on this issue. I'm sure you will not wish to prolong your visit, given the circumstances." She rose. "Safe travels back to London, and give Mother my regards." She left him with his tea.

Outside the door, she paused to take a deep breath. She felt lighter, as if the weight she'd carried all those years had lifted at last. She had been respectful, but she'd refused to bow to his demands, to compromise her ideals or her marriage. That was the woman she wanted to be.

Whoever these men were who wanted John's horses, she didn't fear them. So long as she and John held fast to their convictions and each other, nothing could harm them.

Down the corridor, she saw Major Kensington approaching.

"It seems Caro is keen to return to London," he said as he reached Amelia's side. He was in his dress uniform again, his hair gleaming as brightly as the gold braid across his chest. "So of course I will escort her. I simply wished to bid you farewell, dear Amelia, and thank you for your hospitality."

"Goodbye, Major Kensington," Amelia said, offering him her hand. "I wish you both a pleasant journey."

He took her hand and pressed it against his chest. "I think you know my feelings toward the lady have changed since meeting you."

Why did he persist? Having no battlefield on which to compete, must he now capture hearts instead of citadels?

"And I think you know, sir," Amelia said firmly, "that I want nothing more than a friendship."

He released her hand. "Alas, I feared as much. Will you do me the honor of walking with me to my horse? It would assure me that we part as friends."

She could not count herself a good hostess and refuse. "Certainly, sir." She accepted the arm he offered and allowed him to escort her out to the stable yard.

Grooms and footmen scurried about, lugging trunks, leading horses to training and pasture. Magnum tossed his head at her as he passed. Major Kensington paused

on the steps as if savoring the view, then he turned to
Amelia.

"Forgive me, Lady Hascot," he said. "I am a man
used to being under command, and I have orders to
secure three of your husband's horses. If reason won't
persuade him, perhaps the threat of scandal will."

Before Amelia knew what he was about, he'd taken
her in his arms and lowered his face toward hers. He
was going to kiss her, right in front of everyone! They'd
all think she'd betrayed John. And the major thought
she'd be too meek to resist!

He thought wrong.

"Stop this instant!" she ordered, shoving him back
and turning her face away.

Kensington hesitated, then his arms tightened. "Help
me in this," he murmured against her ear, "and you
won't be sorry."

She was sorry already, that she'd ever laid eyes on
the man! Worse, across the stable yard, she saw trouble
coming. Magnum whipped his head about, yanking his
lead out of the groom's hand. Then he turned to thunder toward her, nostrils flared and eyes narrowed, as if
he knew he had her at his mercy at last.

John strode through the stable, where he'd demanded that Major Kensington's horse be made ready.
He couldn't believe the pleasure he'd felt a few moments
ago at the sight of the equipages, both Caro's and Lord
Wesworth's, being loaded. In less than an hour, he'd
have his horses and his home to himself once more.

And he and Amelia could look to the future.

Her confession of love last night still humbled him.
He had done nothing, in his mind, to merit it, yet he felt

as if he'd do anything to keep it. He was bound to her in a dozen ways, yet he'd never felt more free.

He'd folded his carefully worded note from last night and left it on the desk in the library. He wasn't certain when he would find the right opportunity to give it to her, but the thought of how she might respond left him feeling as if he'd walked through a patch of thorny thistle.

Caro was waiting just inside the main stable door. Her black travel dress and veiled top hat were severe, as if his refusal had plunged her once more into mourning. Seeing him, she advanced down the aisle, head high and beaded reticule swinging from one arm, bringing the cloying scent of roses with her.

"There," she said, stopping him. "I am leaving, just as you asked."

John inclined his head. "A wise choice."

"So you insist." She sighed. "Is this really necessary, John? Can we not be friends?"

"You are the one who cannot leave it be," he replied. "If that changes someday, you will be welcomed back."

Her smile trembled around the edges, as if he'd given her hope. "Please, tell me this visit hasn't diminished your affections for me." She tilted her face, once more offering her cheek for his kiss.

Would she never learn? "I have no affections for you, Caro," John said. "You are my brother's wife. I owe you only support."

Her smile tightened as she straightened. "How kind. As a member of your family, allow me to support you in turn." She leaned closer. "Watch out for Amelia, John. I have reason to believe she and her father are conspiring against you."

She pulled back and eyed him, clearly waiting for his response.

"You are mistaken," John said. "In a great many things. Goodbye, Caro."

She raised her chin and marched out the door.

Why had he ever been enamored of her? She would do anything, say anything to achieve her own ends. Was it fear of privation, of losing her place on the *ton,* that drove her? Or was she merely so headstrong she could see no other way but her own? Regardless, he was thankful he'd never had a chance to propose.

Instead, he'd married Amelia. Sweet, kind, beautiful Amelia.

She made his life better, encouraged him to be the best, supported his convictions, shared his dreams. And because of her gift, there was nothing he would not do for her.

Thank You, Father. The prayer came easily this time. *I didn't know what to say to reach her heart, but You knew. You prepared the way for me, and I will be forever grateful.*

John stepped out of the stables into the sunlight and had the oddest sensation that the world had frozen. The footmen were standing, trunk halfway into the baggage wagon. Grooms stared at the house rather than the horses.

On the steps leading to the rear door, Amelia was in Major Kensington's embrace, and Magnum was rearing over her, hooves flashing.

John ran.

Chapter Twenty-One

"Magnum, down!" Amelia commanded, and the stallion's hooves came crashing down on Major Kensington's shoulder. The hero of Waterloo crumpled onto the steps, even as Magnum bowed over him, blowing a breath of warning in his face.

Amelia put out a hand and touched the black on the shoulder. "Easy, now. It's all right. I'm safe."

The groom who had been leading the stallion arrived at her side only a moment before John did. She expected her husband to reach for the horse first, but he leaped onto the steps and took her in his arms.

"Tell me you are unhurt," he demanded.

"I'm fine," she assured him. "Just a little shaken. Major Kensington tried to kiss me, John, to cause a scandal, he said. And he might have succeeded against my best efforts if Magnum hadn't defended me."

John kept Amelia close with one arm while reaching out to pat the black with his other hand. "Well done, my lad. You finally realized where Amelia stands in the herd." His embrace tightened. "At my side." He nodded to the groom, who managed to lead the stallion away.

Below them, Major Kensington groaned even as Dr. Fletcher pushed his way through the waiting servants, Caro right behind him.

"What happened?" the veterinarian asked.

"Davy!" Caro cried, rushing to the major's side and cradling his head against her. "That vicious brute of a horse! Speak to me! Are you injured?"

The cavalry officer's uniform was torn across the shoulder, and his manly bearing had become decidedly crooked as one arm hung limp beside him. The dazed look on his face told Amelia he wasn't sure what had just happened.

"See what you can do for him," John told Dr. Fletcher. "And if it involves bleeding, so much the better."

The veterinarian frowned, but he hurried forward to check on the major while Caro stood by, wringing her hands. Ordering a footman's help, Dr. Fletcher brought Kensington into the house.

"What happens now?" Amelia murmured to John as they brought up the rear of the procession. Just having her husband near made her erratic pulse slow, her breath come more evenly. Small wonder he was so good with the horses!

"I hope Fletcher can bring him around swiftly," John replied, "if for no other reason than I'd like to knock him down again."

"I'm more interested in what he can tell us," Amelia replied, stopping John just short of the door to the library, where Dr. Fletcher had the major sit on the chair, with Caro perched opposite. "He said he was under orders, John. He and his master seemed to think that kissing me would cause a scandal and coerce you into selling your horses. I don't understand."

"I do." His face was grim again. "I may not recognize certain actions, but I know betrayal when I see it. Kensington could have put it about you wanted his attention. Anyone knowing you would be unlikely to believe it without proof. He gambled on servants talking."

Amelia shuddered. "And Caro knew about why we married. Apparently it's the talk of London."

John shook his head. "All the more reason for people to accept I wasn't a devoted husband. Kensington would have given me a choice—continue to see your name blackened, myself made a fool, or exchange my horses for his efforts to protect your reputation." He frowned suddenly.

"What is it?" Amelia asked.

"The pattern reminds me of another situation," he said. "Don't be concerned. I'll deal with it."

"My lord?" Dr. Fletcher called, and Amelia saw that Major Kensington appeared to have recovered his wits, for he touched the side of his shoulder and winced.

"You, Lady Hascot," he said as John and Amelia moved to Fletcher's side, "have a wicked right."

John broke from Amelia and hauled the major to his feet. "You haven't felt mine."

Kensington didn't flinch. "Go ahead. I won't fight you."

"Why?" Amelia demanded, taking a step closer. "You were quite willing to fight me."

Caro hopped to her feet. "What is all this about? You make it sound as if Major Kensington is the villain when I assure you he is the victim." She shook her finger at John. "You should have that brute of a horse put down, John. He cannot be controlled!"

"Caro," John said, "return to your coach. Now."

She stiffened. "Well, I like that! You, sir, will beg my forgiveness before I speak to you again." She raised her chin and stalked from the room.

John's crystal focus was narrowed on the major. "Who put you up to this?" he demanded.

Major Kensington glanced at Amelia, then back at John. "Might we keep this conversation between gentlemen?"

"How?" Amelia said, hands on her hips. "Only one of you is a gentleman!"

John pushed him toward Dr. Fletcher, who caught the major and kept him from falling. "Bind his wound and lock him in the cellar," John ordered.

Dr. Fletcher eyed the major, who was easily a stone heavier in muscle. Just then, Mr. Hennessy, who had at least two stones on either of them, stepped into the room, and the veterinarian smiled.

"How long shall we hold him?" he asked John, beckoning to the butler.

"Until I am satisfied I have answers." John moved toward the doorway. "There are others I must question."

Amelia waited for Major Kensington to protest Caro's innocence, but he looked away and submitted himself to the butler's less-than-gentle ministrations.

She hurried after John. "Let me come with you."

He stopped in the doorway and looked her in the eyes. His dark gaze was once more solemn, the planes of his face sharp enough to cause damage.

"I'll have Mr. Hennessy send you Turner and Reams," he said. "Stay here and lock yourselves in."

Amelia raised her brows. "Do you expect a siege?"

"I don't know what to expect," he said. "But I won't

allow you to come to harm. Open the door only to me, Mr. Hennessy or the doctor."

She would have thought she was a queen in enemy territory, or one of his horses being made safe in a boxed stall. "Surely this isn't necessary."

"Perhaps not," John said. "But until I am satisfied I have an answer, I will take no more chances."

John found Caro waiting impatiently, pacing back and forth beside the carriage, the passing of her skirts raising a dust. Seemingly oblivious to the scene that had just been enacted, Lord Wesworth had already climbed inside his own carriage, and a groom was folding up the step in preparation for closing the door.

John moved to stop him, motioning Caro over with one hand.

"Major Kensington is a dastard," he pronounced when he thought he had both of their attentions. "He attempted to make me believe he was having an affair with Amelia. I want to know which of you put him up to it."

Caro put her hands on her hips. "And how can you be so quick to put the blame on him? He can be quite charming, unlike other men I know."

"Lord Hascot has no understanding of how things are done in Society," Amelia's father said to her. "Or he would not presume to speak this way to either of us."

"Society." John shook his head. "You cannot use that excuse this time. Whatever Society appears to condone, I know Amelia would never betray me."

Caro dropped her arms and shut her mouth.

"Amelia is nothing if not loyal," Lord Wesworth agreed. "You will remember, however, that I warned you she would feel the consequences of your decision not to sell your horses."

"And I trust you remember my warning, John," Caro added quietly with a nod toward Amelia's father.

"Warning?" Lord Wesworth replied. "Yes, I warrant a warning is needed. Amelia is an innocent, whereas you, Lady Hascot, have a history of manipulation."

"How dare you!" Caro started, chin going up in defense.

"How dare you, madam?" Lord Wesworth countered. "It is clear to me, as it should be clear to Lord Hascot, that you came here intending to poison his relationship with my daughter."

"That is not the point," John argued, but Caro would not be silenced.

She glared at the marquess. "And if I did, it was only at the instigation of someone much higher and more powerful."

"Who?" John demanded, turning on her.

The marquess was not willing to wait for her answer. "And why would you need encouragement to do what you do best? Remind me, how did you convince your husband to marry you when you were all but engaged to his brother, here?"

Now John found he could not intervene as Caro glowered at Amelia's father.

"Do not imagine you know my feelings on the matter, my lord," she told him. "You have never faced privation."

Privation? There had been rumors her father was a profligate, but John had never paid them any mind. And he still could not fault her for being swayed by the promise of the title and all that went with it.

"My imagination is not nearly so vivid," the marquess returned, yet he was watching John, not Caro. "But I believe Lord Hascot's is. Can you see her for her true self, my lord? Devious until the very end."

John waited for Caro to rail at the marquess, to deny his sneered allegations. Instead, she blanched and took a step back, fingers clutching her reticule. She was backing down, running from fear. And what did she fear?

Only the truth.

"Was it a lie, Caro?" he murmured. "Did you care nothing for me?"

She glanced between the marquess and him, biting her lip.

"You see?" the marquess said. "She will not even defend herself."

"Neither would your daughter, sir," she cried, "and look how ill you used her!"

He stiffened, but she rushed up to John. "It was him, John. You have to see that. Yes, I used you to make your brother jealous. Yes, I wanted the security of the title. But I would never order someone to trifle with Amelia! Never!"

How could he believe her? She had set brother against brother, and their rivalry had done the rest. Even now she played on his emotions like a master harper. The woman he thought he'd once loved was a fiction.

But the woman who had won his heart and given him hers was waiting in the house, and she deserved answers.

"Why are you really here, Caro?" John asked. "And no lies this time."

She glanced at Lord Wesworth and clasped her hands before her as if pleading with John to see her side of it.

"I went through James's estate too quickly," she admitted. "There is a cost to remaining at the top of Society, you know. Mr. Carstairs, the solicitor, refused to simply advance me the funds, and as you had recently married without even introducing me to your bride, I wasn't sanguine about my chances of getting more from you. Major Kensington mentioned he knew someone who would pay a pretty penny for a Hascot horse and even reward the person who made it possible. So we came north."

She drew herself up. "But it was only after we reached here that I learned it was Lord Wesworth who put him up to it!"

"Another lie," Wesworth said. "See how easily they roll off her tongue."

"And yours," John said.

The marquess frowned, but John turned to Caro.

"We are finished. I will stand by my note to Carstairs, Caro, but you will have to learn to live within your means. I will not receive you at Hollyoak Farm again."

Her lower lip trembled. "Yes, John."

He was no longer willing to be swayed by the pathetic look. "If you ever attempt anything like this again, Caro, I will have you put on a very short lead. Do you understand?"

She merely nodded. John pointed her to her carriage, and she went without a backward look.

"While I applaud your actions," Lord Wesworth said in the silence that followed, "they do not solve the problem. Your insistence on a childish code of honor put Amelia's reputation at risk. If you cannot protect her, you give me no choice but to take her home with me."

Did he really think Amelia would stand for that? John certainly wouldn't.

"Like my horses, you appear to be a creature of habit, my lord," John replied. "I fear that gambit won't work on me again."

"What are you talking about?" the marquess demanded.

"When I originally declined to join your family with mine," John explained, "you changed my mind by reminding me that Amelia would be the one hurt if I refused. Major Kensington tried a similar approach, but he claimed it was his master's idea. Now you use the same tactic."

"If you feel threatened by the truth," he replied with a curl of his lip, "it is hardly my concern."

"I cannot prove you ordered Kensington to shame Amelia," John admitted. "And for her sake, I would not see you jailed even if I could prove it. But I will remind you of something." He leaned both hands on the windowsill of the carriage and put his face on the level with Lord Wesworth's. Calculation crouched in the pale blue eyes, but John knew he could counter it.

"I told you that you would be given one of my animals if you were able to treat it and Amelia with respect. You have failed. You will have to go far to earn my trust again, my lord."

"Is that a threat?" he said, voice all the more menacing for its quiet.

"It is a promise," John countered. "You are Amelia's father, and I will honor her wishes should she choose to associate with you. But until you can prove to me that you can treat her with the respect she has more than earned, you and anyone you know will never own one of my horses."

Lord Wesworth's eyes narrowed. "You have no idea who you're dealing with."

John straightened. "On the contrary. I am dealing with a man so consumed by the need for approval from those above him that he would sacrifice his only child. How do you think your confederates would feel if they knew? Can a man who lacks loyalty even to his family be trusted in any other matter? Or is there truly honor among thieves, my lord?"

"You wouldn't dare blacken my name," he sneered. "You know it would reflect on Amelia."

"Amelia no longer shares your name," John pointed out. "And I am convinced she would feel less pain should Society shun her than she does now at your callous treatment." He stepped away from the carriage, satisfied that he had made his point.

"So you will refuse me," the marquess said, and something in his tone spoke of surprise and respect. "I would not have thought you had it in you."

"Your daughter has made a new man of me," John told him. "Now collect your lapdog of a major, return to London and carry my regrets to your friends. As for me, I have a great deal to do if I am to show my wife how very much she is loved and admired."

Chapter Twenty-Two

Amelia paced about the library carpet, Turner hovering by the fire and Reams standing by the door as if ready to repel all boarders. She had peered out the window, but the bulky carriages blocked her view of the stable yard. She would have given her household budget to know what was happening outside.

John obviously suspected who had put the major up to his attempt to link her name to scandal. Could it have been Caro? The woman was set on clutching all attention to herself and even to swaying John's opinion on selling his horses, but surely she would not see another woman ruined. And the idea that her father was the instigator hurt too much to consider.

Oh, but she had to take her mind off the matter or she'd go mad! She wandered to the desk, thinking to organize the few papers lying there. But John was an experienced manager, and the staff was competent, so there was little for her to tidy. Then she saw the folded parchment with her name on it. The hand was definitely John's. She'd seen it on their marriage certificate. Why was her husband writing to her?

She picked it up and opened it. He'd written:

My dearest Amelia,
Sometimes I grow so frustrated not knowing how to express what is in my heart. Magnum can tell by the way my shoulders move whether I am happy, sad or angry. But I have not had such luck with the people around me. That is why I wanted to write to you.

I have come to love and deeply admire you. I have never met anyone who can take something wrong and make it right with only a pleasant smile and a kind word. Yet you do this every day, in countless ways. You are like sunlight piercing the gloom of my life. I can never thank you enough for what you've given me.

Hope.

Dear Amelia, you are the world to me. Please never leave me.
John

Tears fell, smearing the ink, and she quickly folded the precious words away. Turner must have noticed her actions, for she ventured closer to the desk.

"Madam?" she asked, head cocked. "Is everything all right?"

Reams was regarding her, too, as if he suspected she'd found something dangerous on the desk. Amelia smiled at them both.

"I'm fine," she assured them. "Everything is fine. I know that now."

And thank You, Lord, for that!

She hugged the note to her heart, smile growing.

She would keep these words for the rest of her life to be read and reread, memorized and pressed upon her heart like summer flowers tucked away in a book. She had made a difference in his life. She was loved. What more could she want?

Someone tapped at the door just then, and everyone stiffened. Reams returned to the portal to unlock it and crack it open, then swung it wider to admit Dr. Fletcher. The veterinarian's curls were in greater disarray than usual, as if he'd run all the way from the cellar to tell them his news.

"It's done," he said with a reassuring smile. "Major Kensington and Lady Hascot are on their way back to London, and so is your father, your ladyship. I took the liberty of requesting that the staff move your things back to your room."

Turner darted forward. "They'll only make a hash of it. Excuse me." She hurried from the library.

"And my husband?" Amelia asked, taking a step closer to the doctor.

"Wishes me to convey a message. He will be busy for the rest of the day, but he plans to dine with you this evening if you will accept his invitation." He held out a folded sheet of vellum.

What could he possibly say that he hadn't already said? But of course, he wouldn't know she'd found his beautifully written love letter.

"I believe he's trying to make amends," Dr. Fletcher said as if he'd wondered at her hesitation.

"There's truly no need," Amelia said, but she accepted the note and opened it.

"My dearest Amelia," her husband had written.

All matters are settled, and I am convinced that Kensington's master, whoever he might be, will trouble us no further. I can see, however, that I failed in a greater duty than to discover our foe. I did not support you in your efforts to entertain our guests; I did not protect you when you needed it. Worst of all, I have not honored you as I should. That ends now. I am planning a special evening for the two of us. I hope you will forgive me and consider joining me.

Your devoted husband.

"What shall I tell him?" Dr. Fletcher asked.

Amelia carefully folded the note, knowing that it, too, would find a safe place among her treasures. "Tell him I am delighted to accept his invitation, Doctor, and that I live in anticipation."

With a smile, Dr. Fletcher inclined his head and left her.

It was an impossibly long afternoon. She directed Turner and the footman on how to rearrange her things, then left them to the matter. She had no wish to treat her staff as if they were incompetent. But if not moving her things, how else was she to fill the time? She was quite caught up on correspondence, except for that letter to her mother that would likely not be written yet for some time, given the current state of affairs. For once, her beloved books held no interest. With no guests to entertain, time seemed to slow. And all she kept thinking about was John.

What would he do? What had he planned? *Oh, please, Lord, show me how to love him, whatever he does!*

She was on her way to her room to change for dinner when Turner met her at the top of the stairs.

"There was a bit of a mess, your ladyship," she said, "as I predicted. Things aren't quite settled. I have everything you need for this evening in the other room."

Well, that was odd. Perhaps she *should* supervise her staff more closely!

"Very well," Amelia agreed.

In the small room, one of her favorite evening gowns lay spread on the covers. It was simple, with white lace at the curved neck and puffed sleeves and a fall of sky-blue satin. She smiled as Turner settled the folds around her.

"I have in mind a different style tonight," the maid confessed. "I think you'll like it, and so will his lordship."

She set about taking down Amelia's pins and combing out the tresses until they shone. Then she pulled them back from Amelia's face to allow them to flow down her back.

"Daring," Amelia said, turning her head to regard the coiffure in the hand mirror. "I like it. I feel daring tonight. But the drape of this gown demands a necklace."

Turner made a face. "The jewel case is still locked up, your ladyship. But I wouldn't worry. You sparkle better than any diamond."

Amelia thought she was right. She felt light as a bubble as she came down the stairs to the dining room. Inside, candlelight glowed on the gilt-edged plates, the crystal goblets. A man stood by the hearth with his back to her, black tailcoat emphasizing the breadth of his shoulders, hair pomaded in place. Disappointment shot through her.

Father, please not another Amble By!

"Forgive me, sir," she said, venturing into the room. "I didn't realize we had company."

"Company?" There was no mistaking that deep, rough voice. John turned and scowled at her. "I specifically said we were not to be disturbed."

Amelia's hand flew to her mouth. His waistcoat was of finest Marcella silk, patterned in blue diamonds on white, but it was open at the neck, showing the skin of his throat. He had refused to wear a cravat.

"Oh, John, please forgive me," Amelia said, going to join him near the fire. "I still find it hard to recognize you when you dress for dinner."

He grimaced. "My fault entirely. A lady has a right to see her husband decked out on occasion." He took her hand and bowed over it. "It is only your due, Amelia. You are the mistress of this house, my wife, and it is long past time I started treating you with the honor you deserve."

Amelia blushed as he led her to her seat. "Thank you, John. You would do justice to any London event."

His mouth lifted. "I'm only thankful we are not there now." He nodded toward her place.

An oblong velvet box sat in the center of her plate. "What's this?"

"Open it," John said, waiting.

She willed her fingers not to shake as she worked the clasp.

Inside lay a perfect set of pearls, each iridescent bead exactly the same size as the others. She knew where she had seen such a set before.

"Oh, John," Amelia breathed.

"Do you like them?" He reached around her and removed them from the box. They brightened in the candlelight. "They were my mother's, and she left them for my wife. It seems she had more faith in me than I did. I wanted you to have them."

Tears were coming, but she blinked them back. She didn't want tears, even ones of joy, tonight. "They're beautiful. But you didn't have to go to such trouble. I found your note."

He had been lifting the pearls from the box. Now he stilled. "It was an early draft. I will do better in the future."

She caught his hand. "You have no need to do better, sir. What you wrote was perfection. Thank you."

His gaze met hers, warmed, even as the planes of his face softened. "May I put the pearls on you?"

She nodded, releasing his hand to sweep up her hair so he could clasp them behind her neck. His fingers brushed the tender skin, and she shivered as he stepped back.

"Beautiful," he murmured, and she knew he didn't mean the necklace.

He went to sit beside her at the head of the table and tapped his glass with a silver fork. At the sound of the chime, Reams brought in a porcelain tureen and proceeded to ladle them each a bowl of mulligatawny soup. Amelia caught sight of Mr. Shanter, Turner and Mr. Hennessy grinning at the door before they respectfully withdrew.

She had taken three spoonsful of the spicy soup when she realized John was merely watching her. She lowered her spoon. "Don't you like it?"

"I'm sure it's delicious," he replied. "I consulted the cook this afternoon, and he assured me it was one of your favorites. I simply find myself less hungry than I expected."

Amelia swallowed, though she hadn't taken another spoonful. "What else did you have planned for the evening, my lord?"

He rested both hands on the pristine linen. "I think we should reach a new agreement, on a number of issues. For one, from now on we are partners, in every sense of the word. I want your opinions on how to manage the stables, what to do with the horses."

Amelia nodded. "You honor me, my lord. We will make all decisions together, then, whether inside this house or out. And neither of us will avoid difficult situations."

"Agreed." He toyed with his spoon but still did not take a bite. "Along that line, I will confess to making a decision without you. I had your things moved to my room. I know some couples do not share, but I'd like us to be that close. I can have a builder cut a door through to the room on the other side so you have your own sitting room and dressing room. What do you think?" He glanced up as if to gauge her response.

He truly was giving her every part of himself. How could she refuse?

Still, he must have read refusal in her hesitation, for he sagged. "I feared I was precipitous. Forgive me, Amelia. It's just that I realize how much I love you, how I have come to depend on you. You are the very air I breathe."

Amelia smiled at him. "Beautifully put, my love. I feel the same. But being here with you, seeing the pains you've taken to honor me, I suddenly find myself at a loss for words, as well. Perhaps there are only three that matter. I love you."

"Amelia." Her name was a prayer on his lips. He leaned toward her, and she met him. The kiss seemed to reach her very soul. This was love, shared heartache, shared joy, a commitment to the future. This was the gift of her heavenly Father. He loved her just as she was, and so did John. She had won her campaign for her husband's heart and given him hers, and she knew her gift would be treasured, always.

That Sunday afternoon, there was cause for much rejoicing at the Conclave. The servants gathered around the large oak table gracing the center of the room and lifted their glasses.

"To Lord and Lady Rotherford," Mrs. Jennings, the Grange cook, declared, her round face beaming. "They are returned from their honeymoon and happy as turtledoves. And I hear that perhaps little Alice will have a brother or sister within the year."

"To their happiness," the other servants chorused.

Next a little maid from the duke's household rose. "My master has returned as well, and with an excellent candidate for bride."

"Can he keep this one?" someone called out.

She blushed. "I believe he can, sir. For he brought back a suitor for his sister, as well!"

Cheers rang out, and more toasts were called.

Not to be outdone, Peter Quimby, the valet to the Earl of Danning lifted his glass, as well. "And here's to having my first holiday in fifteen years so the earl and his bride could have some time alone. And not fishing for a change!"

The others laughed at that.

Dorcus Turner stood up, hand on one hip. "I have you all beat!" she declared. "My lord and lady decided to get married, at last!"

More cheers erupted, glasses clinked and congratulations passed all around. For when the good Lord is involved, all it takes is a little help from the master matchmakers to bring about a happily ever after.

* * * * *

Dear Reader,

Thank you for choosing *The Husband Campaign,* the final book in THE MASTER MATCHMAKERS series. As soon as John, Lord Hascot, rode onto the page in *The Wife Campaign,* I knew he would be the perfect husband for the woman who could capture his heart. I hope you enjoyed seeing how Amelia grew into the woman for him.

Horses were an important part of life in Regency England, for transportation as well as ensuring a livelihood. Hunters like John's were highly prized by their owners for their ability to leap and run across hill and dale. I like to think they, too, had personalities that endeared them to their riders.

If you have a horse story to tell or would like to contact me, be sure to visit my webpage at www.reginascott. com, comment on my blog at www.nineteenteen.com, or join me on Facebook at www.facebook.com/author-reginascott.

Blessings!
Regina Scott

Questions for Discussion

1. In the beginning of the book, Amelia isn't certain of herself and her future. What kind of woman did she become?

2. Amelia realized that love cannot be earned. How do we try to earn love today?

3. John felt guilty for his feelings following his brother's betrayal. When is guilt useful?

4. John feels as if God had distanced Himself. How can we know God is near even when we can't always feel His presence?

5. Amelia and John were both moved by songs throughout the book. How can music affect those around us?

6. John and Amelia both saw their horses as friends. What kinds of personalities have you seen in animals?

7. There were several horses in the book. Which was your favorite and why?

8. Turner was uncommonly outspoken for a maid. When should we speak up to colleagues and employers?

9. Dr. Fletcher was more soft-spoken. When are gentle words more appropriate?

10. Amelia's father was obsessed with prestige and position. What place does ambition have in our lives today?

11. John thought Amelia's father and Magnum are jealous of her. Why do we become jealous of people?

12. Caro used her vivacious personality to manipulate those around her. When is flirting appropriate?

13. Caro thrived in London society, while Amelia came to prefer the quiet of Dovecote Dale. Where do you prefer to live—a city or town, or the country—and why?

FALLING FOR THE RANCHER FATHER
Cowboys of Eden Valley
by Linda Ford

Widow Abel Borgard has his hands full raising twins and establishing a homestead. Mercy Newell's offer to care for the children seems like the perfect solution. Will opposites attract when the wild-at-heart beauty helps a single father set on stability?

THE HORSEMAN'S FRONTIER FAMILY
Bridegroom Brothers
by Karen Kirst

The Oklahoma Land Rush is single mother Evelyn Montgomery's last chance at a new life. But Gideon Thornton insists the land her late husband claimed is *his!* Can two stubborn hearts find common ground?

HIS CHOSEN BRIDE
by Rhonda Gibson

Levi Westland has a year to find a bride and produce an heir—or risk losing his inheritance. But when his mail-order bride changes her mind about marriage, Levi must persuade her to give love a chance.

A RUMORED ENGAGEMENT
by Lily George

Years ago, Daniel Hale saved Susannah Siddons from her uncle's scheming with a betrothal—then disappeared. Finally reunited, Susannah has no intention of trusting Daniel again. But when scandal looms—she might not have a choice!

LIHCNM0414

REQUEST YOUR FREE BOOKS!

2 FREE INSPIRATIONAL NOVELS
PLUS 2
FREE
MYSTERY GIFTS

Love Inspired

HISTORICAL

INSPIRATIONAL HISTORICAL ROMANCE

YES! Please send me 2 FREE Love Inspired® Historical novels and my 2 FREE mystery gifts (gifts are worth about $10). After receiving them, if I don't wish to receive any more books, I can return the shipping statement marked "cancel." If I don't cancel, I will receive 4 brand-new novels every month and be billed just $4.74 per book in the U.S. or $5.24 per book in Canada. That's a saving of at least 21% off the cover price. It's quite a bargain! Shipping and handling is just 50¢ per book in the U.S. and 75¢ per book in Canada.* I understand that accepting the 2 free books and gifts places me under no obligation to buy anything. I can always return a shipment and cancel at any time. Even if I never buy another book, the two free books and gifts are mine to keep forever.

102/302 IDN F5CN

Name	(PLEASE PRINT)	
Address		Apt. #
City	State/Prov.	Zip/Postal Code

Signature (if under 18, a parent or guardian must sign)

Mail to the **Harlequin® Reader Service:**
IN U.S.A.: P.O. Box 1867, Buffalo, NY 14240-1867
IN CANADA: P.O. Box 609, Fort Erie, Ontario L2A 5X3

Want to try two free books from another series?
Call 1-800-873-8635 or visit www.ReaderService.com.

* Terms and prices subject to change without notice. Prices do not include applicable taxes. Sales tax applicable in N.Y. Canadian residents will be charged applicable taxes. Offer not valid in Quebec. This offer is limited to one order per household. Not valid for current subscribers to Love Inspired Historical books. All orders subject to credit approval. Credit or debit balances in a customer's account(s) may be offset by any other outstanding balance owed by or to the customer. Please allow 4 to 6 weeks for delivery. Offer available while quantities last.

Your Privacy—The Harlequin® Reader Service is committed to protecting your privacy. Our Privacy Policy is available online at www.ReaderService.com or upon request from the Harlequin Reader Service.

We make a portion of our mailing list available to reputable third parties that offer products we believe may interest you. If you prefer that we not exchange your name with third parties, or if you wish to clarify or modify your communication preferences, please visit us at www.ReaderService.com/consumerschoice or write to us at Harlequin Reader Service Preference Service, P.O. Box 9062, Buffalo, NY 14269. Include your complete name and address.

LIH13R

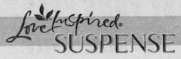
Can an estranged couple find a way to mend fences when they're forced into Witness Protection together?

Read on for a preview of FAMILY IN HIDING by Valerie Hansen, part of the WITNESS PROTECTION series from Love Inspired Suspense.

Grace parked in the shade across from the school and released her three-year-old from his booster seat and looked for her two children.

It wasn't hard to spot her eldest. His red hair stood out like a lit traffic flare at an accident scene when he left the main building and started in her direction. Then he paused, pivoted and ran right up to a total stranger.

The man crouched to embrace the boy, setting Grace's nerves on edge and causing her to react immediately.

"Hey! What do you think you're doing?"

The figure stood in response to her challenge. The brim of a cap and dark glasses masked his eyes, yet there was something very familiar about the way he moved.

Grace gaped. It couldn't be. But it was. "Dylan?"

He placed a finger against his lips. "Shush. Not here. We need to talk."

When he removed the glasses, Grace was startled to glimpse an unusual gleam in her estranged husband's eyes, as if he might be holding back tears—which, of course, was out of the question, knowing him.

"If you want to speak to me you can do it through my lawyer, the way we agreed."

"This has nothing to do with our divorce. It's much more important than that."

Grace's first reaction was disappointment, followed rapidly by resentment. "What can possibly be more important than our marriage and the future of our children?"

"I'm beginning to realize that my priorities need adjustment, but that's not why we have to talk. In private."

"What could you possibly have to say to me that can't be said right here?"

"Let me put it this way, Grace," Dylan said quietly, cupping her elbow and leaning closer. "You can either come with me and listen to what I have to say, or get ready to save a bunch of money, because you won't have to pay your divorce attorney."

"Why on earth not?"

Dylan scanned the crowd and clenched his jaw before he said, "Because you'll probably be a widow."

*Will Grace and Dylan find a way to save
their marriage and their lives?
Pick up FAMILY IN HIDING to find out.
Available May 2014 wherever
Love Inspired® Suspense books are sold.*

Two claims. One future.

Everything Gideon Thornton has worked for is in jeopardy, all because of one stubborn woman. Evelyn Montgomery insists that Gideon's new claim legally belongs to her late husband. Until their dispute is settled, they must share the land. Soon the enemy next door and her sweet young son have encroached on Gideon's heart as well as on his rightful property.

Rumors peg the Thorntons as liars and thieves. Day by day Gideon's thoughtfulness is showing a wary Evelyn the real truth. And it may mean the end of her claim...and the start of a future big enough to encompass all their dreams.

BRIDEGROOM
BROTHERS

The Horseman's Frontier Family

by

KAREN KIRST

Available April 2014 wherever Love Inspired books and ebooks are sold.

LIH28263